"You'll perish from boredom if you marry that man."

"There's nothing wrong with boredom. Why must everyone expect all their days to be full of diversions?"

"You possess far too much spirit to be satisfied with that dullard."

"I've known William all my life. We are quite suited."

"Liar. You. Me. *We* are suited."

She felt her eyes widen. "Rubbish."

"Shall I remind you then?" he challenged, a glint entering his eyes.

She held up a hand to ward him off. "That's not necessary. I don't long for the excitement you offer."

"More lies," he growled. "You *do* long for it."

She shook her head. "You don't know me. I'm not what you think. It was the cordial. It was an aphrodisiac. It altered me. I'm *not* that creature."

"Rubbish," he fired back at her. He stepped so close she could taste a hint of brandy on his breath. She backed away until she collided with the wall and could go no farther. "No aphrodisiac flows through your veins now. No tonic dilates your eyes or sends your pulse fluttering at your throat. That is *all* you, love."

By Sophie Jordan

The Rogue Files Series
THE VIRGIN AND THE ROGUE
THE DUKE'S STOLEN BRIDE
THIS SCOT OF MINE
THE DUKE BUYS A BRIDE
THE SCANDAL OF IT ALL
WHILE THE DUKE WAS SLEEPING

The Devil's Rock Series
BEAUTIFUL SINNER
BEAUTIFUL LAWMAN
FURY ON FIRE
HELL BREAKS LOOSE
ALL CHAINED UP

Historical Romances
ALL THE WAYS TO RUIN A ROGUE
A GOOD DEBUTANTE'S GUIDE TO RUIN
HOW TO LOSE A BRIDE IN ONE NIGHT
LESSONS FROM A SCANDALOUS BRIDE
WICKED IN YOUR ARMS
WICKED NIGHTS WITH A LOVER
IN SCANDAL THEY WED
SINS OF A WICKED DUKE
SURRENDER TO ME
ONE NIGHT WITH YOU
TOO WICKED TO TAME
ONCE UPON A WEDDING NIGHT

Sophie Jordan

THE VIRGIN AND THE ROGUE

❦ The Rogue Files ❧

AVONBOOKS

An Imprint of HarperCollinsPublishers

THE VIRGIN AND THE ROGUE . Copyright © 2020 by Sharie Kohler. All rights reserved. Printed in the United States of America. No part of this book may be used or reproduced in any manner whatsoever without written permission except in the case of brief quotations embodied in critical articles and reviews. For information, address HarperCollins Publishers, 195 Broadway, New York, NY 10007.

First Avon Books mass market printing: May 2020

Print Edition ISBN: 978-0-06-288544-9
Digital Edition ISBN: 978-0-06-288539-5

Cover design by Patricia Barrow
Cover illustration by Jon Paul Ferrara
Chapter opener art © Elena Eskevich / Shutterstock, Inc.

Avon, Avon & logo, and Avon Books & logo are registered trademarks of HarperCollins Publishers in the United States of America and other countries.

HarperCollins is a registered trademark of HarperCollins Publishers in the United States of America and other countries.

FIRST EDITION

20 21 22 23 24   QGM   10 9 8 7 6 5 4 3 2 1

For Sarah MacLean,
for always making everything better.

Are you sure/
That we are awake?
It seems to me/
That yet we sleep, we dream.
> *A Midsummer Night's Dream*
> William Shakespeare

THE
VIRGIN AND THE
ROGUE

Chapter 1

*T*he heavy chimes of the clock resounded on the air, lifting up through the bowels of the house like deep tolls of forewarning. Each strike reverberated deep inside Charlotte like something physical. A tangible beat . . . a tolling clang that coincided with the low pulsing discomfort in her belly—the telltale signal that her menses were coming.

Oh, blast.

If she was given to heavier expletives, this would be the time for it. Once a month would be the time for it.

Now would be the time for it.

Always, it came. Like clockwork, Charlotte endured terrible cramps three to five days before her menses began. The misery. The suffering. The crawl-in-her-bed agony was as reliable as the tides.

It didn't matter when or where. It certainly didn't wait for convenience. The cramping afflicted her whenever it so chose, and unfortunately that was almost never late in the evening when she could lock herself up in her chamber and relegate herself to the comfort of her bed with a hot-water bottle. No, it always seemed to occur at the most importune times.

Such as now.

Charlotte counted the heavy chimes under her breath until they reached seven. It was time. The supper hour. Time to join everyone downstairs. She released a shuddery breath and flattened her hand against her unsteady stomach.

She could do this.

Her betrothed and his family waited below stairs. Her family waited, too. Well, except for Nora, who stared at her expectantly, one hand propped on her hip, the other hand extending a small cup to her.

"Are you certain this is not something else and not your usual monthly discomfort?" Nora asked with arched eyebrow. "Not some other *thing* bothering you?"

Charlotte did not like the question one little bit. She knew what *thing* her sister referred to and she did not care for the implication. Her sister thought her stomach was unsettled at the prospect of dinner with her betrothed and his family.

"It's not because of *that*," she snapped. Indeed, it was not because of *them*. The suggestion was as insulting as it was absurd.

Charlotte snatched the cup from her sister's hand, telling herself the cordial would help. Her discomfort was only mild this time. She would get through the evening. She could do this. To-morrow she could lounge about, shrouded in cozy blankets, sipping tea with hot-water bottles on her belly to help ease the ache.

Now was not the time to let any discomfort get the best of her.

Nora made a face, apparently determined to make her point and not leave it at mere implications. "Are you certain you're not simply dreading this dinner and looking for a reason to beg off?"

"Of course not." Indignation flared in Charlotte's chest. "Why should I dread dinner with Billy and his family? We've taken dinner with them many times."

"Exactly." Nora rolled her eyes. "You know what lies ahead."

"Be kind, Nora," she admonished.

"William is unobjectionable, I suppose. Decent enough. A bit of a dull bird, but . . ." She shrugged as her voice faded away. She looked

Charlotte up and down and her thoughts were perfectly transparent.

Nora thought Charlotte was dull, too.

It was a fair assessment. Charlotte didn't begrudge her for it. She knew she was the uninteresting Langley sister. The *boring* one.

The mouse.

She lacked the fortitude and grace of her eldest sister, Marian, and all the boldness and wit of Nora. She was unexciting—just like Billy. It was that simple.

They were two dull birds, which made them a good and comfortable match. Nora knew it. Charlotte knew it. Everyone who knew them knew it.

Charlotte had known Billy since they were children. She, like everyone else in Brambledon, had always assumed they would wed.

Nora continued, "But his parents are perfectly wretched, Char. How can you abide them?"

"I'm not marrying his parents," she countered evenly.

Nora snorted. "Aren't you?"

Charlotte ignored her and rotated the cup in her hand, looking down at the murky contents. Flecks of herbs spotted the inside walls of the cup, resembling bits of dirt.

She wished her younger sister could be a little more supportive and a little less outspoken. A little more like Marian, who supported Charlotte's decision to marry Billy. "They're good people, Nora, and highly respected in the community."

"Very well. If you insist on doing this, heed my words. I'll miss you dearly, but move away once you've wed—and not around the bloody corner from the Pembrokes—"

"Nora, language, please!"

"Move far from Brambledon," she continued. "You'll not want the Pembrokes constantly interfering in your life."

Charlotte didn't bother to debate the matter of where she would reside once she and Billy were married. It was already decided. They would remain in Brambledon. Naturally. It was the only home they knew. The only place they wanted to be—the only place Charlotte wanted to be. Diving into the unknown was an intimidating prospect. One Charlotte had never wished for herself. Not when home was such a pleasant and comfortable place.

No, they would not leave. There was no need.

They were born in Brambledon. They grew up here. Of course they would stay here as a married couple.

She would remain where all was familiar, where everything was secure and within her experience. No surprises. Nothing out of the ordinary. No risks. A tidy and contented life. She'd leave the world outside Brambledon for the adventurers.

Shaking her head, she lifted the cup to her lips.

If she wanted to stave off her pains and get through this evening, she needed whatever help she could get. She needed to be in top form for an evening with her future in-laws.

She grimaced as the foul cordial went down her throat in a sluggish slide. She resisted the urge to gag and choked it down. She'd never tasted anything like it before, and she was no stranger to sampling her sister's many concoctions.

"Blech. Nora." She licked her lips and worked her mouth, hoping to rid herself of the bitter taste. It did little good. The stuff was awful.

Never had she doubted her sister's competence as an herbalist. Nora had worked side by side with their physician father for years before he expired over two years ago. Twenty-nine months to be precise, not that Charlotte had been keeping track.

It was only that Charlotte was well aware of the day her father had died. She'd been beside him, holding his hand as the light left his eyes. A person did not forget something like that . . . watching a loved one die. When the light had gone from his eyes, some of the light had gone from her world, too.

Papa had placed a great deal of trust in Nora. Several people in the community of Brambledon still did, coming to Nora for draughts and poultices to ease their aches and ailments. Papa had believed in her. Charlotte had no reason not to trust her remedies.

Except the unfamiliar taste of the cordial combined with the curious way Nora studied her sent the tiny hairs on the back of her neck into prickling alert.

Nora nodded in satisfaction as she took the empty cup from Charlotte. "There now. You'll feel better in no time."

Charlotte narrowed her gaze on Nora, wondering if her tone wasn't just a fraction forced. As though her sister was attempting to persuade herself of that fact, and not just Charlotte.

Nora moved away, her skirts swishing as she set the cup down on one of her worktables. Nora had arranged several tables about the space, all littered with vials and weights and instruments. Herbs were scattered through the room in pots and hanging from twine. One would not even know it to be a bedchamber if not for the bed and large wardrobe on the other side of the room. Other girls her age were interested in routs and their marriage prospects. Not Nora, however.

They'd been here a little over a year now, and Nora had made herself at home at Haverston Hall and put her mark on the elegant room. Well, not that *elegant* described it anymore, as it had all the appearance of a scientist's laboratory now.

Charlotte was quite the opposite. She still felt like a visitor at Haverston Hall even all this time later.

When Marian had asked Charlotte and Nora to move in with her, it had seemed like the thing to do. When Papa died, Marian had given up everything and returned home to care for them. No easy task as they were destitute and every creditor in Brambledon was hounding them. It had all seemed rather hopeless for their family before Marian married the Duke of Warrington.

Charlotte had assumed she would enjoy living in the duke's fine manor house with its multitude of servants and rooms a person could get lost in for days. Who wouldn't enjoy that? It was the stuff of fantasy.

She had been wrong, though. Unfortunately, she didn't enjoy it.

Charlotte still felt like a guest in Warrington's house. Yes, it was her sister's house now, too. Marian had certainly put her stamp all over the place, bringing in furniture and papering the walls of several rooms.

Charlotte often found herself taking strolls and walking past the modest home she had grown up in, staring at the now-vacant cottage and marveling that she no longer lived beneath that familiar gabled roof with its scalloped trim.

She lived somewhere else now. In an enormous

house with too many rooms to count and servants that far outnumbered the people occupying those rooms. It was absurd.

She felt like an imposter.

She told herself things would feel more natural once she was married to Billy. She would again live in a comfortable house. Nothing like the ducal splendor here at Haverston Hall.

She would return to a modest existence. A quiet life. That day couldn't come soon enough.

Charlotte waved toward the cup. "That tasted vile." She worked her tongue in her mouth, still trying to be rid of the foul taste. "It isn't like the stuff you usually give me."

Nora always gave her a cordial to help ease her stomach. It only took the edge off. Unfortunately nothing ever entirely saved her from her woman's pains, but she appreciated whatever her sister could do. One day of the month she kept to her bed until they passed. She curled herself into a tight ball and attempted to sleep through the worst of it. She'd accepted this as her lot in life, but Nora, ever the born healer, had not given up. She was always searching for a way to mitigate Charlotte's pain.

Nora waved a hand airily. "Oh, it was the usual ingredients."

Charlotte gave a dogged shake of her head. "It was different."

Nora shrugged. "Well. I might have altered the measurements a fraction to better improve its effects." She picked up her quill and scratched some notes down in her ledger.

Charlotte nodded. "Well, I suppose that accounts for it then. It was more vile than usual."

"What's vile?" Marian asked as she breezed into the room looking resplendent in a gown of deep emerald green, her hair piled atop her head in soft golden waves.

Marriage suited her eldest sister. Or perhaps it was being daft in love with her husband that suited Marian. She had been married a little over a year now, and the shine had not worn off. Marian glowed with happiness.

"'Tis nothing. Merely Charlotte's monthly cordial," Nora quickly responded as she tidied up her table.

"Oh, dear." Marian looked at her in concern, tsking in sympathy. "Are you unwell, Charlotte? What poor timing."

"Nothing too severe," Charlotte assured her. "I am quite well enough to go down to dinner." At least so far. The twinges in her stomach had only just begun. She'd make it through dinner.

Marian exhaled deeply, and Charlotte understood the origin of that sigh. Marian had no desire to be stuck entertaining the Pembrokes without her.

Marian looked at their youngest sister. "Are you ready, Nora?"

Nora removed her dirty pinafore, revealing her gown beneath. "I suppose. If I must. At least it shall be a grand supper. Cook always outdoes himself when we have guests. I'm certain the fine meal will more than make up for the company." She sent Charlotte what could only be considered a pitying glance.

Nora didn't need to explain the meaning behind the look. Charlotte was well aware that her future in-laws were tedious people. Marian was polite enough not to say so outright, but Nora never minced words. She'd let Charlotte know on several occasions that Mr. and Mrs. Pembroke were reason enough not to marry Billy.

Charlotte didn't disagree with her assessment of Mr. and Mrs. Pembroke. She did not especially enjoy the pompous blowhards, and she knew the only reason they now approved of her marrying their son was because Marian had married the Duke of Warrington. It was that family connection alone that made her worthy in their eyes. They cared nothing at all for her on a personal level.

Billy was reason enough to endure them.

She'd grown up with the lad. He was kind and gentle and nothing like his parents. He didn't care for position or where he fell in the order of

Society. Billy had wanted to marry her even before her sister had married Warrington. He simply couldn't go against his parents. Not unless he wished to be renounced by his family, and who would want such a terrible fate? She would not have expected him to make such a sacrifice for her.

But now the Pembrokes approved of the match.

She and Billy would build a life together. Certainly she'd have to suffer her in-laws now and then, but not every day. Charlotte was a patient person. If she had to sup with them once or twice a week, it was a small sacrifice in order to be married to a good man and living in a home of her own.

"Shall we go down to supper?" Marian turned and led them from the room.

"It smells heavenly," Nora exclaimed as they wound their way down the stairs. "Not even the prospect of listening to Mrs. Pembroke pander to Nathaniel can sour my excitement."

"Nora, do try to put on a good face and do not act like you're there merely for the food," Marian advised.

Charlotte trailed after her sisters, pressing a hand to her stomach and taking a slow and steady breath.

It would only be a few hours, and she wouldn't have to talk very much. She never did when she was with the Pembrokes. Her future in-laws did most of the talking. Little was required of her. Often, she felt they did not see her at all when she was sitting in their midst.

For once, this would serve as a comfort. She could sit in silence as they dined, battling her discomfort, and they would think nothing of it.

True, lately this was a point of consternation. She was becoming a member of Billy's family. Shouldn't she have a voice? Shouldn't they care about her thoughts? Shouldn't they care to *know* her?

As her wedding date neared, she had begun to consider this more. She had begun to consider it might be *nice* to have a rapport with Billy's parents. That or Nora and her ongoing commentary on the disagreeable nature of the Pembrokes was beginning to take root.

She shook off her internal monologue. It was self-indulgent. Her in-laws were fine people. They approved of the marriage. They accepted her. It was enough.

She tensed as a twinge passed through her stomach.

Tonight, at least, their disinterest in her would be most convenient.

Chapter 2

Kingston was not himself.

The signs were all there. Glaring and indisputable. *Unwanted.* He didn't wish to be this way, and yet . . . he simply was.

He avoided all his usual haunts. His clubs. Tattersalls. The theater. His favorite bawdy houses. The gaming hells. The parties and routs in Town that lasted until dawn. The dissolute country parties that occupied his winters. The endless stream of women.

He eschewed it all.

Not only did he ignore his friends, he ignored his family, too. Well, the meager few in his life he could call family. It was a loose application. He did not have a family in the traditional sense.

Yes, he had a father. One who enjoyed having him around for some extraordinary reason. He knew it was irregular. Most noblemen did not want their bastards hovering about, but his father had never sired a legitimate child, so his favor was perhaps not startling.

Not that his father was the manner of man to care much what Society thought of him. The Earl of Norfolk was no gentle retiring middle-aged aristocrat. He still played as hard as he had when he was a young man fathering bastards about the countryside. Kingston should know. He was one such bastard, after all.

His stepmother was no demure lady either. She enjoyed all the same pursuits as his father. That was why they were so well-suited. Their parties were some of the most dissolute in the kingdom. His father and stepmother called their gatherings salons, but in truth they were little more than orgies.

They always invited Kingston. He had once reveled in their attention, feeling even—dare he say it?—loved when they included him in their lives.

Except now he did not feel like being included. Their sordid lifestyle no longer suited him. A year ago it had, but now . . .

Now, suddenly, it did not. None of it suited him.

Perhaps the most significant change of all was that Kingston had not been with a woman in thirteen months. Over a year. A record, for certain. Not since he'd visited his mother's bedside. He'd known she was ailing before he called upon her, but being presented with the reality was an altogether different thing.

There was knowing and *knowing*.

Now he knew.

Now he had seen his mother ravaged by disease—a disease too ugly to name—and it had changed him. Soured him to his usual pursuits.

He did not like it.

He did not want this change in himself, but he could not shake this pall that hung over him.

His father did not understand this change in him. Nor did his friends. Not that he had explained it to any of them. He did not talk about things of a deeper nature with his friends or father. He was not about to start doing that now.

He could scarcely explain it to himself.

Avoidance was far simpler.

He had taken lodgings the last fortnight in the Cotswalds. Scenic, but there were far too many nosy guests about. The proprietor's daughter was perhaps the nosiest of all. She was always cornering him and pelting him with questions and prying into his affairs in a poor attempt at flirtation. His monosyllabic responses did little to dissuade her.

He'd cut his stay short on the last night after arriving in his rooms to find the bothersome chit naked in his bed. He'd been abstinent for over a year. She was hardly the woman to entice him from his self-imposed ban on shagging. He didn't know what woman could entice him, if any at all, but it was not the garrulous innkeeper's daughter.

He'd tossed the lass from his rooms and departed the next day for the one place he knew no one would find him. Not his father or stepmother. Not any of his licentious friends.

He took himself off to see his bore of a stepbrother. If he could even call Warrington stepbrother. There was no love lost between them. Warrington couldn't abide him. He'd merely tolerated him during all their forced encounters.

However, his father's stepson seemed the perfect solution. Warrington lived like a hermit, eschewing Society. Never once had he attended any of Norfolk's parties. Kingston assumed he'd find all the peace and isolation he craved at Haverston Hall where Warrington resided. Assuming the duke didn't toss him out. It was quite possible that Warrington would slam the door in his face.

When he arrived at Haverston Hall, he was braced for a dubious welcome.

The last thing Kingston expected to find was

his brother married and saddled with a gaggle of females in his house. Respectable females. A wife and her sisters.

Even more shocking, Warrington was entertaining guests—dinner guests—on the very eve of his arrival.

Indeed, he had not slammed the door in his face. Warrington had grudgingly welcomed him inside. Not warmly, certainly, but Warrington's young wife had made up for that with her genial manner.

The young Duchess of Warrington was exceedingly comely and undaunted by her husband's scowls. She invited Kingston to stay as long as he liked.

Although Kingston doubted that would be very long. Warrington wasn't leading a hermit-like existence anymore. Unfortunately. And that changed all his plans.

He would, of course, stay the night, but tomorrow he could take his leave. He didn't know his destination. Perhaps it was time to acquire his own residence. Then he would no longer be dependent on others for anything.

He had never bothered to obtain his own dwelling because there was no need. He'd never felt inclined to set roots down before.

He had never craved solitude—never a bedchamber or home of his own.

He'd enjoyed a nomadic lifestyle, moving from house party to house party or to any one of his father's properties. There were too many invitations for him to even accept. He had his pick of places to go, and people who wanted him as their guest.

No more.

He'd had enough of his hedonistic ways. He might not be as rich as his stepbrother, but he was a man of comfortable means. It was time he put down roots. He could afford to do so. Then he could be alone whenever and as often as he wanted.

For tonight, however, he would suffer Warrington and his new family *and* his guests. He'd made the mistake of coming here. He would bear it for one night.

Standing in the well-appointed drawing room, Kingston peered out the window overlooking the front landscape. Leaning one shoulder against the frame, he watched as dusk gathered outside, streaking the sky in deep grays and purples with a hint of orange.

He listened to the others around him conversing with only half an ear, planning his escape the next day and contemplating where he might like to go next.

He'd never been to Shetland. The islands sounded appealingly remote to him. There had to be a nice little fishing village with a cozy cottage available for him there.

It wasn't as though Warrington would miss him if he ducked out tomorrow. His expression had twisted into a grimace the moment he clapped eyes on Kingston today. There had never been warmth or affection between them.

Kingston was well aware the duke held him in contempt. He'd never cared what Warrington thought about him as he could scarcely tolerate the man either, kinsman or no. In fact, it amused Kingston that his presence so irked the bloody nob.

"Kingston, something so fascinating out on the lawn? Why don't you join the conversation, my good man?"

He turned at the question. It came from an older gentleman in a bright plum-colored jacket. Kingston forced his gaze from the jacket. Much like the sun, he could only glance at it briefly.

He had already forgotten the gentleman's name. The man's wife sat nearby on the sofa, her considerable frame rigid as a slat of wood. She wore an elaborate turban adorned in peacock feathers. She fanned herself impatiently with a colorful fan, fluttering the feathers.

Warrington's wife had left her moments ago to see what was keeping the other ladies. The ladies being her sisters. Young, unattached females. The precise variety of female he avoided. Marriage-minded and inexperienced chits were vastly dull.

The turban-bedecked matron's pinched lips

proclaimed her unhappiness at being abandoned so early in the dinner party. She had clearly come here ready to socialize.

Kingston gave a slight shake of his head.

Not only had Warrington saddled himself with a wife, but he now found himself with two sisters-in-law and a brother-in-law away at school somewhere. All this he had gleaned upon his arrival. The newly minted Duchess of Warrington was quite forwarding with information.

It was difficult to imagine the once-hermit duke in such a domesticated situation. In addition to Warrington being burdened with a sudden family, he was now entertaining the local gentry—mind-numbingly tedious as they were.

It was hard to conceive. And yet Kingston's eyes did not lie.

Warrington was here . . . sitting just across from him.

Kingston had been to his fair share of dinner parties—not all wonderful, of course, but his usual dinner parties did not consist of proper and decent and perfectly boring people such as those in attendance tonight.

He looked around the elegantly fashioned room with a suffering sigh.

There was indeed one thing worse than a dinner party of depraved and debauched individuals, and it was a dinner party full of good and proper members of Society. Quality people. Ugh. People like these. God save him.

Somehow his stepbrother had joined their ranks, as incredible and unlikely as that seemed. Somehow Warrington had become good and decent and . . . and boring.

He downed his drink, relishing the spicy, warm slide of bourbon, and then poured himself another.

He was in a bad place. He didn't enjoy the company of his usual consorts and he didn't enjoy the company of those fit for good society. Confusing, to say the least.

So where did that leave him?

The answer was glaring. *Alone.* It left him alone.

The idea had merit. Anything was better than this.

Clearly he needed to sequester himself away until he emerged from whatever tedium had seized him and he could return to his usual friends and his usual haunts and the usual him.

Him—Kingston, connoisseur of vices.

He fought back his internal cringe. This strange ennui that had taken over him was only temporary. He'd embrace his old ways in good time.

Except here he was, stuck now at this dinner party. Bored to the point of pain with no relief in sight. Bad decision on his part, to be certain. He would simply have to stomach it though.

The excessively purple gentleman stood in front of him drinking his fourth glass of whisky. He was listing sideways and looked as though he might topple over as he extolled his many connections in the Cotswalds. After having learned that Kingston had just come from there, the man was convinced that they must have mutual acquaintances.

"The Pringleys?" He stabbed a finger toward Kingston insistently. "Are you familiar with them? You must be for Mrs. Pringley is a cousin to Viscount Loughton."

Kingston shook his head, eyeing the drawing room and all its occupants and wondering when they would finally go in to dinner. They had not even started supper and he was already desperate to escape—a fact that did not bode well for the remainder of the evening that stretched so very interminably.

"Now, Mrs. Pringley was quite taken with my wife." He nodded across the drawing room, where his stern-faced wife sat. "Understandably so. Bettina has a way with people."

Kingston glanced at her again. It was difficult to imagine that to be true. The woman wore a perpetual scowl quite at odds with her frivolous turban. She did not seem capable of smiling as she sat on the sofa, her mother, an elderly woman with nearly translucent skin who sat ensconced in a wooden wheelchair, parked beside her.

"People are drawn to Bettina," Pembroke continued to boast. "They've great respect for her opinion on matters of housekeeping and gardening. She has impeccable taste and style, too. She gave Mrs. Pringley much sound advice on millinery, another subject she knows a great deal about . . . whilst we were on holiday there several years ago. They still correspond to this day." He lifted his glass in the air and shook it for emphasis, whisky sloshing over the sides and dribbling down his fingers. "To. This. Day."

Mrs. Pembroke was fussing with the cap upon her mother's white hair as her husband extolled her virtues. The old woman stared vacantly ahead and Kingston couldn't help but wonder if that was because her faculties were impaired or because she, like him, had gone mind dead.

"I can't imagine what is keeping your betrothed," Mr. Pembroke proclaimed loudly, looking at his son reproachfully, as though he were to blame for his betrothed's tardiness.

Kingston had almost failed to notice the couple's son.

Unlike his father, the young man was quiet, a wraithlike shadow where he sat in a corner, his slight hands gripping the arms of his chair.

"Where *are* the other ladies?" Mrs. Pembroke sniped as she finished fluffing her mother's cap. "It's quite, quite . . ." Her lips pressed tightly as though biting back an ugly descriptor. One of those ladies was the Duchess of Warrington, after all. It wouldn't do to insult her hostess. She finally arrived at a suitable word. "It's quite *unusual* of them to keep us waiting this long."

Kingston's lips twitched. It was almost amusing. The woman clearly wanted to call the duchess and her future daughter-in-law any number of less than flattering things for keeping her waiting, but she restrained herself.

"I'm certain they will be down soon," Warrington replied, looking pained. Apparently he did not enjoy these people either. However, as one of his sisters-in-law was engaged to the Pembroke lad sitting mutely in the chair, the duke was stuck with their company.

Poor bastard. If Kingston actually liked his stepbrother he would feel sorry for him.

"Ah!" Warrington clapped his hands together in a gesture of resounding relief. "They've arrived."

Everyone turned their attention to the doors to greet the ladies. Kingston fought down a heavy sigh, feeling none of Warrington's relief as he prepared for the niceties of introductions.

He had no fondness for proper country misses,

but he'd wear a smile and suffer through the evening. He might be a bastard, but he still found himself the target of matchmaking mamas. Hopefully the duchess's sisters did not see him as a matrimonial candidate . . . and then he remembered.

At least one of them would not fawn over him. She was already betrothed.

Chapter 3

Kingston had already met Warrington's pretty wife upon his arrival, but this evening she truly looked the role of a noble duchess. With her golden tresses piled upon her head and attired in an evening gown of resplendent green, the duchess swept into the room even lovelier than when he had first clapped eyes on her.

He supposed if one had to marry, she was a fine choice—although Warrington was not a man who had to marry. It still made no sense to Kingston why he should have done so.

Her sisters trailed behind her. Both were clearly younger. Their golden locks mirrored their older sister, but there the similarity ended.

One was fuller of figure and shorter, her eyes

lively and cheeks pink as though she had just stepped in from the sunshine.

The other one was taller, slender as a willow reed, her features pensive and her skin pale as fresh cream. Nothing about her was lively as she strolled into the room to very correctly and somberly accept the proffered arm of young Pembroke.

Obviously she was the betrothed. A fitting match for the Pembroke lad. Kingston would have guessed her the one even before she joined her betrothed. The other sister was too vibrant to be bound to such a dullard.

Warrington's duchess performed quick introductions. The younger sister, the lively one, looked him over with interest. It felt familiar. He knew his assets. His parents were both handsome people and had passed on such attributes to him. He winced at the thought of his mother. His mother's claim to beauty might not be a point agreed by all anymore. It was one of many things lost to her.

"A stepbrother?" the younger sister exclaimed. "How remiss of you not to mention you had a stepbrother, Nathaniel."

The duke shrugged unapologetically at the reprimand. "It must have slipped my mind."

Kingston snorted. More than likely it never

crossed Warrington's mind because Kingston was nothing to him. Not family. Not a friend. Not anyone who mattered.

Not anyone to talk about to those who did matter to him.

It should not have stung. He tossed the remainder of the bourbon in his glass down his throat, welcoming the warming slide.

It should not sting. And yet it did.

It only asserted how very few people he had in his life. He considered that a moment. Perhaps he had no one really.

Kingston looked away from the youngest Miss Langley and her bright-eyed gaze to the other Miss Langley. The quiet one affianced to the dullard with the bombastic parents. She spared him only the most cursory of glances before settling her lackluster gaze on her betrothed.

No matter their status, most ladies gave him more than a cursory look. He knew what the gentlemen of the *ton* offered. Most of them were balding with rotting teeth and faces bloated from too much drink. By and large, they also had a penchant for dousing cologne over their bodies to disguise their less than pleasant odors.

Kingston was blessed with all of his own teeth and hair and did not stink. He could carry on an intelligent conversation. That put him considerably ahead of other men, even without his handsome mien. He might be illegitimate and without roots, but that had never impeded the ladies from admiring him. It was simple self-awareness and not arrogance. A bastard without title or inheritance had to know his strengths.

The drab middle Miss Langley was immune apparently. Or perhaps she was simply so very enamored of her young man.

Soon they all filed into the dining room. At least he was one step closer to being able to retire to his chamber for the night.

The duchess seated him beside Warrington, who sat at the head of the table. Unfortunate, that, as it put him between the duke and the Pembrokes.

The good country gentleman and his wife wanted nothing more than the duke's attention and they spent the majority of the meal talking *over* Kingston in an attempt to gain it.

The lively Miss Langley eyed him speculatively as she tore bits off her bread. "I am most interested to learn all about you, Mr. Kingston . . . Nathaniel's mystery brother."

"Ah, actually I am his stepbrother," Warrington corrected in the midst of Mr. Pembroke's dialogue about his recent purchase—a curricle he was eager to race.

"Do you have any other relations hidden

away?" the youngest Miss Langley pressed, eyeing him intently even as she directed the question to her brother-in-law.

"Nora, you pry," the middle Langley sister murmured, reaching for her glass. She took a long silent sip, the perfect representation of modest and respectable womanhood.

It had been the first words he had heard from her since they sat down to dine.

Nora rolled her eyes, clearly unaffected by her sister's rebuke as she reached for her glass. "Asking after my brother-in-law's family? I hardly consider that prying, Charlotte."

Charlotte. That was her name. A very proper English name for a proper English miss. He could throw a rock and hit a Charlotte in this country. They abounded like tea and biscuits throughout the kingdom.

"It's not prying," he agreed. His gaze locked on the very commonly named Charlotte where she sat, surmising she was every bit as common as her name, unfortunately.

She ducked her pretty blue eyes, staring in fascination at her plate, her chin practically buried in the linen of her matronly fichu.

She was a fair maid with fair eyes just like any other fair maid he spied on Bond Street or standing in the shadow of her mama at the rail station. England was rife with them. All very drab creatures. He'd never spoken to any of them, and he'd never felt the lack.

Apparently he would not have a verbal exchange with this one either.

She ignored him, treating him as though he had not spoken.

"Have you met our parents yet? The Earl and Countess of Norfolk," Kingston asked with forced levity to the table at large, but mostly to the duchess.

"We have not had that pleasure," Warrington's wife answered genially.

"I should love to meet the earl and countess," Mrs. Pembroke eagerly chimed in, her gaze flitting back and forth between Kingston and Warrington.

"Hear, hear! We should very much enjoy that," her husband seconded, saluting the table's occupants with his umpteenth glass of whisky. "One can never have too many friends of influence and with proper pedigree, I always say!"

"I've an idea! Perhaps we should invite them to the wedding." Mrs. Pembroke looked to the duke searchingly, beseechingly, as though it were his decision and not the pair who was in fact getting married and were seated at this very table.

Kingston turned his attention to the happy couple, curious at their reactions.

The Pembroke lad was using his bread to sop

up all the juices on his plate, not even appearing aware of the conversation.

Charlotte Langley reached a trembling hand for her glass again, drinking deeply, her eyes briefly looking up at her future mother-in-law before darting back down to the contents of her cup as though that was more interesting than the discussion of her upcoming nuptials. That shaking hand was telling, indicating that she was not perhaps as unaffected as Kingston would have thought. Curious, indeed. He wondered what was truly transpiring behind those cool blue eyes of hers.

"Er, I thought the guest list was already decided weeks ago," the Duchess of Warrington interjected, speaking when her sister clearly did not seem capable.

Mrs. Pembroke waved a hand. "We can always make changes. Where shall I direct the invitation?"

The young duchess looked across the table to her sister and young Mr. Pembroke. "What would you prefer, Charlotte? William?" she asked, her voice tinged with hope and a dose of encouragement, as though she willed them each to put an end to the matter of the earl and countess being invited.

The lad blinked at being addressed, wiping

the back of his hand and catching the buttery dribble that ran down his chin. "Beggin' your pardon?"

"Oh, William cares not at all about the wedding," his mother insisted with another wave. "Well, aside from the menu, of course. He might be thin as a rail but he had a hand in organizing the menu. Do you care for custard tartlets? You can thank him if you do, for he's requested copious amounts."

Kingston watched as the lad cleaned his plate as if he were a soldier heading into war and this might be the last meal of his life.

"Charlotte did not want a large affair, as I recall," young Nora contributed, having no difficulty using her voice.

"Charlotte?" Mrs. Pembroke echoed, her expression one of distaste as she looked at her soon-to-be daughter-in-law as though she had forgotten her existence. "I was not aware you had an opinion on such matters, my dear." The "my dear" felt like an insult and not the gentle kindness the words would indicate. Indeed, the statement was rife with accusation and challenge. The older woman glared at the young woman, daring her to contradict her.

Everyone, in fact, looked to Miss Charlotte Langley, awaiting her response.

Kingston was no different.

He stared, too, vastly interested, for some reason willing the chit to find her backbone and address the old dragon with some mettle and remind her that it was *her* wedding and she would say who was and was not to be invited.

Come on, lass. Find your tongue.

The young woman cleared her throat and spoke meekly. "I am certain whatever you decide is acceptable, Mrs. Pembroke."

Shaking his head, Kingston looked away, disappointed, though he wasn't certain why. He did not know the chit. She was Warrington's responsibility.

Kingston would be gone tomorrow and not think again of the lass. She'd wed and lose herself in marriage to a gluttonous bore and an overbearing mother-in-law.

Mild-mannered and weak-willed chits were aplenty. What was one more? He should not feel one way or another at her existence.

He should not feel this compulsion to shake her until she came to her senses and asserted herself as any self-respecting person ought to do.

If she wanted to be a doormat that was her concern.

"That's settled then," Mrs. Pembroke said with flourish. "You shall invite your parents, Your Grace."

Nora Langley muttered into her soup bowl.

Even the duchess looked displeased, although she managed to say, "Splendid."

Warrington inhaled and exhaled out of his nostrils.

Kingston knew there was nothing *splendid* about it and that was precisely what Warrington was thinking, too. Additionally, his father and stepmother were vain, shallow hedonists. They would enjoy nothing *less* than a country wedding.

Warrington would be in misery every moment of their visit.

One thing was for certain. Kingston would be long departed from this place before the wedding *or* the arrival of his father or stepmother.

After all, there was only so much wretchedness a person could endure.

Chapter 4

*S*omething was not right.

All throughout dinner the sensation, the aching discomfort, only grew.

Following dinner, Charlotte excused herself and managed to make it to her bedchamber, where she hastily shed her clothes as though they burned her skin and climbed into bed.

It was bad. Terrible. The queasiness was unlike any other time.

The symptoms were different. More . . . pronounced.

She curled into a ball and dragged the pillow between her legs, hugging it tightly. Usually she endured the twinges of pain until they passed.

The slight cramping that was improved by hot-water bottles and Nora's tonic. She would keep to bed for twelve hours until it passed.

This was *not* like that.

This did not feel in any way endurable.

She was vaguely aware of her bedchamber door opening and closing and footsteps approaching her bed.

She inhaled and exhaled in slow, even drags of air, her fingers digging into the soft linen pillowcase.

Her sisters' voices carried to her ears. Even in her current condition, there was no mistaking the agitation in Marian's voice floating above her.

"What did you do, Nora? She does not look right at all."

"It was simply a draught, Marian. A cordial of various herbs. Nothing I haven't prepared before . . . just not in that precise arrangement. And I might have added a few new ingredients. You know I'm always trying to improve my tonics." Nora waved a hand weakly in Charlotte's general direction.

Her words penetrated the dull fog of her brain. Charlotte lifted her head from the bed and focused on her sisters. "She's poisoned me!" she managed to spit out between her teeth, pushing the pillow harder, deeper between her thighs, as though that might quench the growing ache there.

"Oh, don't be so melodramatic." Nora tsked. "I gave you nothing dangerous and the doses were all well within reason."

The throbbing in her abdomen gave a deep tug, almost seeming to belie her sister's words. Charlotte curled up tighter and moaned.

"Nora!" Marian said in sharp reprimand, waving to Charlotte on the bed. "Look at her!"

"She's not dying," Nora insisted, but there was a wobble of uncertainty in her voice that Charlotte did not miss even in her agitated state. "It was merely a remedy to help relieve her women's pains."

"I *am* dying!" Charlotte insisted as she pressed the pillow ever deeper between her legs.

Marian frowned down at her. "Well, let's make some tea for her. Papa always insisted on the importance of fluids to help flush the sickness through one's body."

Nora nodded and left the room. Marian sank down on the bed beside her and pressed a hand to her forehead. "Oh, dear. You are a bit warm."

Charlotte whimpered and looked up at her sister. "Marian . . . this is wretched."

"I know, dear. Just close your eyes. Sleep is healing. I'm sure you will wake refreshed in the morning."

Charlotte managed a weak nod.

Marian was right, of course. She usually was.

Please, please, let her be correct.

She would sleep. Yes. And when she woke up in the morning she would feel refreshed.

She would feel as though this had all been a bad dream.

CHARLOTTE WOKE ALONE to a silent bedchamber.

Logs smoldered in her fireplace, emitting a low glow, saving her from complete darkness.

Beside her bed, her long-cold tea sat. Her sisters had forced a cup down her throat and she had soon managed to fall asleep after that. The hour was late. An inky darkness swelled between the crack of her damask drapes. It was the kind of darkness that only existed in the quietest, loneliest hours of night. Her sisters had clearly gone to their own beds.

Now Charlotte was awake. Achingly and miserably awake. Sleep could no longer shield her. It could not suppress the wild fury that roared within her, singeing her blood.

When she had fallen asleep before, her body hurt.

At least she had thought her body hurt.

Now she knew true misery.

Her body was afire.

Usually her discomfort was centered in her

abdomen, low in her belly, but this time it was different. Vastly different. Terrifyingly different.

All of her hurt. Every fiber and pore. Her body was a plucked and vibrating string, humming out her pain.

She couldn't make sense of it.

The only thing different this time around was the tonic Nora had given her. It had tasted different, and Nora admitted it was different.

Maybe she truly was dying. She turned her face into her pillow and released a muffled sob as her stomach twisted.

Nora.

She was responsible for this. She could fix it. She had to fix it. Otherwise, Charlotte would die. She felt certain of that. Nora was the only one who could help. *Dear God.* She had to *stop* it.

She could not tolerate another moment of this.

She swung her legs over the edge of the bed and sucked in a deep breath. It didn't help. If anything, it made the burn worse.

She knew she should make the effort to reach her dressing robe across the room where it draped over the settee, but she couldn't be bothered. The struggle to reach the bedchamber door was great enough. Besides. It was late. The entire household was asleep. She would not be bumping into anyone in the corridor who might see her attired in her nightgown.

She managed to stagger from her room without collapsing. With one hand pressed against the wall of the corridor, she dragged herself down the hall toward her sister's room. Each step was an act of labor. The hardest thing she had ever done. *Walking* had become a challenge.

Good heavens, she was in trouble.

All the more reason to reach Nora's room.

She pressed on.

Her palm skimmed the wood paneling as she advanced, the cool texture under her skin doing nothing to ease her full-body burn. There was no way she could move any faster. Her legs felt leaden. The fever was too great . . . the throbbing in her stomach clawing now. She choked back an undignified sob.

"Are you unwell?"

The deep masculine voice shot through her like a bolt of lightning.

She jerked with a whimper, flinging her body against the wall, arms wide at her sides in a gesture of surrender.

She froze, pressing against the paneling as though she could somehow meld herself into the wood where she would be protected.

Her gaze found the owner of that voice. *No. Not him.*

That dreadful man from dinner. Nathaniel's stepbrother.

His expression at dinner had alternated between boredom and contempt. She'd felt his judgment keenly. He hadn't been impressed with her. With any of them. Clearly they did not meet his sophisticated tastes. She was relieved when, at the end of dinner, he had announced he would be leaving the next morning.

Now his expression was one of mild concern. She'd prefer he look bored again. Right now he looked far too interested in her. She did not want his interest. She wanted him gone.

Especially considering her physical state.

For some reason the throbbing between her legs tightened and twisted as he approached, closing in on her.

She shook her head. *No. Go away.*

The closer he drew, the greater the agony. She bit her lip until she felt the wash of blood against her teeth—and still that pain was nothing compared to her body's torment.

Her condition seemed to be worsening the closer he drew to her. She had to get away.

She held out a hand in an attempt to ward him off—and that was its own form of anguish because she had the awful and completely foreign impulse to grab him, pull him in, bring him closer.

It was horrifying, but so was the completely out-of-control way she felt.

Her body was in rebellion—its own master. Rejecting her thoughts . . . her will, her commands . . . willing her to do terrible things, impulses she had never even known existed.

Like touch a man. Burrow her nose in his neck and breathe him in.

Taste him.

He stopped in front of her, his gaze fixing on the hand she held out to stop him and then flitting back to her face.

She knew. Deeply. On a primordial level. He could not touch her. She would not survive that.

"You don't look . . . well, Miss Langley."

Oh, she was not well. She was in hell. It was an unladylike thought, but she could feel no shame or regret for it because it was the truth.

She pressed herself harder into the wall, twisting in on herself to resist the urge to arch her spine and thrust out her chest.

She wanted to feel him even there. Against her breasts.

How could this be?

This had to be hell. All the fiery descriptors she heard from the pulpit every Sunday could only be this.

He took another step closer, and she slapped her hand on the air. "Not another step closer," she warned weakly.

His eyes widened—whether at the command or the hoarse quality of her voice, she did not know. Whatever the case, he ignored her. "Come. Let me assist you. You do not look well. Would you like me to fetch your sister?"

He dared to take hold of her elbow to guide her from where she plastered herself to the wall. It was the gentlemanly thing to do. He could not know the torment he inflicted on her with that circumspect touch.

She hissed at the weight of that hand on her arm, at the stinging heat of him singeing her through the barriers of their clothing. It was only the most prudent of touches, but it felt more. Much more. Intimate and penetrating. A breach to her person.

He lifted his hand from her arm at her reaction. "Did I hurt you?"

She shook her head wildly and turned back for her room—where she could die alone and in peace, without a too-handsome, sophisticated gentleman watching her like she was some manner of bug beneath a magnifying glass.

"Miss Langley?" he called after her.

"Leave . . . me . . . alone," she ground out

between tightly clenched teeth. She feared unclenching them would loose the scream she kept tucked inside.

She staggered away, clawing at the wall and doors for support as she passed. It was too hard, and her room loomed so far away. She couldn't do it. She couldn't reach it.

"Miss Langley," he tried again.

His hand brushed her arm and she moaned as though he'd taken a hot poker to her. No. Not a hot poker. A poker would hurt.

This was pleasure. So profound and intense that it made her lose her mind.

He pulled back his hand and held it aloft, fingers spread wide as though showing her he was unarmed.

She bumped into a door latch. A quick glance down confirmed it was the library. There was a large sofa in there. Perfect. She could go die on that sofa just as easily as her own bed.

She struggled with the latch. Yes, struggled. No longer would she take such simple things for granted. Assuming she lived, of course.

"Miss Langley?"

Ugh. He was still here? "Go 'way," she tossed over her shoulder.

"Have you been imbibing?"

Imbibing? Indeed she had. Only not spirits. She had been imbibing one of her sister's fool remedies.

Never again. She was finished taking anything Nora gave her. Again, assuming she *survived*, she would never again take one of her sister's tonics. Clearly Papa had been too trusting in her proficiency.

Success! She finally managed to turn the latch and passed into the room, but for some reason she tripped over her own feet. Or perhaps her legs simply gave out. She didn't know, but she landed hard on the Aubusson rug with a moan. She rolled onto her side and curled into a ball.

It appeared to be her preferred position.

Her gaze fastened on the man towering over her. He wore an expression of alarm—and then he was bending over her, scooping her up in his arms with nary a grunt. This evidence of his power triggered a deep tug between her legs.

"I have you," he murmured, and the husk of his breath near her ear shot sensation straight to her groin. She moaned, squeezing her thighs together, attempting to assuage the throbbing ache.

No!

She shook her head even as she couldn't resist curling into the delicious hardness of his body. Twisting at the waist, she pushed her breasts into the firm wall of his chest, instinctively seeking the comforting solidness, enjoying the pressure against breasts that felt achy and heavy. Strange, that. Her bosom was small and never much cause for notice. Now, though, the twin mounds were as sensitive as the rest of her and felt as heavy as melons. Weighty, swollen melons.

His arm felt so hard and strong under her thighs and she wiggled against its sinewy length as she wrapped her arms around his shoulders, indulging the very impulse she'd been denying herself. She burrowed her nose into his neck with a force that sent him stumbling. He stopped when he hit the book-lined walls.

"What—" he stammered, "are you—"

She growled, tightening her arms around his shoulders and nuzzling deeper into the crook of his neck, breathing him in. He smelled *so* good.

His hand at her back tightened, fisting into the fabric of her nightgown. "What are you . . ."

Her tongue darted out, tasting him.

All of him froze. Air hissed out from between his lips.

That didn't stop her, however.

Her outrageous behavior didn't even bother her. There were stronger things at play right now. Greater forces. Gale-wind forces she could not resist.

She tasted more of him, licking, then closing her lips and sucking, pressing against him, seeking pressure.

Her throbbing body needed the weight of him, against her, over her, *in* her.

She didn't understand it, but she knew. Intuitively, she knew.

Rubbing against him made it both better and worse. Worse because the more she rubbed, the more pressure she needed. She couldn't stop.

It wasn't enough.

She twisted and writhed against him. He let go of her legs. She slid down his length with a sigh. *Better.* All of her could feel him now. His bigger, taller body was aligned with hers.

She pinned him in place, moving and grinding against him wildly, her hands clawing at him. He wasn't wearing his jacket. Only his waistcoat. She growled in displeasure and seized it in both hands, ripping it open, sending buttons flying.

He cursed, but she kept moving, a fury of motion, her hands sliding under the fine lawn of his shirt so that she could feel his skin.

"Bloody hell. You're in heat, woman."

The words didn't give her pause.

Nothing did.

Nothing could.

She was all frenzied motion. He slid to the floor and she went with him, straddling his lap.

Ahhhh. Yes. This.

She wrestled her nightgown up to her hips until her bare sex was sitting atop his crotch. His manhood bulged beneath the fabric of his trousers.

"Christ," he gasped, his eyes wide on her. "You're wet."

She didn't know what that meant.

She only knew that her womanhood felt swollen, and she might perish if she didn't answer the pulling throb.

She flattened a hand against the edge of a bookshelf near his ear and pushed herself down on his hardness with a strangled sob. *Yes.* That helped.

She moved more, grinding against him until she was riding that bulging swell.

Clumsily. Without skill, but hard and fast and with the single-minded purpose of alleviating the hurt. Feeding the ache. Although it was a good ache now. A sweet pain. A beautiful torment. She understood that now. She knew how to satisfy it, and it was by doing this.

He cursed again, watching her in awe. His hands settled on her hips and she covered them with her own hands, forcing him to squeeze her through the nuisance folds of her nightgown.

Her body didn't need gentle. It needed satisfaction, and *gentle* wouldn't achieve that.

"What are *you*?" he muttered in an awe-tinged voice.

She arched, pressing her breasts into his chest, loathing the barrier of clothing between them. Her skin burned and demanded skin-to-skin contact. The graze of material on her breasts aggravated, chafed and irritated her, taunting and stinging her flesh.

She let go of his hands and went for the wide neckline of her nightgown, wrenching the fabric low so that her breasts popped free.

His eyes glowed with a feral light as they feasted on her, gazing at her like she was a five-course meal and he a starving man.

He groaned as her hands molded to the small mounds, squeezing and fondling as she worked her hips over him. She found her nipples, noticing with a sharp gasp that the distended tips were tender. She seized them and twisted the tender peaks. A rush of moisture sprang between her legs directly where she most pulsed and she released a keening cry.

His hand flew to her mouth, his long fingers covering her lips. "Shh." His gaze darted for the library door.

Even the hard hand on her mouth excited her.

She bucked and rocked on his bulging crotch, reveling in the friction. The harder and faster she moved against him, the greater the ache grew, pulsing, clamoring, demanding relief.

A full-body tremble started to overtake her.

"That's it." He nodded once, his voice tight, as strained as his expression. "You're close, sweet girl. Take what you need."

His words were like their own caress—touching something hidden deep inside her.

She let go then, screaming into his palm, the sound muffled as she shuddered over him, all the coiling tightness in her body snapping.

She slowed, stilling over him, her scream dying against his hand.

He eased his hand from her mouth, his fingers trailing down her throat in a fiery burn.

Their eyes were on perfect level with each other, and even in the shadows she could see the gold flecks in his brown eyes, peering so deeply at her. The astonishment was still there—as it had been ever since she first started climbing all over him.

Oh, no! What had she done?

To the duke's stepbrother, no less!

She was betrothed to be married . . . and she'd just attacked a strange man as though she were an animal in heat, just as he had claimed.

Heat swamped her, but this time it was shame and not the ache of desire. Bone-deep shame.

She'd never kissed a man—not even Billy—but she had just mounted this man and rode him like a well-seasoned female. *Goodness!* Her breasts! Her hands shot to her gaping neckline, tugging it back up over her bared and tender breasts.

He glanced down and then looked away, as though he, too, were embarrassed. And that only made her feel more shamed.

"My a-apologies," she muttered, clambering off him in horror, lifting her hands away so as not to touch him again. Her gaze dropped to his crotch and she froze, a fresh wave of mortification rippling through her as she saw the evidence of their tryst in the form of a wet spot directly over his crotch.

It was all too awful. A living nightmare. No. Worse than a nightmare. She'd lacked the knowledge or experience to even dream up such a thing. She had no idea the pleasure that could be had between a woman and a man in such a way. That it could be so profound. That it could shatter her so completely.

Such wicked abandon had only just now been revealed to her.

Naturally Billy was too much of a gentleman to attempt anything improper. And up until tonight she had been too virtuous to engage in licentious activities.

He followed her gaze, looking down at himself where she'd left her mark on him.

She didn't wait for him to look back at her face. Hopefully she would be gone before she had to endure that.

She shot to her feet, smoothing her nightgown down her shaking legs and tossing back the loose strands from her face. Her plait had come loose and the long strands were a wild nimbus about her.

Her body hummed pleasantly. A dull throb remained, but nothing like before. Nothing like when she had attacked him, mounted him and worked herself to a shuddering climax.

The torment had subsided and the pulling, persistent ache had fled. Vanishing like smoke. There was that at least.

She exhaled, glad for that relief. She was not dead after all.

She only wished she was dead as she felt his gaze pinned tightly on her.

He pushed up to his feet, drawing attention to the fact that he stood several inches taller than Charlotte, and she wasn't a short female. She was the tallest of her sisters. They might have more meat on their bones and flattering curves (never could they claim to possess a small bosom), but she stood several inches over both of them. In fact, she stood several inches over most of the men in her acquaintance.

But not him.

This man was big. She herself had felt just how strong he was when she'd used his sinewy body to satisfy her needs. Even straddling him, riding him, swept away in her own desires, she'd been acutely aware of the size and breadth of him beneath her.

What had come over her? She could not fathom it.

The day had started out as any other. When she'd felt the warning twinges of her menses coming, she had taken Nora's tonic—like she had done dozens of times.

Except the tonic was not the same one she had taken dozens of times.

She twisted her fingers together until they felt numb, bloodless. "I . . . um. I don't know what came over me. Please don't speak of it to anyone."

His expression hardened then. "It's not my custom to carry tales of my dalliances."

Dalliance.

It seemed such a small word. Insignificant. Paltry. It certainly did not convey the magnitude of what just transpired—the *betrayal* she had just perpetrated against her betrothed.

She nodded jerkily, blinking against her stinging eyes. She would not cry. *She would not cry.*

The hardness eased somewhat from his features as he considered her. "Are you . . . well?"

No. Clearly, she was not well.

She inhaled a deep, fortifying breath. Only moments ago she had thought she was dying. Now she was alive. She would cling to that.

Not dead was good. Not dead was everything. Even if she had behaved abominably.

No. She had not done anything wrong. It was all Nora's doing. She could not fault herself. She had been under duress. The tonic, the agony had compelled her to act so wantonly.

It was the tonic. It was not Charlotte.

And it would never happen again.

"Th-thank you for your discretion." Turning then, she fled before she could say or do anything more damaging.

It was difficult to imagine what she might do to surpass her actions of this night, but she did not trust herself. She did not know if she was free of Nora's elixir. She would take nothing for granted.

She hastened to her bedchamber and flung herself down on her bed, and there, in the privacy of her room, with her face buried in the counterpane, she wept.

Her body still hummed with the aftermath of her release.

She sniffed back her tears, dashing them off her cheeks with the back of her hand.

Unbidden, her hand crept down her body to press between her legs. The ache was still there, a dull, pulsing throb now. It didn't feel like clamoring death anymore, but it was still there. Hopefully it would soon fade.

She supposed she should be grateful that Kingston had not taken advantage of her vulnerability and ravished her. In her condition, she would not have protested. No, it had been the opposite. *She* had ravished *him*. He had permitted her advances but made none of his own, simply let her use him for her own titillation.

Charlotte stared into the darkness, wondering what her blasted sister had put into that wretched tonic this time around.

Nora had admitted to experimenting with it. In her quest to make it better, a more effective form of pain alleviation, she had toyed with it. Blast the girl! She should have left well enough alone. She'd meddled with the usual cordial and created a tonic that had turned Charlotte into some feral creature.

She fell back in bed, half determined to go wrench that sister of hers from her bed by the hair. That would give her maybe *some* satisfaction.

Tomorrow would be soon enough to have words with her—and any necessary hair-pulling. Right now she didn't want to brave the corridor again. Not after the last time. Even if her body seemed to be under her control again, she would keep to her chamber and her own bed until morning.

No one would get seduced that way.

Chapter 5

*I*t was at least half an hour before Kingston found the energy to make his way back to his room. It took him that long to gather his thoughts and composure. That long to even find the will to make his legs function.

He had lingered in the library, staring at the cracked door through which Miss Charlotte Langley had fled.

Fled was no exaggeration. The lass had run from the library after stammering out an apology. An *apology*?

Kingston could make no sense of it.

What had just happened?

The girl had attacked him. That, too, was not an exaggeration. One moment he had been helping her to her feet and the next thing he knew she was straddling him and riding him like a Tattersalls racehorse. She took her pleasure without requiring anything from him—well, aside of his body. His fully clothed body. He could not recall a time in his life when a woman had ever so greedily used him so that she could achieve her own release.

Most surprising of all, perhaps? He had not minded one bit.

That was some shock. He'd been abstinent for over a year and was just fine with his status. He was not at all determined to end his streak of self-denial.

No female had tempted him to steer off his course. He could scarcely even remember the last woman to share his bed. He didn't miss it. He didn't miss women.

At least he'd thought that was the case.

Clearly a certain female had changed his position on the matter.

The female he'd encountered in the corridor hardly resembled his dinner companion from earlier. The Miss Charlotte Langley who sat across from him at the dinner table had not piqued his interest—at least not in a carnal fashion. She'd hardly spoken at all, and when she had opened her mouth to talk he'd almost fallen asleep in his soup from boredom. He'd thought her insipid. There was no hint of passion under her starchy veneer.

How wrong he had been.

Upon returning to his chamber, he undressed himself, pausing to admire the damage she'd done to his waistcoat. That was the last he'd see of those buttons.

She was a bewildering creature, without a doubt.

He stretched his length out in bed, tucking his arm behind his head. He doubted sleep would come any time soon. His thoughts were alive with her . . . as was his cock. He reached down to adjust himself. It did no good. He was still hard. For her. For a chit he'd dismissed as dull only hours ago.

Yes, she might bewilder him, but he knew one thing.

He was *not* leaving tomorrow.

CHARLOTTE DID NOT know how long she slept. She woke suddenly, lurching upright, her body feverishly hot. The bedchamber was still dark. She slid from her bed and padded barefoot to the window. Parting the drapes, she observed it was still dark outside, but there was a faint purpling to the air. Dawn was close.

Her belly twisted and she gasped, clutching the window frame for support.

Oh, no! Not again.

The fiery arousal was back. Or perhaps it had never fully gone away. Perhaps her encounter with Kingston had granted her only a reprieve from it. That shattering release hadn't cured her of anything . . . it had merely appeased the beast for a time, and the beast had returned.

Moaning, she paced the length of her room, but it did nothing to help. The throbbing was so intense. The heat made her want to rip off her clothes . . . dive into a frigid pool of water.

The pond.

No one was awake yet. She could slip from the house without anyone noticing. She quickly undressed and delved into the back of her wardrobe for one of her simple dresses. One of the plain frocks she owned before she'd moved into the duke's house following her sister's marriage— before she was granted a new wardrobe.

Dressed humbly, feeling more herself in that regard (if not in the terrible arousal twisting like a serpent through her), she fled the house, departing via the back servants' stairs. Thankfully, undetected. She had no wish to come face-to-face with anyone, yet again, in her present condition.

She rounded the house and cut away from the

pebbled drive, crossing the stretching slope of grass until she entered the copse of woods surrounding her brother-in-law's estate. Her legs churned beneath her skirts. The exertion only exacerbated her condition—made her blood burn beneath her skin.

The air was murky but not impenetrable to the naked eye. She knew every bit of Brambledon and the surrounding area. She could find her way even if it was pitch-black at night.

She moved just short of a run. Her feet led her to the narrow path that routed directly to her pond.

Very well. She knew it wasn't *her* pond. None of this belonged to her. It was Nathaniel's and now her sister's. She didn't have anything. Not until she married.

The soft burble of water reached her ears moments before she broke out into a small clearing. She had to slow down and carefully mind her steps down the rather steep decline that led to the banks of the pond. She didn't need to break her neck. That would cast a definite pall over the strange events of this day.

The deep pool of water was the result of where two streams converged. She was well acquainted with the pond. With the cool sensation of crisp water on her skin, with the soft moss under her feet, with the smooth shape of time-eroded stones beneath the twin waterfalls.

Her pulse pounded in her ears, matching the deep, pulling throb between her legs.

What if it never went away? What if her sister had poisoned her for all time?

She shook her head. *No.* It could not be. It simply needed time to run its course. Like any fever. It couldn't last forever.

The glass-like surface beckoned. Despite her sense of urgency, she forced herself to pause and glance around, peering into the dark shadows. Not that anyone would be here at this hour.

Satisfied and reassured with that reminder, she disrobed, her movements hasty as she removed her dress and tossed it over a nearby bush. She slid off her stockings and shoes and yanked her chemise over her head.

She sighed in relief once she was free of her garments. Her heated and too-tight skin already felt better.

Wearing nothing at all, she charged ahead on her bare feet. The sharp prick of stones and pebbles beneath the soles of her feet felt actually good—a welcome distraction from the primal urges engulfing her body.

She didn't ease into the water hesitantly. She rushed in to her waist and then plunged the rest of the way in until she was submerged up to her shoulders.

With her hair coiled and pinned atop her head,

the cool water lapped deliciously at her neck and shoulders, helping to relieve the fires.

And yet it did not bank them entirely.

The throb was still there between her legs. Her breasts were heavy and tingling as she stretched her arms and sliced through the water, feeling as free as a mermaid. At least she always imagined a mermaid would feel free. No societal pressures or expectations.

It was scandalous, she supposed. Swimming naked in the great out of doors.

No one would ever guess she was capable of such behavior. Not even her sisters. They would never say so, but she knew they thought her boring and predictable.

This was her secret. Something that was hers alone. In addition to what she'd done with Kingston earlier.

She winced. He was departing today. At least there was that. She would not have to worry about confronting him any time soon.

Shaking her head, she turned and floated on her back, letting her arms fan out at her sides in rhythmic strokes. Closing her eyes, she ignored the pulling ache in her body and tried to melt and relax into the gentle current.

Water lapped at her sides, splashing over her bare breasts. Air flowed over her chest, pleasantly cooling all her wet skin.

A bird chirped in the distance, signaling the impending dawn, and she knew she'd have to leave soon and make her way home. She couldn't risk lingering much longer.

She was no daring heroine, unfortunately. *No.* Not unfortunately.

Her sisters were bold heroines. Outspoken and adventurous. She had never aspired to that. As much as she admired them, she did not envy them. What they had . . . what they *were* . . . it was not in her.

Only here, alone, reveling in the privacy of this pond, she felt decadent and free. For once she felt like a bold heroine.

But it would have to end.

It was Sunday. They had church to attend. Unless she begged off because of illness, she would be expected to go. Billy and his family would be there. She had promised to take afternoon tea with them.

She must make an appearance with a smile on her face, all misdeeds put firmly behind her.

KINGSTON STARED WIDE-EYED into the darkness, one arm tossed over his brow, his breathing still much too labored for a man who should be easing into slumber. But there was no ease. There'd be no slumber.

Not this night.

Of course not. After that encounter? After Charlotte Langley had shattered him so thoroughly? How could he sleep?

He was as awake and alert as when he first returned to his chamber a few hours ago. Sleep was impossible. His pulse thrummed hard and fast at his neck.

He stilled at the sound of movements outside his door.

Footsteps.

He assumed the tread belonged to Charlotte Langley.

Strange as it was, he felt acutely attuned to her. His nostrils flared and his pores contracted as though sensing her just beyond the door.

Impossible, he knew, but she had already proved herself to be someone who kept late hours. And did outrageous things in those late hours.

It had to be Charlotte. Who else could be up at this hour in the family wing of the house? This wing of the house boasted the most luxurious chambers and was only for the privileged few— the duke and his wife and the Langley sisters. The list was short. He did not expect to find himself included on it. It certainly was not his stepbrother's doing. If it had been up to Warrington, he would likely be sleeping in the barn with all the animals. No, the lovely Duchess of Warrington had had her hand in this. Her generous hospitality had seen to this arrangement.

Her tread faded away. She was moving quickly.

He could not stay put a moment longer.

Climbing from his bed, he dressed quickly, determined to follow her and see what mischief she was up to now.

He told himself he was concerned.

She had been distraught when she left him earlier. There'd been something in her eyes. A wild-eyed glazed look that seemed to go beyond the passion of their liaison. He couldn't entirely credit it, but he could still see it clearly in his mind. It was troubling.

As he emerged out into the hall, the distant squeak of hinges below alerted him that she had moved downstairs. He took himself below, marching down the corridor and bypassing the kitchens until he reached the back servants' door.

He opened and closed the door carefully, mindful of the noisy hinges. When he stepped outside, he spotted a flash of her pale dress in the distance against the murky air, disappearing into the tree line.

Where was she going?

He followed, sticking to the narrow path that led through a thick copse to a pond. He stepped out on the bank warily, glancing around. He didn't see her.

The burbling little body of water was secluded. Even in the predawn darkness, it was covered by the shade of several large oak trees, blocking out most of the moonlight.

Was she meeting someone? Her betrothed? Someone else?

An uncomfortable sensation spread through him, almost as though a great weight was pushing down on him. He rubbed at the center of his chest, hoping that might alleviate the strange discomfort. It did no good.

He knew so little of her. Other than that she felt ripe and yielding in his hands and moved like the sweetest seductress.

Dropping his hand, he turned to go, telling himself that whatever she was up to was of no matter to him. Charlotte Langley was not his mystery to solve.

The sound of water splashing stopped him. Turning, he looked back out at the water and spotted her.

The air trapped in his chest.

She floated on her back, those teacup breasts she had displayed for him so eagerly earlier now perched and bobbing above the water as she glided, silent as a raft.

She swam in the nude? The chit lacked all decorum . . . all modesty.

And he'd never been so intrigued in his life.

His concern ebbed at the sight of her. She looked so peaceful, floating with her eyes shut. Not at all distraught.

He cleared his throat to gain her attention, but she did nothing that indicated she was aware of him. She didn't hear him with her ears underwater apparently.

He considered her for a moment, glancing around at the quiet woods surrounding them. Looking back at her, a small smile curled his lips. Drifting through the water like a woodland sprite in the softly purpling air, she seemed more magical than real.

This whole night felt unreal to him.

Perhaps it was all a bit of fantasy. The memory of her most sensual assault, her body riding him in hungry vigor . . . Perhaps it was all imaginary, an illusory whim invented within the secret longings of his mind.

A dream.

A dream where anything could happen. Where impulses could be followed with no fear and no consequence.

Certainly none of the wanton images of her matched up with his memory of the girl from the tediously dull dinner party.

She'd come across as so very boring. A dull, vapid creature alongside her dull, vapid betrothed. He'd dismissed her as one would the wallpaper of a room. Something that existed . . . something one was consciously aware of but could not be counted upon to recount in any degree of detail later.

Except now he could not forget her. Not the feel of her. Not the sight of her.

Especially not *this* sight of her.

His skin felt overheated again. The water beckoned, tempting him—almost as much as she tempted him.

Of course, he wouldn't dare. Despite their earlier intimacy, he would not be so bold as to join her in the pond. Not without express invitation. To do so felt vaguely predatory . . . diving into a pond occupied by an unsuspecting *naked* female. It was enough for him to watch her, so vulnerable and appealing and . . . remarkable. She was remarkable and she astounded him.

He'd been wrong about her, and watching her now only reinforced that. She had sparked his interest. His heretofore dormant interest, and he could not look away.

He could not ignore such a turn of circumstances.

She could be the answer to his return to self.

Hope stirred in his chest. He wanted that. He wanted to feel less confused . . . less lost. He wanted to be his old self again—living in carelessness and freedom with no taste of sorrow in his mouth. With no grief in his heart.

He shook his head. It had been a long time since he'd bedded a female.

Clearly too long for one slip of a girl to affect him thusly, even if she was enticingly wet at present and without garments. He was no green lad. He'd seen plenty of naked women before. The sight did not typically undo him. Clearly *this* naked woman was singular in that aspect. *Ah, bloody hell.*

Of all the women for whom he should experience this awakening . . . it had to be a kinswoman to Warrington. And she was betrothed, no less.

She was encroaching closer to the bank, still unaware of him, still on her back, still floating on the surface of the water with her small pert breasts proudly on display.

His mouth dried.

Evidently his tastes had changed and he was only just now becoming acquainted with that fact. From now on, he would know.

From now on, he would know he preferred his women repressed, seething cauldrons of desire ready to boil over onto him. Slender wispy females who looked—*deceptively*—as though they would run at the first kiss.

The purple air softened to a pale gray. He

lifted his face to smell the clean scent of impending day. Dawn would be here soon. People would be about their day. Perhaps not here in this secluded glen, but on the estate. It was time to find his voice and alert her to his presence.

He lightly cleared his throat, hoping this time she heard him. "I had no idea this pond was frequented by mermaids."

Thankfully, his voice escaped in an even tone, reflecting none of the desire shuddering through him.

Chapter 6

Apparently she heard him. She flailed, dunking herself underwater.

Kingston watched as she came up sputtering, water splashing all around her, her mermaid hair sluicing over her face, shoulders and chest, clinging like coils of golden kelp.

"What are you doing here?" She slicked her hair back from her face to gaze at him, blinking spiky wet eyelashes as though she could not quite believe her eyes.

He scanned her water-speckled face, the compulsion to stride directly into the water and lick the droplets from her skin hard-fought. She looked younger, her delicate features fragile as she gazed at him in astonishment.

Licking the water from her face would not be the thing to do right now. Most definitely not.

Splotches of red marked her face. She appeared close to apoplexy.

"I heard you leave the house," he explained.

"So you followed me?" Her bare shoulders bobbed above the waterline as she treaded water, her pale skin gleaming.

"I was worried . . . after earlier tonight—"

"You thought me mad? Unhinged? You thought me in need of monitoring?" She launched the questions at him like arrows, her eyes hot with temper . . . or perhaps it was some other emotion.

That wild-eyed glazed look was still there.

He shook his head slowly, quite certain no other female had ever made him feel so doubtful of himself. With her, he felt as though he were fumbling around in a dark chamber. "I did not say that."

Although it was not far off from his thoughts.

She swept her gaze over him. "You should not be here."

"I merely wanted to assure myself you are—"

"I am quite well," she snapped in a tone that conveyed the exact opposite. As did the stormy look of her gaze.

"I'm happy to escort you—"

She laughed briefly, the sound rather shrill and desperate. "That would be highly improper."

Now she was concerned with propriety? *Now?* Who was this strange creature?

She looked around wildly as though there could even now be a witness to their encounter.

"Have no fear. No one is about," he assured her.

Her gaze shot back to his. "Well, anyone *could* happen upon us at any time." She lifted her chin high above the waterline, stretching her neck, showing off the lovely arch that his lips longed to taste. *Bloody hell.* She was not the only strange creature here.

He glanced over his shoulder to the waiting path, considering granting her request and leaving. Apologizing for intruding and departing. Returning to Haverston Hall and packing up his things. Leaving this place. The stepbrother who wanted no part of him. The family who was not truly his family. And this maddening female whom he had just met but with whom he felt oddly entangled. He should turn and go and wash his hands of her for good.

That would be the sensible thing to do.

And yet he remained. They were alone. This was an excellent opportunity to gain an explanation for what had occurred in the library. She owed him that at the very least.

He cocked his head. "When you accosted me in the library, were you not concerned for propriety then, too? Anyone could have happened upon us. One of your sisters . . . Warrington . . . a member of the staff?"

Her mouth opened and closed several times at what he thought to be a very reasonable question. "Please. Let us not speak of that. And to be clear, I did *not* accost you." She eyed the shoreline as though searching for the best point of escape.

He practically choked at that. "Oh, you think not?"

"No . . . I was under the effects of . . ." If possible, her face seemed to redden even further. "It wasn't me . . . I—I would never . . . It was the tonic my sister gave me."

He could only stare at her as he digested this, turning it over in his mind.

He had not imagined what she might say by way of an explanation, but it had not been this. He had briefly wondered if she was inebriated when she'd seduced him. He winced at the word *seduced*, but was there really any other term for it?

He had quickly dismissed that possibility, however. He'd been around plenty of drunkards. Even been foxed himself on occasion. He knew what it looked like, and it had not looked like Charlotte. Nor had she reeked of spirits.

As improbable as it seemed, she'd been a woman wild with desire. Perhaps an evening with her future husband and his family had pushed her over the edge. God knew it had pushed him to his limits. Perhaps her limits had been stretched and it toppled her over the edge. Perhaps she had decided to seize passion for herself so that she might have a taste of it—so that she might have the memory of it to keep her through the endless nights of tedium ahead.

He didn't know the reason.

But this explanation? *Rubbish.*

It was merely regret in the aftermath of her actions that kept her from admitting the truth.

"There is no reason to be ashamed." He assumed it was maidenly shame that prompted her into such a ridiculous excuse of denial.

She blinked. "Ashamed?" The word struck him as humorous coming from a woman swimming naked.

"Indeed. Desire is a natural thing."

Again, her mouth opened and shut several times as though groping for speech. She gave her head a slight shake. "Of course I'm ashamed." She made a sound that was halfway between a snort and a grunt. "You're a stranger. You do not understand. I'm . . . I am . . . Charlotte Langley." Apparently that meant something. Something, if he was to infer correctly, that meant she was incapable of desire. "I do not *do* the things I did with you."

To be fair, upon first meeting her he had assumed the same thing. Miss Charlotte Langley was the very image of moral frigidity—of pristine and virtuous womanhood. The kind of woman who went to her marital bed in the dark, buttoned up to her neck in a woolen nightgown.

She continued, her voice insistent, "I am a modest person."

"Modest?" He arched an eyebrow, looking very pointedly around them, his gaze sweeping over the pond and then her person—her very *unclothed* person. *Modest* was not the word that leaped to mind.

He gave a slight chuckle.

Her blush now extended from her face down her throat to her upper chest. "I was warm, overheated . . . I merely wanted to cool off in the water. I assure you this is not a regular occurrence."

"So . . . you said you don't do the things you did . . ." He flattened a hand to his chest. *"With me."*

She nodded, but after a moment, she stopped nodding. Her eyes widened. "Good heavens. I do not do those things with *anyone*, if that is your implication. Not you. Not anyone!"

He grinned. He knew the question would needle her. "Not judging. Merely inquiring."

"Of course you judge. That is what everyone does. Females are judged from the moment of their first breath. But to the point . . . I do not engage in liaisons with strange men—with any man!" She took a deep breath as though she meant to duck below and submerge herself in the water. Instead, she asserted, "Desire had naught to do with what happened between us."

He shook his head, refusing to accept that bit of absurdity. "Desire had *everything* to do with it."

It was that desire that had so shaken him. That had kept him awake.

That had him standing at the edge of a pond at the break of dawn, conversing with a mermaid.

She flinched. "It was not *me*." She lifted a hand from beneath the water and pointed to her face. "Not me. Not me at all. It was the tonic."

Incredible. She was sticking to her ridiculous story. "You must indeed be mad if you believe what happened between us had naught to do with desire."

It had everything to do with desire.

She sank a little lower and shook her head, her chin sloshing water. "It was a chemical reaction. A matter of science."

He chuckled, but felt no mirth . . . only a twinge of annoyance. "Is that what you believe? Truly?"

"My sister is a very accomplished herbalist. You can ask anyone in Brambledon. She mixed together a new tonic to aid me with my . . ." She paused, the tendons of her throat working. "With my aches."

"Aches?" He frowned. "What ails you?"

She looked away, clearly discomfited at discussing the subject of her health. He knew one should not pry into a lady's health. It was not polite, but after this night he considered them well past politeness. The woman had used him to bring herself to climax. That certainly elevated them to intimates.

And truthfully, he felt an odd stirring in his chest. He didn't like the idea of her ill or hurting.

"Come, lass," he said gruffly, stepping closer to the water's edge. "Tell me. What ails you?"

She considered him with those clear blue eyes. She did not look unhealthy. Indeed, the pink flush to her cheeks smacked of health and vitality.

"If you must know, they are pains of the female variety," she finally confessed, and then watched him as though she expected him to turn and flee. "Nothing life-threatening. They merely plague me once a month and my *clever* sister sought to help me."

The way she uttered *clever* indicated she was not very happy with her sister presently.

She continued, "Nora gave me this concoction on countless occasions . . . but this time she thought to alter it . . . to give me a bit more relief. She meant well."

"And that's when you accosted me?"

"Would you stop saying *that*?" she snapped, her hand slapping the surface of the water, sending it spraying through the air. She swam forward, stopping just short of where the water became too shallow. Closer now, she glared up at him. "It makes me sound positively predatory."

He arched a brow. "Does it? Well, that's not an inaccurate description."

"It was not like that!"

"You tore my waistcoat," he reminded.

"I popped a few buttons," she protested. "They're easily mended."

"*If* I was to find them. Right now they're scattered somewhere on the floor of the library—"

"I'm an excellent seamstress," she declared. "I can befit your waistcoat with new buttons. Finer buttons than before."

"Can you now? Fine buttons, eh?" he mocked. "Well, that will go some way toward reparations."

"Reparations?" she echoed, looking quite stunned. She really was easy to unnerve, a fact he found quite diverting. He could discourse with her all day, in fact.

She continued, "You hardly offered protest, sirrah, when I *accosted* you."

He shrugged. "Call me a gentleman. You were in quite a fever and *very* demanding. Who was I to deny you? I did not want to cause you further distress."

Her hot gaze actually burned him. "A *true* gentleman would have turned me away."

He laughed. "No man, gentleman or not, would have turned his back on a fetching, half-dressed woman throwing herself at him."

"You make me sound a . . . slattern."

"Not at all. I respect any woman strong enough to know her mind and claim her own passion. There is no shame in that."

She gazed at him skeptically.

For a moment, he had a flash of his mother, Helene, as he'd last seen her . . . dark hair like spilled ink on her pillow; not a strand of gray even at her age, not even in her condition. She had been stretched out in a bed, a ghost of her former self. So much in pain. Used up and forgotten and forever broken from all the men in her life, his father included.

Kingston didn't believe in shame. It was a construct invented to keep people inside Society's lines—to keep them inside and feeling acute remorse if they ever dared to stray outside those lines.

There was not shame. Only risk.

And the memory of that, of Helene, was enough to kill his good humor.

"Have a care, though," he heard himself saying rather bitterly. "The next man you corner in the middle of the night might not be so kind as to walk away without lifting your skirts and taking his own pleasure."

She flinched.

He saw that other scenario in his mind and it turned his stomach. The scenario of Miss Charlotte Langley with some other man. A far rougher, greedy man uncaring of her needs. Any number of men would have taken her in the library whether she wished it or not. They would not have hesitated to seize all she offered and plunder her, and it left him dazed with anger.

He wasn't just angry at these phantom men. Indeed not. He was incensed at *her*. Incensed that she would risk herself so foolishly.

"I vow to you," she whispered, "what happened in the library was not my customary behavior." Another breath, jagged as a broken bit of glass. "And I told you why."

"Ah, yes. The elixir."

Her face tightened in anger and suddenly she was splashing water at him, soaking his trousers.

He jumped back against the onslaught. The nerve of the girl! "Brat," he muttered, shaking out first one leg and then the other. Even his boots were wet. Fortunately they were made to withstand the elements.

"I speak the truth, and it's maddening that you truly think me some vulgar manner of female who goes about climbing all over strange men like she is eager to . . . to—"

"Rut?" he suggested.

"Oh!" She gasped at his suggestion.

"Apt, I think." He nodded.

"You are a wretched, *wretched* man."

Smiling, he wished he could see her more clearly through the water, but he could only make out her vague shape.

She swam backward from him, her chin bobbing at the waterline as she inched away, her hands working feverishly under the surface.

"You weren't thinking that of me earlier," he taunted after her, the toes of his boots stepping closer, right up to the water's edge.

She released a cry of outrage while still continuing her retreat. "Please come no closer. Stay where you are until I emerge from the water."

"Why?" He looked down at the water lapping the tips of his boots. "Are you afraid of me? You know I could have had you last night. You would have made no protest. I would think that earned me a modicum of your trust."

"You're a cad to fling my ill behavior at me."

"Your ill behavior?" He tsked. "Is this not where you again insist that you were drugged with an aphrodisiac and lacking all control over yourself? The behavior, then, is not yours."

"You continue to mock me." Even as her words vibrated with angry emotion, she ceased to swim away. In fact, she began gliding forward again, toward him, moving as sinuously as an adder.

He shook his head and stared at her with earnest sincerity as she inched closer. "No. I do not mock you. You believe in your rubbish. That much I know."

Her eyes flared, but she did not retreat again.

"Are you not a little curious, though?" he continued.

"About what?"

"The library . . . You blame it on this aphrodisiac your sister invented, but wouldn't you like to know?"

"Know what?"

"If it could be like that again? *Without* your sister's potion?" He was humoring her. He knew it. But he could not forget the way she had shattered in his arms, desire convulsing through her. It was impossible to forget. As impossible as *not* wanting to experience it again.

Impossible, indeed.

"Would you not like another climax?" he taunted. "To see if it's as good as before?"

Those eyes of hers grew larger yet. "I am certain it won't be," she said in clipped tones.

He let loose a bark of laughter. She was blunt. And impertinent. Again, it boggled his mind that he had so vastly misjudged her. How had he ever thought her insipid?

It was gratifying that she'd admitted her climax had been good—even if only indirectly. At least there was that. Especially as she had been denying the authenticity of her desire with the most maidenly airs. In this, she was truthful.

This, if nothing else.

"Oh?" He arched an eyebrow. "You seem very sure of that."

"Indeed I am." She sniffed. "The tonic clearly heightened the experience."

He closed his eyes in a tight, long blink. She was unbelievable. The lass was infuriating. He reopened his eyes to look at her. "Is that a challenge?"

"Simply true."

"Do you not feel it now? The sparks between us?" He motioned across the distance. "I'm standing here, and you're there in the water, but it's still there. The heat between us that has nothing to do with the temperature."

She held silent for a moment, treading in place, considering him with deep scrutiny and her perpetually pink cheeks. She moistened her lips, catching droplets of water with her tongue. His gut tightened at the small action. "All effects of Nora's tonic, I am certain. I don't think it's left my . . . uh, body yet."

The bloody tonic again.

"And how long, pray tell, do you think it will before the effects dissipate? Fully dissipate?"

She shrugged and inched closer. "Days. I don't

rightly know. Who can say? You will be long gone from here before then, though. I am certain of that. A man like you has far more diverting things to do than keep to this little provincial backwater."

It was as though she was a mind reader. That was what he *had* thought, after all, when he had initially planned to depart after the tediously boring dinner.

He narrowed his gaze on her. She was practically crouching now in the pond's shallow edge, her attractive knees poking up out of the water. She seemed to be weighing her options. If she were to emerge from the pond she would be fully naked.

He had already gotten an eyeful of her. At least from the waist up. He swallowed thickly at the memory of her yanking down her nightgown.

She only had to stand and he'd have all of her in his gaze.

"Can you turn around, please?"

"I beg your pardon?" The words felt like marbles rolling around in his mouth.

"Turn. Please."

He snorted. After everything, she would cling to modesty. As though he had not seen her. As though he had not moments ago just witnessed her floating on her back like a water nymph, her perky breasts sticking out of the water, those pebble-hard nipples tantalizing him as they had when she yanked her nightgown down.

Smiling tightly, he obliged.

He listened to the sound of her moving forward through the water, then water dripping and sluicing down her form as she stood, followed by the crunch of her bare feet over the ground.

He had many flaws. Too innumerable to count. As the bastard son of the Earl of Norfolk and a famed courtesan, it seemed he was destined for vice and wrongdoing. His fate had been sketched before he drew his first breath.

But he had never denied a lady's request for modesty.

If a woman said *stop*, *wait* or *no*, he obeyed. In this, he was at their mercy.

Just as he was now at Charlotte Langley's mercy. In the library and here. Right now.

"I look forward to continuing our acquaintance and getting to know the real you without the influence of your sister's tonic," he called, still humoring her insistence that this tonic was the reason for her behavior this night.

"What do you mean?" Branches rustled as she gathered up her clothes. "You were to leave today. You said so yesterday." A touch of desperation tinged her voice.

"I've decided to stay," he announced.

Silence behind him met the declaration.

He risked a look to find her attired again, her dress damp and clinging in several places. She stood still as a marble statue, her shoes and stockings dangling from one hand as she stared at him with horror.

She'd only just emerged from the water, but the tendrils framing her face were already curling charmingly. "You cannot. You cannot mean to stay."

"You needn't look so appalled." He stepped forward.

Gasping, she backed up several steps on the pebbled ground, watching him as he advanced. He strolled toward her, enjoying the sensation of her heated eyes on him.

For all her horror, she could not seem to look away.

A gratified smile played about his lips. He looked her up and down. "You've dressed yourself, but you might as well be without garments. I can see you quite clearly in my mind. Your lovely dusky nipples, the size of a farthing, perfectly bite-sized. I grow hard just at the memory of you."

She gaped like a fish at him as he lowered himself down on the grassy earth at her feet.

"Would you like to see?" he asked.

"What are you doing now?"

She glanced around wildly, clearly assuring

herself that they were still very much alone. Satisfied, she then looked back at him, and he saw the understanding in her scalding gaze.

She knew perfectly well what he was offering.

"Yes," she whispered and then licked her lips, staring at his hands as they lowered to his trousers.

He opened his breeches slowly, still giving her time to flee if she chose, but she didn't move as he freed himself.

"Oh! Cover yourself." The soft words were barely audible between her ragged little pants.

A dragonfly, its wings beating as rapidly as his heart, darted in the space between them, its blue-green body glinting as it hovered, coming dangerously close to landing on her shoulder. All things were drawn to her. He fought a smile at the whimsical thought.

He lay on his back, elbows propped on the soft cushion of grass. He angled his face up to the lightening sky as though he had all the time in the world to lounge naked.

"You're incorrigible." Her breathy words escaped like a caress as her hungry eyes devoured him. He felt them wrap around him in a seductive touch, leaving no doubt that she did *not* want him to cover himself.

"And yet you still stand here." He looked up

at her as he took himself in hand. "Taking your fill of me."

She flushed and shifted on her feet.

It was encouraging. She had not fled in scandalized affront. She remained. She was still that lass—the one from the night before who had boldly mounted him and took her hungry pleasure. Of course, she still believed herself drugged.

Her gaze roamed him freely and he could not help his body's reaction. His cock hardened. He glanced down at his member, noting its deepening color, his prick's flushed head, swollen and ready.

"Curious, is it not?" he asked.

"What?" She moistened her lips.

"How we're made to fit each other. Man and woman. Aren't you a little curious at what it would be like with a man inside you?"

Her nostrils flared as he fully circled his prick and gave it a slow pump.

Her eyes never left him. She watched his hand wrapped around his cock. "I'll have that experience soon enough. I don't need you for that," she blurted defiantly even as her lips parted in unabashed fascination.

His grip tightened on his cock and he felt himself scowling. "With that Pembroke fellow?"

He couldn't stomach the thought.

She nodded jerkily, and he couldn't help marveling at her eyes. The blue was so vibrant, shining around her dark pupils.

"Well, you're not his yet," he grit out as blood rushed to his cock. "Tell me, Charlie—"

"My name is Charlotte. Not that I've granted you permission to use my Christian name. You may call me Miss Langley."

He ignored the ridiculousness of that request. "Have you ever thought about doing the things to Pembroke you did to me? Fantasized about him?"

Her silence was deafening . . . and telling.

And damn satisfying.

He smiled slowly. Smirked, rather. "Of course not."

Pembroke was a proper gentleman.

Thankfully, Kingston was not.

She was a vision, inching closer, her lovely eyes drawn to the sight of him, spread-eagle, his cock arrow-straight and swollen with need. It was very nearly enough to make him spill himself in the grass right then.

She licked her lips, her breathing labored . . . as though she were in the midst of some exertion and not standing virtually motionless.

"I've never even fantasized about doing such wicked things," she confessed.

"And yet you did. And now you stand here

watching me rub one off." He resumed stroking himself then, watching her rapt face hungrily. Her chest rose and fell faster. She was not unaffected by the sight of him.

Her hands played with the collar of her gown, curling into white-knuckled fists as though she wanted to yank it from her body. "It's as I said." Her chin went up defiantly. "The lingering effects of the tonic and nothing more. I would never stand here and watch you otherwise—"

Her words lit a match to his temper. "Tell me, Charlie—"

"I told you to address me as Miss Langley," she said in the sternest tone.

That made him laugh. A hard and dark chuckle that he felt in his belly.

Her lashes lowered to half-mast over eyes that seemed all dark pupils. She watched him fondle himself and yet she insisted he address her formally.

By God, he would not.

He would use her Christian name. "Charlie . . . come here."

Chapter 7

t Kingston's command, she blinked but remained where she stood. Her eyes boldly studied his cock, not at all in the manner of a frightened maid. If he believed in things like love potions he would almost believe she was, in fact, under the spell of one.

But of course, he did not believe in such rubbish. He was not a lad to believe in fairy tales, potions or spells.

"I—I beg your pardon?" she stammered between gasping breaths.

Bloody hell, but she was aroused. Wildly aroused. He could almost smell the desire, the need, radiating from her like something born of earth and wind and the ancient beats of nature.

He did not miss how one of her feet inched closer. Against her will, it seemed, she was tempted.

"If you want this, then get beside me now. Permit me to give you relief," he taunted—although he felt no levity as he got the words out. It felt like only the most serious thing in his life. This woman getting beside him. Touching him. Letting him touch her.

She stared at him for an interminable moment, still watching him working his member. She swallowed visibly as the moment stretched and he wondered what she would do. His gaze drifted to her throat, to the madly thrumming pulse there. It was jumping beneath her flushed skin like a wild drum, like a hammer pushing to break free. It was passing strange. She wasn't exerted and yet that pulse was throbbing, beating, fighting like the wings of a bird at her neck.

"Make a decision. Go or come here," he commanded, at war with himself. Wanting her to go. Wanting her to stay. He simply needed it done one way or another.

She dropped down beside him with an anguished little cry that he felt echo through him as keenly as the twist of a knife's blade.

He wasted no time, flipping her skirts and positioning himself between her thighs.

He dragged her toward him. She slid easily over the slick grass.

His eyes met hers. She looked back and forth between his face and his cock, pulsing and aimed directly for her crotch.

There was a good amount of alarm in her eyes and he wished it gone. He wished to put her at ease. She thought he meant to take her. Ravish her in the outdoors like a rutting beast.

He would not.

He was not that much of a cad. Nor was he keen on deflowering a maid who couldn't even bring herself to own her own desires.

Still, there were other things they could share that did not involve relieving her of her maidenhead.

The open seam in a lady's drawers made it blessedly convenient to access her pretty quim. As a randy youth, he had always been grateful for the mechanics of female undergarments. He had taken many a maid for a quick tumble, neither one of them discarding their clothing.

Even so, he had never been as grateful as he was now.

He studied her pink and quivering flesh in the light of day. She was wet, weeping for him. He could practically smell her desire, ripe and pungent on the summer air.

"You're still suffering the influence of your tonic?" he heard himself asking.

She nodded jerkily.

His gaze dropped to the open seam of her drawers. "Would you like me to relieve you again?"

She nodded, but it wasn't enough. He needed to hear her say it.

"Charlie?" he prodded. "Tell me what you want."

She licked her trembling lips, her gaze landing on his cock. "Make the ache go away."

Nodding, he released a ragged breath. He could take her now. He knew that was as good an invitation as any, but still he withheld himself the pleasure of sinking into her inviting heat. Again, he was *not* a cad.

Instead, he lowered his face to her, inhaling her fragrance and nuzzling his lips in her sweetness, his tongue tasting and finding the tender pearl buried at the top of her folds.

He seized it between his lips, interchangeably grazing with his teeth and flaying with his tongue. Her body bucked under him. His hand found her abdomen, pressing down and holding her as he feasted, working and rolling the little nub.

She began to roll her hips, working herself

against his mouth in abandon. Her hand delved in his hair, her fingers tugging fiercely on the strands as she used him, seeking her release.

Then she found it. She climaxed and the tension in her body snapped.

He drank deep from her until the last wave rocked her.

He fell back, his chest rising and falling as the air shuddered out of him.

This was perhaps not his best idea.

His own arousal raged unabated. His erection jutted out hard before him, unrelenting and unrelieved.

He gripped it savagely, determined to finish himself off before he turned and drove into her welcoming heat, so soft and available and still vibrating with the aftershocks of her release.

He was not a mindless brute, however.

No matter how tempting she was. No matter how many times she used him to take her own release.

He'd not find his pleasure with her until she was in full possession of reality and not hiding behind excuses. Not until she admitted she wanted him strictly for passion's sake and not because of some idiotic aphrodisiac.

Groaning, he dropped his head back and closed his eyes, trying to block out the sound of her gasps as she came down from her release.

Then suddenly her hand was pushing his own hand aside.

His eyes shot open to find her over him, staring down at him with bright-eyed determination. She bit her lip and his gaze fixed on that mouth, hungrily absorbing the way that tiny row of white teeth sank into the deep pink of her lip.

He read her determined expression for what it was. She wanted to return the favor—last night's favor, and now this one.

He shook his head. "You don't have to do—"

"Quiet," she murmured in a throaty voice that brooked no argument. "It's my turn now."

Her touch was by no means expert. Her small hand was uncertain, barely big enough to wrap around him, but the tentative sensation of her slender fingers, so warm and delicate on him, had him sitting up on his elbows and watching her ministrations.

"Harder," he directed after some moments, covering her hand with his own and showing her how he liked it, guiding her once, twice, three times up and down his cock in a pumping motion.

She was a quick learner. He dropped his hand and let her take over.

The sight of her pale fingers around his thickness mesmerized him.

He watched, transfixed as her head suddenly dipped.

She kissed him there. It was gentle and sweet and tentative. Her tongue darted out to taste him. He jerked at the first velvety swipe of her tongue on his pulsing head.

She looked up at him, her lovely lips inches from his manhood. "Is this not acceptable?"

"Oh, it's completely acceptable." He threaded his fingers through her wet hair, piled atop her head in a messy arrangement.

She lowered her head back down and lapped at him with her tongue, her hand still flexing around the root of him.

It took everything in him not to thrust deeply into her mouth. He held himself back and allowed her to lavish him with her lips and tongue and hand.

His balls tightened, rising up, and he reached for her arms, hurriedly lifting her up and moving her away.

With a choked gasp, he turned and spilled himself into the grass, pleased that his ragged breaths matched her own behind him. He wasn't the only one affected. She was every bit as discomposed.

"Kingston?" she said behind him, her voice shaky as a brittle leaf on the breeze.

He turned to face her. She'd covered her legs again, hiding her sweet quim from his gaze. Despite her bedraggled appearance, she looked deceptively demure and not like a chit given to shagging in the out of doors.

And for some reason that irked him.

Even with his body still humming from release, he was irked that she looked so wholly unsuited to illicit trysts.

He could almost believe she was under the influence of a love spell or aphrodisiac or some other such rubbish. If he believed in rubbish, which he didn't.

But she did.

She thought this was inspired by something outside of herself.

"How was that?" he asked. "Better than your last taste?"

Her cheeks went scarlet.

Instead of stopping there, he added, "Lucky for me your tonic was still holding strong."

The softness melted from her face. She turned to hard edges before his eyes. If he tried to touch her, he was sure he would cut himself on one of them.

"You mock me." Not a question. She stated it unequivocally. The sky was up. The ground was down.

And he mocked her.

"Admit it was *you* here." He waved back and forth between them. "You. *You*, Charlotte Langley. Not a female possessed."

She stared at him with her chilled blue eyes—the only sound between them that of the water burbling nearby and the anger pounding in his ears. Anger she could deflate with just a few words.

A few honest words.

Instead, she said, "I should go. Anyone could happen upon us."

"Indeed. You wouldn't want to be compromised with the likes of me."

"No." Her chin lifted. "I would not."

"Have no fear, Miss Langley. You can count on me for discretion."

"Can I?" She looked at him intently, as though truly concerned.

Fear shadowed her eyes. In that moment, she looked so very young. Lost and confused. He had the fool impulse to gather her up in his arms and reassure her, tell her everything would work out for the best—whatever that meant. It was what people said. What men told the women for whom they cared.

Absurd, of course. He needn't go that far. He did not possess such depth of emotion. Not for any female.

"Indeed." He gave a single resolved nod. "I'm not looking for a wife. You may trust this is behind us."

She sighed. Relief draped heavily within the sound. "Very good then."

After a long moment of awkwardness, she turned and fled in the blossoming dawn, snatching up her shoes and stockings in her hasty flight.

He watched, unmoving from where he lounged partially naked on the grass. Honestly, he did not think he could tuck himself back into his trousers. Not yet. That would require more movement than he could manage. His muscles had the consistency of jam, so undone by her untried talents.

His own words echoed in his ears. *You may trust this is behind us.*

He'd said the words, but he did not like them.

He forced himself to remember that she would soon be wed, and he didn't dally with married ladies.

Soon be wed.

But not yet. Not yet wed.

He released a short, tormented laugh. *Brilliant.* He was laughing to himself like a madman alone in the woods, demented and fantasizing after a woman he ought not want.

He knew he should leave her be and cease this senseless pursuit of her. Disaster loomed ahead if he did not. He recognized that. She might be fatherless, but Warrington was her brother-in-law and he knew the man well enough to know he would not tolerate Kingston dallying with her—for the sake of his wife, if nothing else.

He sighed and fell back on the cushion of grass. This attraction, this unfortunate *pull* he felt toward her, was because he had not been with a woman in a long time. He was suffering for it. *It* being a shag, of course. It had nothing to do with *her*. Nothing at all. Nothing to do with the unusually compelling creature that was Miss Charlotte Langley.

He watched shades of pink streak across the sky, splashing through the purple cotton fluffs of clouds.

The chit was not to be shagged. Plain and simple.

She was the kind of lass one married.

Specifically, she was the kind of chit another man was going to marry. *Another* man, not him.

He needed to remember that. That was the critical distinction. As much as the idea knotted his gut, he accepted it. Because whilst she was not for him to shag . . . he was not built for marriage.

He was not husband material. It was not in him. He was not fashioned that way.

He knew himself well enough to know that.

Chapter 8

*H*ours later, Charlotte paced a hard line back and forth across Nora's bedchamber, taking a breath amidst the accusations she was hurling at her sister.

Sunlight streamed in through the windows, doing little to cheer her mood and dampen the barrage of words she launched at her younger sister.

Irresponsible. Reckless. Dangerous. You could have killed me!

When she'd returned from the pond, despite her maelstrom of thoughts and emotions, she had somehow returned to her bed and fallen asleep. She'd dropped into her bed like a lead weight.

Not only had she managed to sleep, but it was perhaps the best sleep she had ever enjoyed since moving into Haverston Hall. She'd slept deeply, the ravages of Nora's tonic melting away with the vestiges of night.

When she woke up to ready for church, her encounter with Kingston felt as illusory as a dream. Gossamer wisps of fantasy.

One of those wildly impossible dreams that faded bit by bit, piece by piece with each passing waking moment.

Except it had all happened. It was no dream.

In the broad light of day, the truth was a maelstrom hitting her in full, unremitting force.

What had she done?

The blue-and-yellow-striped fabric of her skirts swished smartly about her ankles as she moved. It was a new dress. Far lovelier than anything she had owned before her sister married the Duke of Warrington. Almost all her dresses were new now. She and her sisters were regularly outfitted in all the latest fashions. Marian enjoyed clothes. To be fair, so did Charlotte.

Charlotte had a way with needle and thread. Unlike her sisters, though, she actually enjoyed sewing. She had not necessarily enjoyed it when she had been forced to work long hours for the local dressmaker after Papa had died, but there had been no choice in the matter then.

Those days were behind her. Now she no longer slaved away to earn coin to help support her family. With that burden lifted, she actually enjoyed fashion again. Sewing it. Wearing it. She could once again pick up a needle and thread without a bone-weary sigh. She could study the fashion plates and it no longer felt like a chore, like something she must do in order to stay abreast of the current trends.

"What are you accusing me of, Charlotte?" Nora asked indignantly.

"There was something in that cordial last night!" She stabbed a finger toward her younger sister.

"Well, obviously there was something in it," Nora replied smoothly. She was never rattled. Many a time, Charlotte had lost her temper with her and Nora weathered it all with equanimity. "I wasn't giving you a dose of tea."

"Oh! Don't be wippish with me. This is very serious! There was something . . . foul in the draught . . ."

Nora looked her up and down. "Why are you so distressed? Have a seat. Clearly you are well today. Your color is exceedingly fine. You don't look ill. You didn't die. What is amiss, love?"

"What is amiss?" she echoed almost shrilly and then she did something totally out of character. She laughed.

She laughed uproariously, holding her sides until they ached.

Nora's eyes widened. "Dear God. You've gone mad."

Suddenly Marian strode into the room. She stopped and looked back and forth between them.

Nora waved at Charlotte helplessly. "She's gone mad."

Marian tsked and shook her head. "I can hear you two down the hall. Why are you bickering? We're going to be late for church. Can you not choose another time for one of your arguments?"

Nora waved her hand at Charlotte as though that was explanation enough.

Charlotte shook her head, trying to regain her composure, but she couldn't seem to stop the absurd laughter.

"Talk to her," Nora encouraged. "The girl is daft. Look at her, would you? Listen to her!"

Frowning in concern, Marian turned on Charlotte. "Char, are you well?"

Charlotte shook her head wildly. "No," she got out between gasps of mad laughter. "No. I am *not* well. I am not fine at all, thank you for asking." She stabbed another finger at her younger sister. "This idiot poisoned me with an aphrodisiac last night."

There. She said it. It was out.

Aphrodisiac.

The word had been swimming in her head ever since she'd first scrambled off Kingston in the library. Ever since she'd taken her pleasure of him without so much of a "by your leave."

She was a well-read individual. True, perhaps a little sheltered and lacking in worldliness. And yet she knew what an aphrodisiac was. Up until last night she had thought it entirely fiction. A thing of lore. An invention of fantastical works. Something one would read about in a Shakespearean play.

Not real. Not possible.

Except it was.

It was possible.

She knew because she had experienced it.

There was no other explanation for her behavior. It wasn't in Charlotte to accost a strange man and seduce him. The things she had done to him were not even in her knowledge. Her actions had been led by pure primal instinct.

The silence stretched on forever at her declaration until Marian finally found her voice. "Charlotte." She said her name slowly as though speaking to someone slow to comprehend. "Are you still feeling unwell?"

She and her sisters exchanged looks—as though she were some poor demented creature—and that only infuriated her.

"I am not ill," she said in her steadiest voice. "I am of sound mind." *Now* she was at least.

Marian released an uneasy laugh. "Yes, well then. There is no such thing as an aphrodisiac, my dear. That's just absurd. Certainly you know that."

Charlotte nodded. "Indeed. I would have thought the same thing until last night."

"Last night?" Nora's eyes narrowed with suspicion. "What happened? We left you asleep in bed."

Marian's eyes widened. "What could have happened to you . . . in your bedchamber . . . in your bed?" She looked faintly ill as her words penetrated. Evidently her mind was drifting through terrible scenarios.

"Indeed. You left me sleeping in bed. And then I woke up," she snapped, heat firing her body as she recalled waking up and all that had transpired after that. "My body was in a rage."

"A rage?" Marian echoed, her expression wary.

"Because of the aphrodisiac Nora gave me. I could not sleep."

"Stop calling it that," Marian bit out, her composure slipping. She was clearly exasperated. "It's mad. Is it not, Nora? You did not give her anything that could have done such a thing. It's impossible. Tell her so."

Nora winced and shrugged. "I cannot. As I mentioned, the tonic wasn't exactly the same one I usually administer to her, so there was no way of knowing how this combination of ingredients might affect her."

Charlotte nodded, satisfied Nora was at least not denying her assertion that the tonic functioned as an aphrodisiac.

"Well." Charlotte tossed her hands in the air and spoke with great sarcasm. "We know now. Now we know how it *might* affect me."

Myriad emotions flickered across Marian's face. "Let me understand this. You said you woke because of the . . . tonic?" Marian stared at her expectantly, clearly unable to name the tonic for what it was—what Charlotte alleged it to be.

Charlotte had no such compunction.

"Yes. The *aphrodisiac* woke me. I was in . . . agony. I left the room to see Nora." She nodded to her sister. "I thought if anyone could help me it would be the person who poisoned me in the first place."

Nora rolled her eyes at her choice of words.

"Why do you think this tonic was an . . . aphrodisiac?" Marian spit out the final word as though it were something foul on her tongue.

And that vexed Charlotte. Why should it be so difficult for Marian to say it? To utter the mere word? Charlotte was the one who had endured it. Who had gone through the anguish of it and compromised herself with Kingston. Multiple times.

Charlotte angled her head sharply. "Oh, I am fairly certain. For no other reason would I have ravished your husband's brother in the corridor last night."

Silence met her declaration. The loud kind of silence one could actually hear.

Marian cleared her throat. "Nathaniel's step-brother? Kingston?"

Could I be talking about anyone else? She bit back the sarcastic reply and instead nodded.

"Oh, he's a handsome chap," Nora blurted. "Bit of a rogue, from what I understand." Her eyes danced as though this was clearly an enhancement of his character and not a detraction.

"Nora!" Marian reprimanded. "That's neither here nor there."

Nora twisted one shoulder up in a shrug. "I think it's a little bit . . . *here*."

Marian ignored Nora and continued, "And when *you* say ravished . . ."

Charlotte expelled a breath. "I launched myself at him and used him to . . ." This part she did not even know how to explain. The words were not even in her sphere of knowledge. Her face burned in mortification.

Trust Nora, of course, to speak what was on her mind. "Are you still a maid?"

Marian grasped her arm. "Did he hurt you?"

"No. He was very restrained." She gave a

hoarse croak of sound that weakly resembled laughter. "Certainly he didn't have to be. I was very . . . eager." Humiliatingly so.

"Are you a maid still?" Nora repeated, her eyes alight in a way that did not reflect any disappointment if she was not. In fact, perhaps there was even a fraction of . . . *hope* in her gaze.

"Yes, I am, but I thoroughly disgraced myself. I seduced him for my own needs—"

Nora frowned and shook her head, tossing back an errant golden curl that bounced over her eye. "But you're still a maid. I don't understand."

"How can you be so well versed in science and anatomy and not understand?" Charlotte bit out.

Nora's expression remained ever perplexed, her forehead creasing in confusion. "How could you have used him for your needs and still remain a maid—"

"Not now, Nora!" Marian snapped. "I will explain it all to you later." As a married woman, Marian clearly had no such trouble understanding. She stepped forward to take both Charlotte's hands in her own. She squeezed them comfortingly. "You are certain you were unharmed?" Her gaze flitted searchingly over Charlotte's face, and she had no doubt Marian would go to battle for her. If Charlotte even intimated that Kingston harmed her, Marian would have his head.

Charlotte nodded firmly. "He did not hurt

me. I am fine. Better. Much better than I was last night." *Thank heavens for that.*

Marian visibly swallowed, and her thumbs pressed down a little deeper into Charlotte's hands. "Do you want me or Nathaniel to speak to him?"

"No!" she blurted. "That will make more of it, I fear."

She wanted it to be nothing. She wanted it never to have happened at all, which was unrealistic, she knew, but she didn't want her sister or Nathaniel confronting Kingston when she only wanted to minimize the entire encounter.

"Very well." Marian nodded slowly, clearly digesting that. "Can you tell me what the tonic made you . . . feel?"

"Indeed," Nora seconded.

"I felt feverish . . . so very overheated. I was breathless and I ached. When I happened upon Kingston in the corridor, something just came over me." She shook her head, mortified at the memory. She didn't bother mentioning the pond. She couldn't bring herself to share the extent of her wantonness. What she had done in the library was bad enough. "I had these wild impulses I couldn't resist." She shook her head. Even as close as she was with her sisters, she could say no more than that. No more description than that. Her shame ran too deep. She buried her face in her hands. It would be appalling even if she wasn't betrothed to Billy. But she was. She was betrothed to a good and decent man.

She was awful.

Marian's arms were suddenly around her, holding her in a tight embrace. Even Nora was there, coming up behind them and patting Charlotte on the back. "Do not torment yourself. You didn't do anything irreparable. Everything will be fine." Marian pulled back to look at her, a resolute fierceness in her eyes. "Kingston is leaving this very morning. He will be gone from here. You don't have to see him. You can forget him. You'll be married soon and all of this will be but a dim memory."

Charlotte nodded, comforted. A shaky smile chased her lips and she breathed a little easier. It was just as when they were little and Marian always took charge, always made everything better.

"Yes," Charlotte agreed, the rigidity in her shoulders lessening.

"And," Marian added, casting a reproving look to their youngest sister, "Nora will never use that combination of ingredients again. Will you, Nora?" This last bit she demanded with a fair amount of emphasis.

Nora blinked. "Um. Yes. Yes. Of course."

"Nora?" Marian said her name again, clearly unconvinced from Nora's less-than-firm assurance.

"What? I'm a scientist."

"You're an herbalist," Marian corrected.

Nora scowled, clearly in disagreement.

Even Charlotte had to admit, her baby sister was more than an herbalist. *Scientist* might not be far off from the truth. And after last night . . . *mad* scientist might be a more apt description.

"You're an herbalist," Marian insisted.

"Of course I am curious to see if this was a one-time anomaly or whether repeating the dosage would result in the same outcome."

"No." Charlotte shuddered at the notion of enduring what she had to endure last night all over again.

"Rid yourself of such ideas at once! Have you any idea how badly last night could have gone for Charlotte? Fortunately, she wasn't hurt. Nor was she ruined. Let's put this behind us, and that means you will forget all about that dangerous little tonic of yours!"

Nora ducked her head. "Very well," she said grudgingly.

Satisfied, Marian moved her hands down to smooth out the invisible wrinkles in her skirts. "I'm sure the carriage is waiting downstairs. Shall we be off?"

Charlotte swallowed against the thickness in her throat at the prospect of seeing Billy and his family this morning. Her actions the night before cast a dark shadow. It would be some time before she felt like herself again.

It didn't matter that they didn't know. *She* knew. She would know always that she had been intimate with another man. She had not even kissed Billy, but she had mounted another man—a stranger!—and worked herself into a frenzy over him.

"Charlotte? Are you coming?" Nora stood hovering in the doorway, looking back at her questioningly.

Charlotte shook free of her disturbing thoughts. She had to do this. It would be just as Marian said. Fine. Everything would be fine.

Kingston was gone. Last night had not been her fault. She had not been in possession of herself. Her faculties had been impaired. Her actions had not been her own.

She would forget all about it. Put it behind her. Forget and forgive herself.

Starting now.

Chapter 9

*T*he service had already begun when Charlotte, settled comfortably in her pew, was alerted to his arrival.

A ripple of murmurs started behind her, but she dutifully kept her focus on the front of the church. Her reckless ways were behind her. She was herself again. Proper. Modest. A rule follower. The type of person who paid attention in church and tried to incorporate the lessons preached into her daily living.

A shadow fell over her and she looked up to observe Kingston standing in the aisle, staring down at her with those deep, impenetrable eyes.

She blinked several times as though that would clear her vision.

Kingston was here.

Standing in her church. Beside her family pew, looking down at her expectantly.

He was not supposed to be here. Her sister had said he was departing this morning.

He cleared his throat and arched an eyebrow, motioning with a flick of his fingers for her to make room for him.

There was scarcely any room in the family pew—certainly not enough to fit his significant person—but that did not stop him from squeezing himself in directly beside her. Thankfully she was seated at the end of the pew so he did not raise many eyebrows as he sat. The congregation would merely think he was joining his brother's family in the Warrington pew, where he belonged.

For a fraction of a moment she resisted, shoving back at him, determined that he not have his way in this, but then she realized to refuse him would only create a scene and half the village of Brambledon was sitting at her back. She scooted as close as possible to Nora, ignoring Nora's wide-eyed questioning stare that she felt on the side of her face.

"Good morning," he whispered close to her

ear. The skin there immediately turned to goose-flesh.

She clutched a handful of skirts in her lap and tried to ignore how closely he sat beside her. His entire left thigh was aligned with her own. It was indecent!

Indecent was what you did to him last night. She swatted the voice aside.

"What are you doing?" she managed to get out from scarcely moving lips. The vicar was looking directly at them.

"Is it not obvious? I'm attending church this fine morning."

Church? *Him?* He did not strike her as a church-going individual.

"I thought you were departing today," she murmured from the corner of her mouth, staring straight ahead, feigning great interest in the vicar.

"Had a change of heart."

Change of heart?

She pressed her lips into a tight mutinous line. She would not give him the benefit of a reaction. Not here, not now, at least.

Not later either because that would require the privacy of a conversation, and she vowed there would be no private conversations between them. That seemed most inadvisable.

Thankfully, the vicar focused his attention on the congregation at large. She held herself stiffly, willing the minutes to pass quickly, hoping that she appeared unaffected with the duke's sinful stepbrother beside her.

Only, was he the sinful one? Last night he had been the victim of her attentions.

It was a shaming thought. Even if she had been a slave to the tonic's power and not herself.

She was achingly conscious that her betrothed and his family sat only one pew behind her. She could almost imagine she felt Mrs. Pembroke's eyes on the back of her neck.

The sermon ended and they all rose from their seats. She could not put space between herself and Kingston fast enough. She quickly crossed in front of him, closing her eyes in one hard blink as their bodies brushed.

"In such haste?" His voice reached her ears alone.

She ignored him to reach the Pembrokes. Anyone watching would merely think her eager to join her soon-to-be husband.

Billy was waiting for her in the aisle. He offered his arm and she accepted it, returning his smile and trying to squash the surge of guilt she felt for her dalliance with the man only a few feet behind them. The cordial was to blame. She had not been in control, and it would never happen again.

They'd both agreed to that. More or less, he had agreed. So what was he doing here tormenting her?

They quickly merged with the other bodies leaving the church.

She permitted Billy to lead her outside, where his parents waited with the carriage. She usually took tea with them after church. She'd promised to do so today. She would take comfort in the familiar, in the security of her life's rituals.

Still . . . she could not stop herself from risking a glance over her shoulder for Kingston. She caught a glimpse of him—of those bourbon-colored eyes fixed on her before he disappeared from sight, lost in the church crowd.

WHEN KINGSTON STEPPED out into the afternoon sunshine, Warrington was leaning against a tree, waiting for him with his arms crossed and his lip curled in derision.

"What are you still doing here?" he demanded baldly, squinting at him with his usual dislike.

Kingston shrugged and strode past his stepbrother.

Warrington followed, and they moved off to

the side, away from the milling people, several of whom nodded eagerly in the duke's direction.

Warrington even managed to smile back at several of them, tight as though that smile looked upon his face.

"Brambledon agrees with me," Kingston murmured.

Warrington narrowed his gaze on him. "You're a bloody liar."

With their history, the brusque words should not have come as any surprise. The duchess was not here to moderate their exchange, after all.

His stepbrother continued, "What game are you playing at here, Kingston? Is there someone after you? An angry husband? Someone you cheated at cards—"

"I'm no cheat," he rejoined, experiencing a flash of anger. There was no love lost between them, but Kingston had never revealed himself to be a dishonest sort. He'd always known Warrington never cared for him, but perhaps until this moment he had not quite understood how low in esteem he actually held him.

Warrington merely arched a dark eyebrow, unperturbed by his apparent offense. "Angry husband then?"

He felt a fresh stab of annoyance that quickly went away and turned to uneasy discomfort when he considered how he had spent the previous evening—with this man's sister-in-law, doing all the wicked and depraved things one never did with a proper lady. "Is it too much to believe I find myself enjoying your hospitality?"

Warrington snorted. "Yes." He glanced toward the church, where his wife stood chatting with a small crowd of people. She tossed back her head and laughed in delight at something someone said. They seemed a mismatched pair—the curmudgeon duke and the laughing young woman. She was far too delightful to be his wife.

"Well, then not your hospitality. Rather your lovely wife's hospitality. She's been quite welcoming."

Warrington's sharp gaze studied him distrustfully then. "You haven't designs on my wife, have you?"

"What? You don't trust your bride?"

"Oh, I trust her implicitly. Only I won't have you coming at her like a letch. If you do that, then I'll have to thrash you."

He chuckled. "Rest easy. Contrary to your allegation, I've no affinity for married women and I would not insult your charming wife in such a way."

He stifled a wince. No, he would insult her in another way . . . by dallying with her sister.

Seemingly appeased, Warrington fell to silence. In the growing warmth of the afternoon, they watched the villagers mingle and start to disperse from the churchyard.

Kingston searched for Charlotte. He'd lost sight of her when she dove from the pew and latched herself on to young Pembroke.

He spotted her across the churchyard with her arm linked with her fop of a betrothed.

He frowned as they joined his insufferable parents. Together, the four of them made their way toward one of the waiting carriages.

He nodded in their direction. "Where is your sister-in-law going?"

Warrington followed his gaze. He shrugged. "To take tea with the Pembrokes."

Charlotte didn't speak as she was escorted forward. He watched her lips. That mouth he held in such acute fascination did not move. Not in speech. Not in smile. Unlike her companions.

Mrs. Pembroke talked nonstop. The old dragon's husband called out to someone across the churchyard with no thought to decorum, or that he was likely bursting the eardrum of his wife beside him.

"Not exactly charming people."

From the corner of his eye, he noted that Warrington lifted a shoulder in a shrug. "That's Charlotte's burden. She's made her choice, and it's to be the Pembroke lad."

"He's a dullard."

"Her choice," he repeated.

"She should make a better choice," he said, feeling and thinking dark things.

She disappeared inside the carriage and Kingston felt the ridiculous urge to give chase. To stop the carriage and wrench her from it and save her from herself.

She deserved better. He'd only been in her company a short time and in the company of her betrothed an even shorter duration, and yet he knew that.

That mouth of hers deserved to smile. The passion inside her ought to be let out, and that fop wasn't the man to do it.

"By God." Warrington broke into his musings. "It's *her*."

His gaze snapped back to the duke. Only the duke wasn't looking at him. His focus was fixed on the departing carriage.

"What do you mean?" he asked warily.

"She is the reason you're still here. Charlotte."

Instantly he realized his mistake. He should never have asked after the chit. Nor should he be staring after her like an abandoned puppy. Warrington was far too observant. Kingston had made his interest in her much too obvious. Ah, bloody hell.

"Nonsense," Kingston lied, doing his best to keep his tone light and easy. Too much denial would not be the thing either. "I only met her last night."

And last night had been truly incredible.

"And she must have made some impression on you."

Indeed she had, but Warrington didn't need to know all the details of that. He could never know, in fact.

The last thing he needed to find out was that Kingston had dallied with his sister-in-law. If his stepbrother didn't challenge him outright to a duel over that offense, he'd at the very least cast him from his home.

And Kingston had no intention of leaving. Not yet.

Or even worse than those possibilities: Warrington could force him to do the honorable thing and marry her.

That would be a tragedy for both of them. He'd make a miserable husband.

"You're mistaken," he insisted, determined to convince him. "I've no appetite for milksop misses."

"Hm," Warrington murmured, clearly still in doubt. "I must confess, she does not strike me as your brand of female." Kingston bit back that he had not imagined the duchess to be to Warrington's tastes either, but such a response would be much too defensive . . . much too revealing.

"You are correct. She is not to my tastes." Somehow the untruth managed not to stick in his throat and choke him.

"Indeed. Respectable females are not your ilk."

"No," he agreed. "They are not." No sense explaining to him that presently no female was to his taste—respectable or otherwise. Until last night. Until Charlotte Langley.

Warrington considered him for a moment before moving away. Once he was gone, Kingston's gaze returned to the departing Pembroke carriage. He watched it go, cutting through undulating waves of heat rising up on the afternoon air.

He watched until the conveyance was well out of sight, vowing he would be waiting for her on her return to Haverston Hall. He and Miss Langley would have words.

They had much to discuss.

Chapter 10

*C*harlotte plucked at her dress and pulled it away from her chest, hoping to encourage a bit of air flow to cool her skin in the very close and suffocating confines of the carriage.

It did little good. Her chemise and corset remained plastered to her body. What she wouldn't do to be free of her garments and out of this infernal heat and back in the pond again—without Kingston. The winter had been unseasonably cold, and it seemed they were being rewarded with an unseasonably warm summer in recompense.

Billy's voice murmured beside her in a mild, intermittent drone as he returned her home following tea with his family. He was not much for conversation. Nor did he ever expect much chatter from her.

She frowned. She might have exchanged more words with Kingston last night than she had in weeks with Billy. That was a troubling realization.

She shook off the sudden insight and chased away her frown, reminding herself that she *liked* Billy this way. She liked that Billy did not talk to nauseating excess. If he talked excessively, then he would be like his parents. She shuddered briefly.

These days his sporadic commentary centered on the subject of their wedding. They would marry this summer, but they still had much to decide. Mrs. Pembroke was forever telling her that.

Even so, her primary focus was on the passing countryside and not the myriad wedding tasks demanding her attention. She lifted her face, hoping to feel a bit of breeze reach her through the window.

She slid Billy a considering glance. He was attractive in a mild, unassuming way. She covertly assessed his lanky form. Soon they'd be married and sharing a bed. Her thoughts had never strayed to those intimate details before, but now she wondered.

Now she questioned whether there would be passion between them. It had never felt a necessary prerequisite, but she could not help thinking it would be nice. After last night . . .

No.

She would not think about last night or compare it to anything. Not Billy.

The carriage rolled to a stop before Haverston Hall and she inched forward in her seat, eager to be free of the stuffy confines of the carriage. The coachman opened the door and handed her down. Billy followed, taking her elbow and leading her very correctly up the front steps.

Once they were in the foyer, they were spared the impact of direct sunlight, but the lack of free-flowing air made her tug uncomfortably at her collar.

"I will see you tomorrow?" Billy inquired, bending over her hand.

She nodded, trying not to hide her cringe at the reminder. He would be bringing both his mother and grandmother with him for tea.

Charlotte watched from the doorway as he departed, climbing back up inside the carriage. She stood there for some moments as the carriage rolled away, various emotions churning through her chest. Turning back around in the foyer, her gaze landed on the footman. He stood post in the corner, trying to look alert and not a little drowsy in the sweltering afternoon.

She could empathize. She tugged at the cloying and itching fichu tucked into her gown. Escaping to her room, removing her garments and flopping down on her bed for a nap in nothing but her chemise sounded like bliss.

She took the winding steps upstairs. Once in her chamber, she shed her clothing. Dropping down on the bed, she spread her arms wide at her sides, not touching herself.

The memories of last night were too close. Her skin felt new, tender and raw. No longer the skin she had worn yesterday but a new layer. It would take some time for it to fade into something resembling normalcy, she imagined . . . for her to feel like herself again.

Still, the lack of clothing was an improvement in the uncomfortably warm air.

She exhaled and inhaled in several great sighs, futilely wishing that she could have a day without the Pembrokes in it.

A reprieve from Billy's family. A senseless wish. At least until they were married. For now, she was scarcely ever alone with Billy without his mother present.

She really needed to learn a little more forbearance when it came to his family. They were to be her family, too.

She cared for Billy a great deal. She'd known him all her life, after all. That meant she had known his family all her life—even if his grandmother had only recently come to live with them.

Charlotte should be able to find something agreeable about them . . . something to like.

But if she could not, so what?

Where was it written one must get along with their in-laws? She'd have Billy. He had always been a steady and gentle constant in her world. Theirs was no grand love affair, but what they had was good. Friendship would run deeper and last them much longer.

When her mother died, he did not plague her with visits and inane conversation. Because he was kind that way. He'd understood what she needed. Everyone else had fluttered around Papa, dropping off food and lingering, occupying their parlor for hours with no care that they might want to be left alone to mourn. But Billy knew.

He would simply leave little gifts for her. A book. A beautiful ball of yarn. A necklace he had fashioned from honeysuckle vine. He knew to give his distance. He knew how to show he cared.

She had been forever grateful to him for that. She still was, to this day.

When Papa had died and her family's prospects took a grim turn, Billy's parents had put an end to their courtship in true mercenary fashion. She knew Billy had been miserable about it. He'd written her a heartfelt letter, offering to run away with her, but she had quickly killed that notion with a swift refusal.

She'd never told her family. She was not certain why except that it felt too private. Too personal. His offer . . . her rejection . . . it was *her* business. Hers alone. And she didn't want her sisters to know of it. They might have tried to talk her out of it.

As an only child, Billy stood to receive a nice inheritance, and she would not cheat him of that. She had refused to let him make such a sacrifice.

And he had not really thought out the details of eloping with her. Ever the pragmatic one, she saw all the flaws and potential harm if they eloped. She could predict the potential consequences and none were enviable.

He had no means of support aside of his family. They'd have nothing. No income. No home of their own waiting for them. Marian would have welcomed them, of course, but that would have been an additional burden on her sister. Charlotte could not do that.

They'd be married and destitute, and she knew what destitute felt like. It was not a pleasant way to live. If avoidable, it was no way to live at all.

She had declined to subject him to that.

So she'd had to let him go. On reflection, it hadn't pained her very much. She'd told herself it was because it was the right thing to do.

Then her sister had wed the duke.

Everything changed after that.

She and Billy could be together. They could marry. Just when she was getting accustomed to the idea of not being with him.

Once they were married and in their own home, things would be different. Better. She would have her own house, one in which she felt comfortable, and Billy would be separate from his family. He would be his own man. *Her* husband. Things would be better, indeed.

"STOP MOVING," MRS. Hansen muttered around a mouthful of pins, glaring up at Charlotte.

The irony wasn't lost on Charlotte.

A year ago, she was in the employ of Mrs. Hansen, the very same woman who now sat at her feet and worked so diligently pinning the hem of her wedding gown.

Strange how life could turn so quickly. One moment Charlotte was working her fingers bloody with a needle and thread, hoping she was doing enough to help her family, hoping they would not be expelled from their home, hoping they would have a proper dinner that night.

The next she was here, living in an extravagant home. Her sister was married to a duke. And she had entered into liaisons of a lascivious nature with a rogue.

Life, indeed, could turn quickly.

Charlotte had not been keen on using the woman to create her wedding gown. Mrs. Hansen had not been the kindest of employers, and her husband, the repellent Mr. Hansen, often made her feel uncomfortable with his leering ways. The wretched man always seemed to be bumping into Charlotte and the other dressmaker apprentices. She thought of those poor girls now, still working for the Hansens with no end in sight, no relief—just an endless stretch of days bent over their sewing and suffering long body brushes with Mr. Hansen.

But Mrs. Pembroke had insisted on commissioning Mrs. Hansen for Charlotte's wedding gown. Even Marian had to agree that Mrs. Hansen was very talented and knew the business of dressmaking better than any other seamstress in the fife.

Charlotte considered herself in the cheval mirror. They were right. The dress had turned out beautifully. She rotated and turned, observing herself from every side: from the lace cap sleeves to the delicate threading and beadwork across the cinched bodice, it was lovely, understated elegance. No fancy London dressmaker could have done better.

Even Nora looked suitably impressed from where she sat on a chaise in the middle of Marian's dressing room. "Beautiful." She nodded. "Too bad it's your wedding dress."

"Nora," Marian snapped.

Charlotte ignored her, still studying herself in the mirror.

"Let's just see how it will look with this atop your head."

Marian lifted a tiny cap and cascading veil speckled with tiny pearls from where it sat nearby and carefully positioned it atop Charlotte's head, letting the veil drape partially over her face.

Mrs. Hansen rose to her feet, removing the pins from her lips. "Indeed, you're the bonniest bride to ever grace Brambledon. Wait until everyone sees you!"

There were more words, compliments all, talk of the dress, the flowers, the menu for the luncheon to follow the nuptials.

And yet she felt nothing inside.

Charlotte felt utterly hollow as she gazed at herself in the mirror—seeing the bride she would be in a few short weeks, walking down the aisle to join Billy. *William.* Perhaps she should start calling him William like everyone else.

Boys you grew up with were called Billy. Husbands were William. Yes. Indeed. William. Her husband, William.

Husband.

Why did the simple word, the very notion of it . . . the notion of being married to Billy—no, *William*—fill her with such queasiness?

It must be Nora's fault. All her jibes and unwelcome remarks were taking root and giving Charlotte doubts. *Jitters.* She gave an internal nod. That was all it was. Jitters. Perfectly normal. Everyone said so.

Mrs. Pratt had teased her just the other day over that very thing, asking if Charlotte had prewedding jitters yet and then going on about her own long-ago wedding to Mr. Pratt and how she had been so nervous the weeks before. Apparently everyone entertained second thoughts as their wedding day approached.

Everyone.

Except Charlotte had not felt any doubts regarding her marriage to William until Kingston showed up. Blast the man and all his wicked ways.

Wicked ways you fully embraced.

She took a deep breath. The air felt thicker in the room, harder to draw inside her shrinking lungs as she contemplated his wicked ways and her role in them. Her very active and participatory role.

Certainly the first time she could blame it on that blasted tonic Nora fed her, but what about what happened between them at the pond? Was her behavior truly a result of residual effects, as she had claimed to him?

What about now? Just the thought of him made her skin hot. Was that normal?

No.

Certainly it wasn't normal.

She glanced down at her hands. Her arms were covered down to the wrist in fabric. The only part of herself exposed was her hands, but the skin there was puckered to gooseflesh.

It had been a week since the incident at the pond and she had managed to keep her distance from Kingston during that time. It wasn't easy. It mostly involved hiding out in her room until dinner, so then she only had to see him in the company of others, where he could do nothing other than comport himself properly.

Again, it was manageable, but not desirable for any extended length of time. She couldn't hide in her room until the wedding.

Wedding. It felt like a great boulder was sitting on her chest. She couldn't lift her rib cage to suck in air. *Wedding.* Again, the word reverberated through her like a death knell.

Suddenly she was moving, hopping down from the dais where she stood and shaking out her skirts as though that could free her of the confounded dress. Perhaps then she could breathe.

Mrs. Hansen squawked, flapping her hands.

"I have to get this off." Charlotte twisted around, trying to reach for the buttons she could in no way reach—at least not without help.

The other women exclaimed and lunged for her, but she was past reason. She couldn't tolerate one more moment of this dress on her body.

"Char? What's wrong?" Marian cried over Charlotte's ragged gasps.

"It's the dress!" Nora stabbed a finger in her direction. "It's biting her!"

"Rubbish, Nora!"

Charlotte lifted her chest high, desperate, hungry for air.

"Look at her! What's wrong with her?"

"Have a care! Stop! You'll ruin all my hard work." Of course, that was Mrs. Hansen.

Charlotte couldn't stop, though. She couldn't breathe and she was convinced that had to do with the wedding dress suffocating her.

Irrational or not, she twisted and tugged, getting poked by pins. She winced. The pain was justified. Necessary.

The dress had to come off.

Suddenly the room felt too tight. The dress itself was a constricting fist, but the room . . .

Heavens save her, the room was like a coffin closing in.

"Charlotte! Stop!" Marian waved her hands in

the air as though she were trying to calm a wild animal. "We will help you! Hold still!"

Shaking her head, she lifted her skirts and lunged for the door, charging out of her sister's dressing room and through her bedchamber.

Outside. Naturally there would be plenty of air outside. Outside this room full of ladies gushing over her in her wedding finery.

The other ladies followed fast on her heels, complaining loudly.

"Charlotte, what is happening?" Marian shouted.

She didn't know. She only knew that panic was riding high in her squeezing throat and she needed out of this dress, out of this room.

Air. She needed air. Blessed air.

She yanked open the door leading out into the hall and stopped hard. Kingston stood there, clearly surprised to see her. She'd evidently caught him as he was passing by. He must think her mad, charging out like some deranged bride.

If it had been hard to breathe before, now it was impossible. She pressed a hand to her chest, wheezing.

His gaze widened, raking her up and down, missing nothing as he assessed her in all her wedding finery.

"Kingston," she managed to get out in a gasp. As far as greetings went it was fairly pathetic.

His expression altered, flashing to alarm. "Charlie?"

Even in her state of distress, her face caught fire at the nickname he insisted on using. No one ever called her that, and it only added to the sense of intimacy between them—an intimacy that she could not allow to exist.

Suffocated beyond endurance, she clawed at the neckline. Modesty was the least of her concerns when she could not draw breath. At any rate, what would it matter if she tore it off? Underneath she wore a corset and chemise, and he had seen her in those before. In *less* than those.

He seized her elbow and his touch on her bare skin felt like multiple points of fire. "Charlie? Are you unwell?"

She shook her head, her fingers curling inward against her chest, digging into her bodice. "Can't. Breathe."

His gaze flicked from her face to her laboring chest.

She felt the arrival of her sister at her back. "Oh, Mr. Kingston," Marian exclaimed in perfect graciousness even in the present circumstances. Her years as a governess had trained her to keep her composure. "It appears you've caught a sneak glimpse of our bride here."

"It appears so," he agreed even as his eyes remained transfixed on Charlotte.

"I trust you'll spread no tales describing the glory of her dress." Marian laughed lightly as she rested a hand on Charlotte's shoulder.

"You can trust me, indeed. I'll not utter a word of it."

"Splendid! We want Mr. Pembroke properly surprised." She gave Charlotte's shoulder a reassuring pat—as though Charlotte cared about such tattle, as though she were not choking for breath.

"Your Grace . . . your sister does not look well."

Marian stepped around to get a better view of her face. She blanched at the sight. "Char! You're turning red!" Marian pressed the back of her hand to her cheek.

Suddenly Nora was pushing out into the hall with them. "Red? She's turning purple."

"She can't breathe," Kingston exclaimed.

Then it was all a blur.

Kingston spun her about and his hands went to her back.

Over Mrs. Hansen's screeching, Charlotte heard the popping of buttons at the back of her gown. From her peripheral vision she saw several tiny rose-colored buttons launch through the air.

Her dress immediately loosened, sliding down her arms in a whisper.

Kingston's gaze dragged over her. "Bloody corset," he muttered. "No wonder you can't breathe."

There was a tug on her laces and then relief as he undid them, freeing her from the constraints of her corset. Sweet air rushed into her lungs.

Air. Blessed air.

The shouting intensified and suddenly she was being hauled back into the bedchamber, away from Kingston's eyes, as though she must be shielded from view, her modesty protected. That was an almost amusing thought considering that her modesty, in relationship to Kingston, was unsalvageable.

There was a brief moment before the door slammed shut on Kingston's face when she saw his expression. He wasn't looking at her semi-clad body or the wedding dress sagging around her. He wasn't seeing the dress at all. He was looking at her face, and his gaze was full of worry.

He was worried. About her. *For* her.

He didn't care about her torn wedding gown or that she stood in a state of dishabille. Indeed not. He only cared for her welfare and that she could breathe again.

"Come, come. Let's get you to the bed." Marian and Nora guided her to the bed as though she was an invalid. Before settling onto the thick mattress, she stepped out of her dress.

Mrs. Hansen was ready for it. She snatched it into her arms, embracing it like it was a dying soldier. With a moan of distress, she whisked it away, clearly hoping to repair it.

Nora dropped down beside her. "What on earth just happened?"

Marian scrutinized her closely. "Your color seems improved."

"I already feel much better," she murmured, taking a breath.

Perhaps it was putting on the wedding dress. Or perhaps it was the upcoming wedding. Either way, whatever had brought about her distress had passed and she was breathing easier now.

"Was it your corset? Were you laced too tightly? Poor dear." Marian rubbed circles on the center of her back just like their mother used to do.

Charlotte inhaled and nodded. It was easier to let her think that than explain the truth. *The truth.* That she had found herself in some manner of physical upset simply trying on her wedding gown.

If that was indeed the truth, it wasn't something she could understand.

It was unwanted and vastly inconvenient. It couldn't be true.

"Well, then thank goodness for Kingston acting so quickly," Marian added.

"Indeed. He wasted no time," Nora seconded. "Did you see the way he discarded her of her clothing?" Nora lifted her eyebrows as though in awe. "He must have had copious practice at that."

"Nora, hush," Marian reprimanded. "You mustn't say such things."

Her sisters devolved into bickering among themselves and Charlotte took the time to compose herself. She relaxed back into the much too comfortable bed. She rested a hand over her stomach that now rose and fell with gentle, easy breaths.

She was indeed glad to be free of that dress. Certainly her episode had been an anomaly. A protest against her overly tight garments.

After Mrs. Hansen altered the gown and loosened the stays, she would not have another episode. She would not wear her corset so tightly again either. She'd put on a little weight since the first fitting. Her measurements had changed, obviously. Nothing more than that. It was Warrington's excellent cook and all the delicious meals she had been eating, making up for those many months of deprivation.

Nothing more than that.

It wasn't because the dress had felt like a funeral shroud, signifying the end of her life.

Chapter 11

The following afternoon Charlotte departed from her room with a cautious glance to the left and right. Satisfied the corridor was empty, she closed the door to her chamber quietly behind her and hastened forward.

She was done hiding away.

She could not abide another day indoors, counting the minutes until the supper hour.

But that didn't mean she wanted to bump into Kingston. Every single one of their encounters had been fraught with calamity.

Interesting, that. Her life had been so unfettered. Aside of the tragic loss of her parents, she had led a dull and contented existence.

Certainly, she had had a brief taste of tribulation. There had been poverty and deprivation aplenty following Papa's death. The loss of her mother was so long ago she felt it like a dull ache. An old wound or echo of an injury. Nothing too unbearable.

People lost loved ones and bore that grief and carried on. She deliberately focused on the happy times. Small moments of comfort. Charlotte remembered Mama humming as she worked in the garden or in the kitchen. She remembered how a tender smile would grace her face as she played at the pianoforte. Those memories were fond little gems that she would pull out on occasion . . . especially within the walls of her home. *Home.* Not this place.

She missed her old home. It might lack the grandeur of Haverston Hall, but it was more than enough for her. It had always been enough. Always grand in her eyes and never so much as when she had left it behind. As when she no longer possessed it.

It held so many precious memories. When she envisioned her future, she saw herself there. She saw herself with a child or two, tending the garden as Mama had, cooking in the kitchen as she had liked to do. Even when they had staff to do such things for them, Mama had been there, elbows deep in dough.

Charlotte minded her tread, keeping it light and silent as she made her way to the back servants' stairs.

Kingston might have helped her out of a situation yesterday when he freed her from her gown—as awful and awkward as that had been—but that didn't mean she wanted to see him again. She was not ready for that.

Truthfully, she might never be ready for that. She winced. Their encounters often involved a shocking *lack* of clothing on her part.

Cowardly or not, she would continue to avoid him. It was the wisest precaution.

Hopefully, he would take his leave soon. He could not mean to stay forever.

A sophisticated gentleman like him couldn't want to linger in a provincial little hamlet like Brambledon despite what he said to the contrary. He doubtlessly had parties and routs and a flock of glamorous women waiting for him.

She'd also sensed a tension in her brother-in-law. Warrington did not want him here. That much was clear as he sat at the head of the table each evening, chewing his food with a rigid jawline. Marian was forced to carry on the conversation, often glaring at her husband for his sulking manner.

Curious indeed. Charlotte would like to know more of the relationship between Warrington and Kingston, but she resisted nosing about. It was not her business. To inquire reflected poorly on her . . . made her appear too interested.

She descended the servants' stairs at the back of the house and slipped outside stealthily. Lifting her skirts, she very nearly broke into a run to escape the shadow of the grand manor house. Her nape prickled as she imagined any number of eyes watching her from its many windows, tracking her escape. She gave a swift shake of her head. Simple paranoia, that. No one was watching her.

Fortunately today was not as uncomfortably hot as the previous week. Perhaps the hottest days of summer were behind them. She could only hope. She'd voiced concern that a wedding in July might be too warm, but Mrs. Pembroke had insisted on it, overruling Charlotte's concerns. As was her custom.

Still, even with more temperate weather, Charlotte was glad she had worn her bonnet with the widest brim to shield her face. She did not relish Mrs. Pembroke criticizing her nose and cheeks for being overly pink.

Now well clear of the house, she strolled at an easier pace, enjoying the day, letting the fresh air fill her lungs and fortify her.

This evening she was taking dinner with the Pembrokes. She could use a bit of fortification before going into that. While the men took their cigars and brandy, she would be left with Mrs. Pembroke. She would want to talk about the wedding. Incessantly. Exhaustively.

Briefly, fleetingly, it crossed her mind that she *should* want to talk about the wedding. It was *her* wedding, after all. Was wedding planning not something brides lived to do?

She crossed the duke's property and arrived on the main road that meandered past the Pratt farm. The Pratt's property sat between Haverston Hall and her original home. She eyed the Pratt farmhouse as she passed it, grateful that Mrs. Pratt was not outside. The lady loved to talk. Gossip was her currency. Charlotte was thankful to avoid her.

She kept to the road until it was time to cut across toward her house.

Home.

She crested the hill and looked down at it with a lovely unfurling inside her chest. It had not fallen to disrepair since they vacated it. Warrington's groundskeeper saw to the lands. Charlotte visited often, tending to the garden and performing light housekeeping to keep the place up until she moved back in.

It would always feel like home to her. As happy as she was for her sister, as grateful as she was to the duke for taking her and Nora in and never making them feel like unwanted relations hanging about, that would never change. She could not wait to return to this place permanently.

As she passed through the white fence surrounding her house, her heart continued to lighten. She latched the gate behind her and quickly located the additional key they hid under a rock in the front garden.

She unlocked the yellow front door—even faded the color struck her as cheerful—and stepped inside, frowning a bit at the creaking hinges. She needed to see to oiling that.

She stood in the foyer, rotating in a small circle. The house smelled a bit musty, even with her frequent visits. It required a good airing out.

No, it required people. She nodded with certainty. A family again living beneath this roof breathing life back into the place.

She smiled, seeing herself and those faceless children she had yet to meet. Her smile slipped as she attempted to envision William among them, with them. His features were a bit hazy in her imaginings. Indeed, he was rather faceless as he lifted one of those children up into his arms, which didn't make sense. She'd known William all her life. His face was more familiar than her own. She should be able to see him very clearly in this particular daydream.

"Are you feeling better now?"

She whirled around with a gasp at the question spoken behind her, her hand flying to her throat.

Kingston stood in the doorway, limned brilliantly in the sunlight, coatless, cravat loosened at his throat. The handsome sight of the bare skin there gave her a bit of a jolt. His lack of attire might have looked unkempt on another man, but he merely looked casual and breezy and achingly handsome.

She swallowed against her suddenly dry mouth. Apparently her departure from Haverston Hall had not gone unnoticed. Had he followed her?

"Yes, thank you. I don't know what happened. It was a spell of some kind, I suppose. I must have been laced too tightly in my corset."

"You must have been," he agreed, his gaze rather vague, as though he did not entirely believe in his agreement. "I'm glad you're doing much better."

"Thank you for acting so quickly." She let loose a nervous little laugh.

"Even if you did send Mrs. Hansen into a fit when you ripped the dress."

"Did I rip it? I had not noticed."

She released another little laugh. "You tore the buttons off."

His bourbon-colored eyes glinted at her and

she knew he was remembering another time buttons had been lost—only she had been the person doing the ripping then.

He shrugged. "You couldn't breathe. A silly dress was hardly of concern to me. You were my priority."

You were my priority.

She did not think anyone had said such a thing to her before. Indeed, her sisters and brother loved her as they ought to do, as family loved family.

But she did not think any individual, outside of her kin, considered her a priority. Not even William, and that was a disheartening thought. She imagined he would . . . once they were married. Once she was his wife. An uncomfortable sensation swept over her. A disquieting prickling that ran all over her body.

An awkward silence rose up between them.

She wished she hadn't mentioned the *silly* dress. She didn't even want to think about it, much less talk about it.

He stepped fully into the foyer as though she had invited him to do so, as though the matter of the two of them being alone here was of no concern or threat to propriety.

She eyed his lean figure, summoning the words that would demand his departure, but they did not come.

Craning his neck, he peered about them. "So you lived here? This was the dwelling of the infamous Langley sisters?" A devilish smile played about his lips.

She was not certain if he'd been informed of that fact or he simply had inferred it.

"Yes. Up until a year ago."

"Very nice." He nodded, looking around. Even vacant with only a few rudimentary items of furniture, the happy spirit of the Langley family remained, clinging about the place, humming on the air. She felt it and, staring at his thoughtful expression as he surveyed, she suspected he felt it, too.

She moved deeper into the house, pushing open the double doors to the drawing room.

"I'd offer you tea, but the house is not outfitted."

They shouldn't even be here together. It was improper. The kind of thing that could end a reputation. *Her* reputation. And yet the circumstance of finding herself here with him seemed redundant after all that had transpired between them.

They'd been alone together several times now, and every time inappropriateness had abounded. This time she would like to prove, if only to herself, that they could behave and comport themselves appropriately when the opportunity for mischief was present.

She moved to the drapes and dragged them open, revealing through the mullion-paned glass the riot of wildflowers that Mama had planted so long ago. Every year they returned without fail.

"Well, that's a lovely view," he commented, walking up beside her and staring out the window with his hands clasped behind his back.

She held herself still, trying not to *feel* him beside her—trying not to notice the way his body radiated warmth and something else . . . an energy that pulled at her.

"My mother planted those and they still thrive. It's like a part of her is still here every year I see them bloom."

He nodded. "I suppose she is then." He glanced out through the glass at the myriad flowers in full bloom. "I'm sure that gives you comfort."

"My sisters and I would sequester ourselves there and weave coronets of grass and flowers for our heads." She smiled fondly at the recollection. "We had happy times here," she volunteered. "Even after we lost Mama, Papa kept us occupied with our studies and hobbies. Our lives were full." She smoothed a hand along the papered drawing room wall. "There was a lot of laughter in these walls."

"You were very fortunate, indeed, to have such an upbringing."

She smiled and shoved off her sudden over-whelming sense of nostalgia. He didn't need to see her so maudlin. She was no Gothic heroine under the dark cloud of pervasive threat. Indeed not.

Charlotte lived in a grand house and was preparing for the finest wedding the shire had ever seen. She lived a life of comfort and privilege and had a doting betrothed.

With a smile fixed to her face, she inquired, "Is there someplace like that for you? Where you grew up?"

"I was sent to school at age four. Our instructors were not the sort to encourage frolicking in wildflowers."

"Four? Is that not very young?"

"I imagine it is. Childhood goes to die in places like that."

She shuddered. "Sounds awful. Will you send your children away to school so young then?"

He hesitated. "I don't imagine I will ever have children."

She angled her head thoughtfully. "Why not?"

"I don't anticipate marrying, and although I was born outside of wedlock, illegitimacy is not something I'd wish on any child." His face grew tight as though he was somewhere else right then, lost in some memory.

"My brother is away at school," she volunteered, hoping to lighten the mood and distract him from somber thoughts.

"You have a brother as well?"

"Yes. But he did not go away until he was twelve." She laced her fingers, twisting them together slightly. "We had many good years with him."

He smiled. "A proper age for a young man to be sent to school." His gaze dropped to her fingers and she forced them to stillness.

"He seems to enjoy it from all his letters. And he visits at every holiday. Each time we see him he's grown another half foot."

"That's the way with lads. They grow like weeds until suddenly they are lads no more."

She drifted through the room until she sank down on the settee. It appeared the thing to do as they were having a normal conversation with no buttons flying.

Very civil and acceptable, as it should be—as it should have been from the beginning.

"Did you not go home for holidays when you were at school?"

He lowered down beside her, the springs protesting slightly as he rested his hat on his knee. Her gaze skimmed over that knee encased in his well-fitted breeches, and then darted away, up to his face—another manner of distraction there, for certain.

"I would visit my mother, yes," he answered. "I would not say I ever went *home* as she was rarely ever at the same place. She moved around often. Very few places stand out in my memory. Certainly none were home." Pause. "I've never known a home."

"Oh." She tried not to reveal how very sad Kingston's life sounded to her.

Her heart softened as she imagined the small, adrift boy he had been, and she felt the wild urge to touch him, of all the ill-advised things to do. Pat a hand on his arm or shoulder. Ridiculous and dangerous. She should certainly stay any impulse to make physical contact.

Except she could not help thinking: *He was a boy without a name or a home.*

She curled her fingers into her palm until her nails cut deep. She had no doubt if she were to look at her hands she would see tiny half-moons carved into her skin. She didn't care, though. She'd gladly take the pain. Anything was better than touching him.

Chapter 12

The proximity was too much to bear. Sitting close to him felt a precarious thing. Charlotte surged to her feet, determined to put some space between them before she bled all over her skirts from digging into her palms.

"Shall I give you a tour?" she asked abruptly, striding away from him, ahead of him.

"Very well." He followed her up the stairs.

While keeping a safe, respectable distance, she showed him each sparsely furnished room, trying not to reveal how very nervous he made her. She supposed that was natural given their history with each other, but, again, she wanted to prove herself strong. Not a slave to her impulses. She was not under the influence of Nora's tonic, so she could behave properly.

As she moved through the house, she witnessed everything through his eyes. She saw the shell of a house he must now see.

They'd sold off several pieces of furniture after Papa had died. Before Marian married Warrington. It had been necessary, but she was hoping she could locate some of those items and buy them back once she and William married.

"Nice light in here," he commented as she showed him the master chamber.

The bed was still there—a lovely mahogany four-poster bed that had belonged to her grandparents before her parents. All three of her siblings and Charlotte had been born in that bed.

She realized the sight of the bed and Kingston in proximity to it should have struck a chord of alarm within her, but why should one mere bed strike her with anxiety? They'd never been near a bed before, and that had not stopped them from succumbing to lascivious behavior. No, if they had surrendered to passion in the library at Haverston Hall and out beneath the wide-open skies on a summer afternoon, then any environment could be conducive. If she so chose. If she was weak again. Which she was not.

She was in full control of herself and all impulses. She had nothing to fear.

"I've always thought so," she agreed, moving past the bed to the double balcony doors. Unlocking them, she pushed them open, allowing the afternoon air inside. "It overlooks my mother's wildflowers."

Kingston stepped onto the balcony and peered down. "The world can't be too bad whilst waking up to such a view."

"Indeed not," she agreed, feeling more relaxed.

She rather enjoyed the ease of talking to Kingston. *Kingston.* Did he not possess another name?

Turning from the view, she faced him. "Does everyone address you as Kingston?" She'd never heard Nathaniel or Marian call him anything else. Charlotte hadn't the slightest clue as to his Christian name.

"Ever since I was a lad, yes. Even my own father calls me Kingston."

"That's rather . . . perfunctory."

A corner of his mouth lifted. "Are you asking me for my Christian name, Charlie?"

She stiffened at the intimate moniker on his lips. She supposed digging around for his name invited that. "Yes, I expect I am." She forced the rigidity from her frame. They were having a perfectly normal interaction and she did not wish to ruin it.

"I'm not certain anyone even remembers my name," he mused, staring out into the trees, resting a hand on the railing.

She gazed at him a long moment, wondering if he was simply jesting. His sober expression hinted at no such thing.

"Certainly your mother," she supplied.

A shadow fell over his face. "I would not rely on that."

She fought against a frown. What manner of mother forgot her child's name? The wretch. Charlotte immediately felt a keen dislike for the faceless woman. Perhaps disproportionately so. And yet she could not help envisioning, yet again, the handsome man before her as a little boy, lost and yearning for a mother's love.

Kingston continued, "My mother is not well these days. I suspect her illness precludes her from remembering a great many things."

"Oh." Now Charlotte felt the wretch for thinking poorly of an ailing woman. "I'm very sorry to hear that." She moistened her lips and pressed, "What is your name?"

He sent her a small smile. "You know my name."

"Kingston is a surname."

"It's all anyone ever calls me."

She frowned. "I'd like to call you by your name. Your true name."

"You'd be the only one to use it."

The only one.

At that, she hesitated. She knew she should let the matter drop. It would be far too intimate to be the *only* person using his Christian name. She didn't want that intimacy to exist between them.

Still, she heard herself saying, "I don't mind that."

After several beats of silence, he answered. Over the chirping of birds and wind rustling in the branches, he said, "It's Samuel. Sam."

"Samuel. Sam." She tested it on her tongue. "It's a nice name . . . makes you seem more human. It's certainly less imposing than Kingston."

At that, he grinned. "Perhaps that is why I never tell people. A bastard is better served if he comes across as a little imposing."

She flinched at the ease in which he called himself *bastard*.

"You knew that, of course?" he asked. "I am the Earl of Norfolk's bastard."

"Yes, I knew that." She gave a perfunctory nod. He smiled humorlessly. "People talk."

Indeed. She knew that, too.

He moved from the railing with a crisp turn. "So what are the plans for this place?" he asked in what felt, to her, an obvious evasion or, at the very least, an effort to change the topic from his mother. He strode to the center of the chamber and stopped, turning idly to examine the room.

She released a sigh. "For now, Marian is holding on to the property, on the chance that one of us might choose to reside here some day."

Charlotte chose to be deliberately vague. She did not feel inclined to speak of her future in that moment—specifically of her future here, in this house, with William.

Yes, she was counting on residing in this house again. It was decided. It was what she wanted and William had agreed.

It felt in poor taste, however, to speak of it with Kingston, a man with whom she had recently shared intimacies, however ill-advised those encounters happened to be . . . however much they would *not* repeat on those mistakes, however much she battled the shame of her actions.

Even if she believed herself unable to resist, she still battled with shame.

"Ah. Might you then? With Pembroke?" Despite her prevarication he saw directly to the matter. He stared at her politely, patiently waiting for her response.

"Well, actually . . ." No sense lying. Perhaps it would be a good thing for him to realize how very much their paths diverged.

He stared at her mildly. Apparently he felt no reaction over the mention of her impending marriage. Something pinched near her heart at that. Relief, she supposed. What else could it be?

"Yes," she admitted. "William and I have decided to move in here after we're married."

She studied him then. Was it her imagination or did he look affected at this announcement? For the briefest moment did the line of his mouth compress?

"I am certain living here will make your marriage more palatable." He delivered the words so politely it was not easy to detect the offense given at first. Until she did detect it.

Until she heard and felt the remark for all its intended sting.

She pulled back her shoulders in affront. "My marriage will be palatable no matter where we reside."

His look turned pitying. "Do you think so?"

"Oh," she puffed in outrage. "Are you deliberately insulting me?"

"Does the truth offend?"

"It's not the truth," she insisted.

Again came a pitying look. "If your impending marriage to this Pembroke fellow was right for you, then you would not care where you lived as long as you were together."

"Well, o-of course, that is true," she stammered.

"Is it true, though?" he queried, one eyebrow arched in skepticism. He motioned about him. "I think you love this house and the idea of returning to it more than the man you're to wed."

"Oh!" Heat swelled up from her chest to burn her face. She opened her mouth, wanting to deny him further, but she was too busy digesting his words.

Was this house more important to her than William? Could that be true?

He pressed on. "In fact, I don't think you love your betrothed at all."

She sputtered at the accusation, pointing a trembling finger to the door. The man did not know when to cease. "I think you should leave, Mr. Kingston."

"*Mister* Kingston, is it? What happened to Samuel? Or, if you prefer, Sam?"

He strode closer, his tread falling on the bare wood floor in steady thuds. The plush Aubusson rug that once covered the floor was another thing gone, another thing sold off. "If you felt even a fraction of love for your Mr. Pembroke you would never have touched me . . . never have let me touch you. Even now, you would not look at me the way you do."

Dear heavens. What way did she look at him?

She must have asked the question aloud because he was answering her with a slow smile
that belied the gravity in his voice.

"You are looking at me as though you would
like to continue where we left off at the pond.
You're looking at me," he repeated, his voice an
erotic rasp, "as though you can still taste me . . .
the way *I* can still taste you. With the morning
light on your skin. The summer air wrapped
around you."

She was in trouble. Deeply. Tragically.

His words were dangerously seductive. And
quite dangerously, possibly, true.

Growing up, whenever she had heard hushed
gossip of young ladies that toppled over the
brink into ruin, she had thought herself unlike
them. She had never understood how they could
succumb and give up all propriety.

Now she did. Now she understood.

Now she knew she had been a small-minded
prig lacking imagination because she entirely
and wholly understood how one could surrender to desire.

Now she understood how a man's words could
turn a woman giddy.

This close to Samuel, his words were a warm,
heady husk on her skin. She felt intoxicated,
drugged again, although that was not the case.

This time she could only blame herself for the

way she melted beneath the sensual assault of his words.

She closed her eyes in a hard squeeze. This was wrong, and fair to no one . . . but especially not fair to William. He deserved the loyalty of a good woman, and presently she felt like neither of those things. Not loyal. Not good.

This had to stop.

Her eyes flew open. "We cannot continue to consort this way," she said in a feverish rush.

"Why not?"

"I'm betrothed. I'm not free to . . . to do *this*." She waved a hand back and forth between them.

"I'll take you as you are. I'll have you any way you'll permit. Betrothed or not. I'm not an honorable sort."

She blinked. He did not appear to be jesting. There was no pride or shame in his voice—no inflection at all. He uttered the words solemnly. Matter-of-factly.

Only she could agree with him.

He'd been respectful toward her and exhibited admirable restraint . . . even if he was offering to seduce her now.

He wasn't a perfect man, but there was decency in him. She would even say . . . *honor*. She'd wager on it.

"I see you considering my words. You do not agree?"

She lifted her chin. "You are not the complete cad you would have me believe."

The gold flecks in his eyes sparked. "Oh, you are far too trusting."

"I'm not—"

"If you could read my thoughts you would not be so quick to defend me." He laughed deeply and the sound was dark and rich, wrapping around her like the warmest, most luxurious fur. "It's absurd, is it not? I'm being honest in that my intentions toward you are dishonorable . . . and you don't believe me. Promise me you'll stay in this provincial little hamlet forever and never venture to Town. The place is swimming with sharks ready to devour sweet chits such as yourself . . . even as they utter kind things to your face."

She took a steadying breath. "I'm only saying you judge yourself too harshly. You have . . . limits." Clearly, there were boundaries he would not cross. She knew that from their first encounter . . . and their second. "You would not—"

"Oh, don't be so certain I wouldn't." His gaze warmed, the golden brown turning molten. "You have to feel it, too, between us. You know it's there."

Her breath caught.

Madness. He spouted madness. Tempting and impossible.

"It's just . . . the tonic . . ." she whispered brokenly, desperately reaching for it, for something to explain this hopeless thing between them. She dragged her gaze away, hoping to hide anything that resembled longing in her expression.

"To hell with that bloody tonic. It has naught to do with the fire between us!"

Her gaze shot back to him, rattled, unable to breathe. Her body was afire.

Without touching her, she felt touched. Raw and exposed, vulnerable.

"You need to leave," she blurted, pleased to hear the firmness in her voice.

"Evidently the truth offends." He turned and sauntered toward the door.

"It is not the truth you speak."

In response to that, he tossed a smirk over his shoulder.

It was too much. At the infuriating sight of it, an epiphany struck her. She charged ahead and seized him by the arm, forcing him around.

"And what if it is the truth? What if I don't love him?" She felt as though she'd just emerged from a deep pool of water and took a gulp of fresh air after long deprivation. Her fingers tightened around his forearm. "*Should* I feel bad about that? Should I regret what is standard in our society? What is normal? Has marriage ever necessitated love?"

"True." He slowly nodded in agreement,

looking down at her hand on his arm and back to her face. "Love and marriage rarely go together."

She yanked her hand away as though burned, appalled that she had surrendered to emotion and grabbed him.

He stepped closer. "But you are not in a position where you have to marry anyone unless you want to. Unless you are in love."

"Don't presume to know me or my *position*. You know nothing of me."

His face was so close now that she could detect the dark ring of brown surrounding his lighter irises. His smile deepened. "Oh, but I *know* a *few* things about you. Do I not?"

His words robbed her of all air. His implication seemed clear . . . full of dark and naughty things. Unspeakable things.

Her lungs ceased to move as she held his gaze, studying his face and the starkly intent way he looked at her. All of those things, memories of taste and touch and pleasure, surged between them.

"Leave me be . . . and leave this house," she managed to get out in a whisper, desperate for him to go, for space between them.

Desperate to hold strong. To do the right thing.

He lingered for several moments, holding her gaze before he obliged and turned, striding from the chamber.

She listened to the thud of his feet on the stairs.

She listened as the front door opened and clapped shut.

She listened until there was nothing more to hear.

Until there was only silence and the beating pulse of her heart in her ears.

Chapter 13

Kingston strode out of the house, his biting steps perfectly matching his ire. He could not recall ever feeling so exasperated. So annoyed. So . . . *rebuffed*. Certainly no female had ever provoked such emotions in him before.

She'd ordered him from the house. Clearly she refused to acknowledge the attraction simmering between them as anything substantive. *Bloody hell.* She refused to acknowledge it as anything that existed in truth at all.

Delusional chit.

She still blamed the tonic . . . and she was still planning to marry Pembroke.

He didn't know what was more ridiculous. A

magical elixir? Or marrying some bore when no one was forcing her to do so?

She was not being commanded by parents. No controlling papa was forcing her to the altar. She was not in dire financial straits that *required* her to wed.

Countless unfortunate females all over the kingdom, all over the world, were at the mercy of family and society. His own mother had been one of them. She was left an orphan and penniless shortly after she turned sixteen.

On holiday from school, during one of his occasional visits, his mother had offered him this glimpse into herself, sharing bits of her history with him.

He knew so little of her upbringing until that moment. He'd been curious. He'd never met his maternal grandparents. No aunts or uncles or cousins. As far as he knew, his mother was alone. There was no other family. Just him.

His mother's father had been a tailor, operating a small shop in London's East End. Kingston's grandmother had passed away when his mother was still in leading strings. At his grandfather's death, she had been left alone with very little funds. She could not even secure a marriage for herself. She was too poor and too lacking in connections. She'd utilized the only resource available to her—her considerable beauty.

Charlotte Langley did not suffer even remotely similar circumstances. Indeed, there was no pressure of any kind as far as he could determine.

He did not look back at the house as he strode away.

He did not want to see it again.

He had walked through each and every room alongside Charlotte, forcing a polite expression and courteous words, imagining her inside its walls, beneath its roof. With her husband and future children.

His feelings on that were complicated. Jealousy was not an emotion in which he was accustomed to, but he could not help wondering if what he felt was not that very thing.

The thought of her rubbing herself all over the Pembroke lad in the same manner she had rubbed on him? Doing the things that would result in the begetting of those children? *Intolerable.* It was intolerable.

He wished he could rid himself of the images from his mind.

He had seen enough of the home she was planning to share with Pembroke. It was a nice house. It would serve as a nice home for someone.

Only not Charlotte. Obviously, she didn't know that, but he did.

He did not believe she would find the contentment she sought within its walls.

He knew something of feigning contentment. Of passing each day as though there was nothing amiss. He'd watched his mother play that game . . . and lose.

Reality had a way of catching up with a person. Eventually. In his mother's situation this had become true in the very worst way.

Did Charlotte think she was going to find happiness with Pembroke? No house could fix what was broken . . . or what was never right in the first place.

It was stone and mortar and timber. Nothing else. Nothing more. It was no cure for all the little hollows and disappointments in life.

A skeleton. Bones. A shell. That's all that house was. An echo of what was once living and pulsing. She thought she could reclaim it. She was trying to recapture the past. Only that was the problem—or blessing—with the past. The past was gone. Only memory. Impossible to re-create.

He was walking a hard line across the countryside, scarcely paying attention to his surroundings as these many thoughts churned through him.

"You there! Sirrah! Over here! Over here, please!"

He stopped at the desperately shouted words and scanned the landscape, immediately spotting the tidy little farmhouse to his left and the older woman outside it, tugging on a cow that appeared impervious to her efforts. And her efforts were considerable. Her cheeks were red with exertion and tendrils of gray hair fell from her bun to straggle in her face.

The cow was tethered, but the good woman did not possess the strength to budge the tan and white beast who was happily munching the flowers in her front garden.

"Help!" she squawked. "She's eating my poppies!"

Kingston hurried to her aid, running lightly through knee-high grass and hopping over her fence in one easy motion.

The woman eyed him distrustfully as he approached, he noted with some irony. A smile played about his lips, his mood lifting. She was calling him for help, but she eyed him as though he were a highwayman come to rob her.

The cow eyed him, as well, but with less distrust. In fact, the large brown eyes appeared generally unimpressed.

"Come now, Buttercup," the lady in distress chided, grunting as she renewed her efforts to remove her cow from her garden. "Poppies aren't good for you," she said, continuing to speak to Buttercup. "Nora said too many can make you sick."

Nora? Charlotte's sister? He turned that over

in his mind, recalling Charlotte had said her sister was an herbalist of some repute in the community. The woman must be referencing her.

"Well, are you going to assist me or stand there gawking, young man?" she snapped at him.

"Oh, yes. My apologies." He lunged forward, reaching for the rope.

"Of course my Mr. Pratt is inside having himself a fine nap right now." She glared at Kingston as though he were somehow responsible for that. "Claims his back is aching him again. His back has been aching him since the morning after our wedding. Forty years ago!"

"That's . . . a . . . shame?" Kingston murmured, presumably to Mrs. Pratt, uncertain what was expected of him in this moment. What should one say when a complete stranger was complaining about her husband?

Kingston seized the rope the older woman clutched whilst the cow continued its contented chewing, one long stem with a bright red poppy the size of his fist jutting from her mouth.

Buttercup worked her jaw until the poppy disappeared in her great maw. She then dipped her head and tore off more flowers as though two humans weren't standing nearby pestering her.

The woman made a sound of distress as more of her garden was lost to Buttercup's ravenous appetite.

"Do something!"

He closed both hands around the rope and yanked, forcing Buttercup's head up. She issued a long low of protest.

"Stubborn old girl." The country dame swatted the cow's considerable rump. "I feed you enough. You're as big as a house. Leave my flowers be!"

Buttercup clearly did not care for her treatment. She tossed her head to the side, striking Kingston in the chest. Hard. The force caught him off guard and he dropped back a step to keep his balance.

Buttercup took full advantage of his suddenly lax grip and bolted faster than he would have thought an animal her size capable. She barreled past Kingston, knocking him to the ground.

He landed in the garden with a muffled epithet, rolling in soil that smelled of pungent dung.

"Ack!" Mrs. Pratt fluttered her hands helplessly, staring after the rebellious creature and not sparing him a concerned glance. "She's getting away! We need to get her back in the pen." She finally looked down at him with an expression of exasperation. "Young man! You're crushing my flowers. Up with you, sir."

Kingston hopped to his feet with a mutter, ignoring that he was now covered in manure. He gave chase, but Buttercup was surprisingly spry. She cut turns sharply like a sheep dog, evading all his lunges for her tether.

"Kingston?"

He stopped abruptly at his softly uttered name and located Charlotte. She passed through Pratt's gate, staring back and forth between him, Mrs. Pratt and Buttercup with wide eyes.

"Miss Langley," he returned.

Her gaze skimmed his length and he resisted the urge to look down at himself. He didn't need to see himself to know he was covered in filth. He only need inhale to confirm it. He could smell the stink of Mrs. Pratt's garden all over him.

"You two know each other?" Mrs. Pratt suddenly looked intrigued. Then she shook her head as though she had no time to cave into her curiosity. She pointed to her cow. True to form, amid everyone's distraction, Buttercup trotted merrily back to the flower garden.

"I was trying to assist Mrs. Pratt," he explained, motioning to the frazzled-looking woman.

"Buttercup!" Mrs. Pratt howled, waving her hands in the air. "Oh, would you look at that? She's back in my poppies now. There will be none left!"

"Not to mention, they are bad for her," Charlotte reminded in a polite voice.

"Yes. And that," Mrs. Pratt agreed.

Kingston caught up with the beast, easily seizing the tether this time. He tugged on the rope, but the overfed bovine resisted with a long braying low.

"She's like dead weight," he grumbled.

"Mrs. Pratt," Charlotte calmly inserted. "If you will pardon me?"

Mrs. Pratt blinked. She and Kingston tracked Charlotte as she marched across the yard and disappeared inside the farmhouse.

She was gone a short time, returning moments later with a cluster of carrots in her hand.

She glanced at Kingston as she passed him, and there was something smug in the look. "Did Mrs. Pratt fail to mention that Buttercup often escaped onto our property?"

The older woman shrugged rather defensively. "I've been telling Mr. Pratt he needs to see about replacing the fence around the pen."

Buttercup must have caught the scent of the carrots. Clearly it was a treat she knew well . . . and enjoyed.

Charlotte was not even in proximity before the cow whipped its head in her direction and charged toward her. She held her ground even as it looked as though the animal might plow over her.

At the last moment, Buttercup pulled to a hard halt.

Charlotte extended one of the three carrots she'd appropriated from somewhere inside the

Pratt house, permitting Buttercup to delicately pluck it from her. Charlotte started walking backward. Buttercup followed her, still chewing her carrot, the long green stems dangling from between her teeth.

Just before Charlotte rounded the house, she offered a second carrot to the cow.

Kingston followed. Rounding the house, he spotted Charlotte as she offered the final carrot, simultaneously securing Buttercup in her less than secure pen.

Kingston circled the pen, examining it. A stiff wind might send the whole thing crumbling. It was a surprise that hadn't already happened.

"She gets loose all the time, bumping against the gate and dislodging it, but she knows where home is. She always returns," Charlotte volunteered as though she could read his mind.

He nodded.

"Thank you so much, Charlotte," Mrs. Pratt called from behind them, hastening forward rather breathlessly, walking in her uneven gait. "You are always so good with her."

Charlotte shook her head. "She merely likes carrots."

"She merely likes *you*." Mrs. Pratt glared at him with a *hmpf*. "I suppose I should thank you for your *attempt* to assist me, sirrah."

He inclined his head in acknowledgement of

his failure. "You're welcome . . . for whatever it is worth, madam."

Charlotte studied him as though he was some mystery, a puzzle she could not quite piece properly together. "It was very kind of you to stop and offer assistance."

He shrugged, feeling a little uncomfortable from the praise.

She pressed on, "Most gentlemen would not roll through all manner of muck and take on a cow to help . . ." Her voice faded away as she shot a quick glance to Mrs. Pratt.

To help a humble country dame.

She did not finish the words, but he could infer, and he would have to agree. Most *ton* gentlemen would fear mussing their garments. He possessed no such airs. Kingston knew what he was, and it was not a man with a sense of self-importance.

He wasn't too good to roll around in shit.

He'd spent a lifetime surrounded by it, after all. He had not been raised with any real moral compass. Whatever code he possessed, he'd had to fashion it on his own.

"Always happy to help a lady in distress," he said gruffly. "You should know that." He could not help the last meaningful prod. He meant it only in jest, but her eyes flared wide and she shot a horrified glance to the matron, as though she feared Kingston would reveal their liaison to her.

Mrs. Pratt did not even seem to hear his remark, or if she did, it did not strike any significance. Her eyes narrowed on him. "I've never seen you before and I know everyone in these parts." She slid a suspicious glance to Charlotte. "And how is it you know my Charlotte here?"

"Mrs. Pratt, may I introduce you to Mr. Kingston? He is kin to His Grace."

"Kin? How so?"

"Warrington is my stepbrother," he replied.

Her eyes widened slightly. "Oh, indeed?" She looked him up and down, no doubt assessing his person—which was still covered in manure. "Well, it is very fine to meet you, sir. How long will you be visiting up at Haverston Hall?"

Kingston and Charlotte spoke simultaneously.

"Oh, he won't be here very long—"

"I've not yet decided."

Charlotte's cheeks pinkened.

Kingston went on to say, "I believe I shall stay a while and enjoy all the delights of your lovely village."

"Ah." She nodded, measuring him with her veteran gaze. "Brambledon does boast unique riches."

"I can believe that." He could not stop his gaze from traveling over Charlotte.

The pink in Charlotte's cheeks deepened.

Mrs. Pratt tittered. "You are a charming young man." He resisted rolling his eyes. The old dame had not been of that opinion before she learned of his relationship to Warrington. "Perhaps you will take a shine to our young Nora? Marriage and a few babes will curb her restless spirits."

"Mrs. Pratt," Charlotte admonished. "Nora is much too young for courtship . . . and there is nothing amiss with her spirits."

"Rubbish." She waved a hand. "She is no little girl anymore. I wed Mr. Pratt when I was only ten and five. The lass needs to occupy herself with something other than her experiments and herbs and books." She looked Kingston over with renewed interest. "I am certain you are quite appealing when you don't reek of dung."

He chuckled.

Charlotte pressed her lips into a mutinous line. Naturally courting her younger sister would be awkward given he and Charlotte now had a history of shared intimacies.

Not that he would court Nora. He had no interest in her, however vivacious and interesting she might be. Unfortunately, the only Langley sister to capture his interest was the one who stood before him . . . the one he could not have.

"It was a pleasure, Mr. Kingston, but go on

with you now." Mrs. Pratt waved a hand, gesturing in the direction of Haverston Hall. "You need a proper bath. Make yourself presentable and consider my words. Nora Langley." She nodded emphatically. "She might seem a bit unruly, but she will make a fine wife. Just needs a bit of domesticating."

Domesticating? As though she were a feral beast that required breaking. He winced.

Charlotte snorted in patent disapproval.

An awkward silence fell. Charlotte glared hotly at Mrs. Pratt who was oblivious that she had given offense.

Kingston inclined his head in acknowledgment, ready to put an end to the exchange. "Good day to you, too, Mrs. Pratt."

Charlotte muttered a muted farewell.

As Mrs. Pratt turned for her house, they fell in step side-by-side. He kept a careful distance from her as they strode from the Pratt farm lest he offend her with his odor. They walked for several moments before she blurted out, "You stay away from my sister." Emotion shuddered in her voice.

He nodded and then recited, *"Stay away from you. Stay away from your sister.* You're very free with your commands, Charlotte."

"I mean it."

"I have no interest in your sister. Have no fear. I won't trouble her with my attentions."

Yes. He would leave Nora Langley alone. He deliberately made no promises when it came to Charlotte.

Again, he knew himself. He knew what he was.

He was not a perfect man, but he had never been a liar.

He would not become one now.

Chapter 14

*T*he following day, Charlotte paced Nora's bedchamber, or rather her laboratory, with the restless energy of a caged cat.

It was almost as though her skin felt too tight and no longer fit her frame.

There had been no proper night's sleep since *he* arrived. She had tossed and turned in her bed and even when awake, as now, she could not hold still. There was no peace to be found.

She *should* feel triumphant over yesterday's encounter. She and Kingston had not touched. No inappropriate physical interaction had occurred whatsoever. That felt like a cause for celebration. It was a relief, to be certain. Even if the conversation had grown heated between them and their dialogue had become overly intimate, there was no more repeat impropriety between them.

She'd felt this restlessness ever since her conversation with Kingston . . . *Samuel* . . . at her house. Ever since she saw him smelly and covered in filth. All to help Mrs. Pratt, the old busybody. He possessed a generous nature. She had not expected that.

Charlotte tried to imagine her betrothed rolling up his shirtsleeves to help any of the villagers. It was a struggle to envision. Her husband-to-be was a kindhearted man, but not the type to get his hands dirty. He was much too genteel.

She had not succumbed.

Her sister's bed was covered in books. Charlotte motioned to it. "How do you even find room to sleep?"

Nora glanced distractedly at the bed. "Oh, there's room enough. I just stack the books to the side when I'm ready to go to sleep."

Shaking her head, Charlotte acknowledged there was some irony with her being so concerned with her sister's sleep habits whilst she had spent the majority of last night tossing and turning and wide-awake. She could not forget Samuel's words. His voice played over and over in her head.

But you are not in a position where you have to

marry anyone unless you want to. Unless you are in love.

She'd never considered the matter of a grand love affair. It was not something she wanted or expected for herself. She wasn't like Marian with her duke. Passion was not in her makeup.

At least it had not been before Kingston. Now her body came alive in his presence, fairly burning—

No.

She gave herself a swift mental slap. It had naught to do with Kingston. She did not burn for him specifically. It was merely the tonic. It woke her to certain physical needs.

If she had taken the tonic and stumbled on her William in that corridor she would have assaulted him, too.

She idly examined all the various herbs and materials littering Nora's worktables, sniffing at the pink contents of one glass cylinder.

"You should never do that," Nora scolded.

Wrinkling her nose, Charlotte set the cylinder back down.

Her sister moved about the room briskly, snipping some herbs with a pair of scissors where they hung near her window. With a sprig in her hand, she moved back to her worktable and began to grind it with mortar and pestle, biting her lip in concentration.

Charlotte moved to the window and peered outside through the collection of herbs. Rolling green parkland stared back at her as she contemplated the mire her life had become. Clearly, Mr. Kingston appeared in no haste to depart, despite her hopes.

She released a breath and spun around to face her preoccupied sister. "Clearly, I should kiss him," she blurted.

Of course she should. It seemed so overdue now. Especially after her interactions with Kingston.

Normally, she would have happily waited until her wedding day. Partly because decorum dictated she wait . . . and partly because she had felt no overwhelming compulsion to kiss William.

"Kiss who?" Nora blinked and looked up from her mortar and pestle.

Charlotte puffed out a breath in annoyance. "William, of course. The man I am betrothed to marry. Who else would I be talking about?"

Nora looked at her mildly and shrugged. "Never quite certain with you these days. Who can tell?"

"Oh! The cheek of you! You know the only person I dallied with is Kingston, much to my regret! I would never do so again. And it wasn't my fault. If it was anyone's fault, it was yours."

Nora cocked her head to the side consideringly. "Is that true, necessarily? Would you have assaulted dear eighty-year-old Chester in the corridor if he were the man you happened upon? I do believe a modicum of basic attraction is likely necessary."

"*Likely* necessary? You have no notion if that's true."

Nora looked at her crossly. "I'm working on figuring that out. Perhaps you should take *some* responsibility and stop blaming me?"

Charlotte curled her hands into fists at her sides.

Her sister had no notion, no concept, of the power within that tonic. It was concerning. Her sister had created a powerful tonic and she appeared to lack all respect for that fact. In that regard, she was very like Samuel. He had no appreciation for the tonic's capabilities either.

"There are so very many things wrong with what you just said, Nora. Firstly, I object to the word *assaulted*." *However close to accurate it might be.* "And I don't think we know enough about your infernal tonic to be making any assumptions. For all we know I very well could have pounced upon Chester." She nodded even as the idea of seducing their ancient butler struck her as ludicrous. She could not imagine doing to him the things she had done to Kingston.

Nora looked skeptical. "I think you are attracted to Kingston and it has naught to do with anything I did."

"Rubbish!" Charlotte's face burned. It was almost as though Nora knew of her encounter with Kingston beside the pond and her complete lack of inhibitions.

It felt like salt in the wound, and seemed to only encourage Kingston's voice in her head.

You are looking at me as though you would like to continue where we left off at the pond. You're looking at me as though you can still taste me . . . the way I can still taste you. With the morning light on your skin. The summer air wrapped around you.

She'd been playing those decadent words over and over in her mind and that certainly didn't help matters.

"The only man I should be talking about kissing right now is my betrothed," Charlotte insisted. William should be the man to fill her thoughts, not Kingston.

Nora nodded slowly. "Of course. Naturally. William. You should kiss *him*." The words were coming from her mouth, but Nora did not seem especially enthusiastic or even sound very convinced at the suggestion. "I can't believe you haven't done so already. If I were betrothed, you can be assured I would have sampled my fiancé's lips by now. I mean, not that I ever plan to get married."

"You might change your mind on that score."

"Doubtful. It's not necessary. I need not wed for position or income."

Charlotte nodded. That was true enough. Marian had wed well—remarkably well. Doing so had afforded them the power to choose their fates.

"You might marry for love," Charlotte suggested.

"As you are?" Nora quickly shot back, shaking her head ruefully.

Charlotte couldn't find her tongue to respond to that, but fortunately she didn't have to. Nora continued, "There's no man with patience enough for me . . . and no man I would find more interesting than the task of working in my lab or herb garden."

She had no doubt her sister spoke the truth, and she envied her self-assurance.

"Still . . ." Nora angled her head and looked heavenward thoughtfully. "If I was betrothed I would most certainly have done a certain amount of exploration, starting with my betrothed's mouth. I wouldn't wish to climb into the marriage bed completely ignorant, after all. For research's sake, it would be necessary. I would want to guarantee that what was to come is satisfactory."

Charlotte felt her face heating. Thanks to Kingston, she would not be slipping beneath the sheets of her marriage bed in ignorance.

"For goodness' sake, Charlotte. You've been sweethearts all your life. Well," she amended with a considering pause, "I actually *can* believe it." She grimaced. "Mama Pembroke probably advised him against it. Kissing before marriage . . . that old dragon would frown on such a thing." She tsked. "He does seem to excel at following her bidding."

Charlotte did not feel up to arguing the status of William's biddableness to his parents. She knew he could take a stand when necessary. He'd offered to elope, after all. Only she had not accepted his offer.

William was simply a respectful son. It spoke well of him. Things would be different once he and Charlotte were married and living in their own house.

A long stretch of silence filled the chamber as Nora continued working and Charlotte considered the task of kissing Billy. *William.*

No. Not a *task*. It wasn't a chore. Kissing the man she would spend the rest of her life with was not a burdensome chore. It was something she looked forward to doing.

When and *where* and *how* . . .

The potential logistics whirled through her mind.

"Are you sure you want to?" Nora asked idly

as she added a pinch of the pink powder into her mortar.

Charlotte bristled. "He's my betrothed. Of course I want to kiss him. I *chose* him."

And because she chose him, because she was going to marry him and share a bed with him, she'd best get accustomed to the notion of kissing him. As well as doing other things with him— the manner of things she had done at the pond with Kingston. *And beyond that.*

A traitorous shudder ran through her body.

Blast it. She should not be shuddering at the idea of intimacy with her husband-to-be.

In all truth, she had not considered the physical side of marriage until Kingston came along.

Perhaps that had been naïve of her . . . to not contemplate the marriage bed with her future husband. Now, however, matters of intimacy plagued her and kept her from sleeping. The problem, of course, was that William was *not* the man she was thinking about in these scenarios, and he should be the man.

He should be the one.

She had to *make* him the *one.*

"Do you truly?" Nora persisted, remaining doubtful.

She sighed in exasperation. "Truly what, Nora? Do I want to kiss him . . . yes, I—"

"No," she cut in, her gaze intent on Charlotte. "Do you really want to choose him? To marry him? I mean . . . that's forever, Char. There's no coming back from that. Once it's done, it's done." She shook her head somberly.

Charlotte swallowed thickly and glared at her sister for cutting to the heart of it so quickly. She was sincerely starting to hate the way Nora insisted on questioning her and prying so deeply into her thoughts. Why could she not be supportive and accepting like Marian? Why must Nora make her doubt herself?

"Yes," she snapped. "I really do believe he is the one."

It was already done. She'd agreed. She'd said yes. *If you didn't want to marry William, you should have never accepted his offer.*

At any rate, how did one reverse such a course once it had been set?

Simple. One did not. Not without a great deal of awkwardness and shame and scandal. It was not done. Not if one possessed a shred of decency.

Nora considered her for several more moments before arriving at, "Very well then. Perhaps you simply need some courage. I mean, if I had to kiss William I would need some, er . . . encouragement in that endeavor."

Charlotte looked at her blankly. "Encouragement?"

Nora elaborated. "Come, come. Don't be ob-
tuse. You know my meaning . . . the tonic?"

"Again?" Charlotte demanded. "You want me
to endure that wretched misery again?"

"It ended well enough the last time."

"Did it? Did it end well, Nora? Truly?" The
last time had resulted in Charlotte seducing the
duke's black sheep of a stepbrother. Theoreti-
cally, it had led her to seducing him twice. Their
encounter at the pond could only be attributed to
Nora's infernal tonic, after all.

Nora, however, didn't seem to sense her outrage. Or she didn't care, which was probably
closer to the truth.

Charlotte took a steadying breath. "I don't
need your potion to kiss the man I'm going to
marry. Take your witchery elsewhere."

Nora sniffed. "I don't appreciate being called
a witch. Especially since witches have a habit of
being burned at the stake historically. I'm a scientist, Char. Not a witch."

"Well, I don't need your particular brand of
science interfering in my life. I can kiss my fiancé
without your assistance. The old-fashioned way
shall suit me just fine." She wagged a warning
finger.

"Very well then. So when do you plan to
launch this *old-fashioned* seduction of yours? His
mama scarcely leaves you two alone as it is."

Charlotte shrugged. "I said nothing of seduction. Merely a kiss. And I have not thought that far along yet. The next time I see him shall be as good a time as any, I imagine." She nodded decisively. "Yes. Yes, indeed. The next time I see him."

"If you can get him alone."

"I can get him alone," she retorted, a touch defensively. "We often take strolls alone, as you well know."

Nora made a humming sound rife with skepticism.

It only made the determination burn hotter in Charlotte's chest.

Kissing William seemed rather important right now. *Critically* important.

More important than ever.

In all her intimate encounters with Kingston, they had not kissed. Incredible as it seemed, they had somehow managed to skip that part of intimacy and had instead jumped headlong into a firestorm of passion.

She had not kissed Kingston.

Her mouth tingled as if it heard the thought and now wanted to change that fact.

Treacherous lips.

There would be this, at least. She had not given her first kiss to Samuel. That was still hers yet. Hers to give. Hers to choose with whom to share. At long last. Her first kiss would be with William.

This one thing she would reserve for her future husband . . . the way it ought to be done.

Chapter 15

*C*harlotte failed.

She couldn't do it.

The opportunity presented itself when William called on her for afternoon tea. His mother and grandmother accompanied him as usual, but they remained in the drawing room whilst she and William took a turn about the gardens.

Marian was the far greater draw to Mrs. Pembroke anyway. It didn't matter who her sister used to be. She was the Duchess of Warrington now. That was the only thing that mattered.

Aware of her mission to kiss William, Nora joined them for afternoon tea as well. A rarity. When the Pembrokes called, she usually concealed herself somewhere and didn't emerge until they'd departed.

Intent on helping Charlotte, Nora had come prepared, clearly ready to distract Mrs. Pembroke by sharing her letters. Her sister knew that woman's weakness well. The moment Mrs. Pembroke learned Nora was corresponding with an army colonel who happened to be a kinsman to the Duke of Birchwood, she was riveted as Nora relayed the contents of their correspondence.

It was remarkable. Charlotte knew those letters to be full of boring material, mostly consisting of medical jargon between Nora and the colonel, but Mrs. Pembroke leaned forward as though Nora was reading the most titillating gossip from the latest scandal rag.

The colonel had read a paper Papa published and reached out to him, but too late. Papa had already passed away, but Nora had answered his letter, and the two of them had been writing ever since.

Nora's colonel was vastly interested in pain mitigation just as Nora was. It was natural, Charlotte supposed, as he had witnessed so many soldiers sustain ghastly injuries in wartime. He hoped to alleviate their suffering. If Nora wasn't working in her laboratory, she could be found penning a letter to him.

In any case, Mrs. Pembroke was very preoccupied thanks to Nora. Charlotte and William wouldn't be missed.

The tall garden hedges were convenient, shielding Charlotte and William from prying eyes, if any happened to be about, as they strolled. They had just passed a lawn of wildflowers Marian had planted the previous season. She had thought the stretch of grass could use some color, and instead of keeping it the same perfectly manicured green as before, Marian had followed in Mama's footsteps and planted a variety of seedlings.

That was her sister, always pushing boundaries and being extraordinary. Oh, very well, planting wildflowers mightn't be extraordinary, but it was one piece of the *whole* that made up her extraordinary sister.

Marian could have married when she was eighteen if she set her mind to it, but she had instead chosen to become a governess and leave their small corner of England and see the world. She had only returned out of necessity upon Papa's death.

Charlotte was not so bold. She knew that.

That was why she and William were perfectly suited. Two dull creatures. Neither one extraordinary in any way. Both content to lead a tamely quiet life in Brambledon.

Samuel intruded on her thoughts then, as he did so often.

She had a flash of them together—entangled against the library wall. Then of Samuel's head buried between her thighs in the bright out of doors.

Nothing tame or quiet in either one of those scenarios.

Perhaps a little excitement was acceptable. At least in regard to intimacy. A token amount of excitement was acceptable. She could have that with William hopefully.

And yet when she turned to face her perfectly matched betrothed in the privacy of the garden, she could not bring herself to initiate the much-planned kiss. She lifted her chin, urging herself to stretch to her tiptoes.

He was a gentleman. They were betrothed. He would be receptive. The simple act would not offend him.

She was overthinking the matter. She simply needed to do it. Get it done.

And yet planting her lips on his felt an unnatural task. She could not do it. It would be like forcing herself to quit breathing. It was most disturbing.

He must have read some of her alarm. He patted her hand nestled in the crook of his arm in an almost paternal manner. "Is anything amiss?" he asked as they turned and headed back toward the manor house.

She glanced at him from beneath her lashes.

He was so close. Close enough to kiss if she so chose. *If* she could simply gather up her nerve and do so.

Except, apparently, she did not choose. She could not do it.

She did not choose William.

Her stomach twisted in on itself. If she couldn't bring herself to kiss the man, how could she marry him?

It was most troubling. She could almost visualize Nora nodding smugly at her. Perhaps it was time to consider that she and William might not be as well suited as she had always thought.

She faced forward again and gave an affirming nod of her head as they approached the back of the house. "Everything is splendid."

The word *splendid* failed to ring convincingly even to her ears.

Apparently William thought so, too. He stopped and turned to face her, taking her hands in his.

She ducked her gaze to stare down at their linked hands. It was the most familiar they had ever been. She frowned. She had known him all her life and this was the most intimate act ever shared between them.

"You seem distracted of late, Charlotte."

For some reason she felt surprise over his observation. William had never been the most perceptive soul. Even as children, he viewed everything at surface value. He never dug too deeply, never dared to pry into her feelings. If she wasn't willing to volunteer information, he never probed. She'd thought she liked that about him. He was uncomplicated, and she preferred things to be uncomplicated.

Except everything felt suddenly complicated.

She gave his hands an encouraging squeeze. "I'm fine."

He stared back at her dubiously.

Tinkling laughter drifted toward them, floating on the air. Charlotte turned as a pretty maid emerged on a path leading to the kitchen. She recognized her as one of Cook's assistants.

The girl wasn't alone, however. Samuel walked beside her, his arms bulging impressively in his jacket as he carried a basket full of vegetables, presumably for Cook's assistant.

She did not think most gentlemen could be bothered to help a servant. Certainly, he was not like most gentlemen. She already knew that much about him. Even in their short acquaintance, she judged him to be kind enough to assist a female of any station.

And yet she couldn't help wondering . . . was

he helping this particular servant because she was pretty?

A flash of jealousy rushed through her. She fought back the hot wave of emotion. It was wrong. She had no right to harbor such feelings in relation to him.

Still, her gaze followed the pair avidly. They had not yet noticed Charlotte or William. They talked amiably, their words undetectable across the distance. Charlotte's face burned to think their conversation might be half as suggestive as what passed between Charlotte and Samuel.

The girl laughed anew at something he said, reaching out and brushing a hand along his arm.

The hot blade of jealousy forced a small whimper from her throat. Senseless, she knew. Inappropriate. She had no right to feel jealous of Samuel.

"Charlotte?" William queried.

She didn't turn to look at him. No, she froze, prey caught in a hunter's sights as Samuel's gaze found her just then.

He'd spotted her.

She swallowed, forcing back any further sound.

William followed her gaze. He lifted a hand in greeting. "Hello there, Mr. Kingston," he called out cheerfully, oblivious to the tension stiffening her. She resisted the unladylike impulse to kick her betrothed for calling attention to them. He was only being polite.

Samuel paused, his gaze skimming over William before coming to rest on her. He missed nothing. Certainly not their joined hands. His eyes narrowed there. She attempted to swallow again, but a boulder had inconveniently taken residence in the middle of her throat.

She sniffed and squared back her shoulders. How dare Samuel look so very . . . disapproving? She was doing nothing wrong. At least nothing wrong to Samuel.

Poor William was the one she had betrayed.

She was merely standing with him, her husband-to-be, her hands very chastely clasped in his. It was completely acceptable.

Except . . . it *felt* wrong.

Across the distance, Samuel's bourbon eyes took measure, probing, making her suspect he knew her feelings. Ridiculous, of course. He couldn't read her mind. He couldn't know of her intended kiss.

The kiss that had never happened because she couldn't do it.

She couldn't force what was not there.

She'd dallied with another man but could not bring herself to kiss William. How was that fair to William? Guilt plagued her.

Clearly her betrothal was a damaged thing . . .

now she simply had to decide if she needed to officially end it. What was the proper thing to do here?

"Mr. Pembroke. Miss Langley," Samuel called in return with a nod of his dark head. A tremor bolted through her at this first sound of his deep voice.

His manner was utterly circumspect. Laughable, when she considered how very *not* circumspect he had been with her on almost every occasion.

Those bourbon-hued eyes clung to her before returning his attention to the eager young maid beside him. The girl beamed up at him as they resumed their way toward the kitchen.

And that was it.

She stared after him, feeling unaccountably . . . *dismissed*.

The wretch.

"Charlotte?" William inclined his head toward the house. "Shall we return to the drawing room?"

"Yes. Of course," she hurriedly answered, looking away from Samuel and the cook's assistant. The girl was welcome to him. He was a bachelor, after all, and virile. She knew that firsthand. If he was interested in another female—*a female who wasn't her*—then all the better. Perhaps he would cease his inappropriate advances on Charlotte. Yes, indeed. That would be welcome.

If the thought produced a little pang in her chest, she ignored it.

Facing forward, William tucked her hand in his arm again with a small pat and went up the winding steps that led to the drawing room balcony.

Soon she was seated in the drawing room again, surrounded by the Pembrokes and her sisters, the same unkissed woman she had been when she departed for her stroll with William. Her shoulders slumped.

She could not kiss William.

All was not well.

Chapter 16

$\mathcal{K}$ingston had scarcely taken three strides down the corridor from his bedchamber when his stepbrother materialized before him.

"Kingston?" Warrington's voice matched his somber expression.

In fact, his stepbrother's tone and mien reminded him of when he had been called into the headmaster's office as a lad.

He crossed his arms and lifted his chin once in a semblance of a nod, not about to be daunted. "Lying in wait, were you, Your Grace?"

"A word, please?"

Kingston had retired to his room after spotting Charlotte with Pembroke—holding hands. The pair of them had been holding hands. A growl rumbled from somewhere deep inside his chest. Even now, remembering it, seeing it in his mind, made him feel . . . hell. It made him *feel*.

The sight of them together in such an easy, familiar way had caught him like a blow. It shouldn't have. She and the lad were betrothed. He knew that, but somehow he continued to forget it. Because it was something he wanted to forget.

Mere hand-holding should not have jolted him so much. Not when he had done far more intimate things with Charlotte. He had no right to feel this possessive toward her . . . but he felt it nonetheless.

Warrington strode ahead and opened one of the double doors leading into the library. He entered the room, clearly assuming Kingston would follow.

With a glance up and down the empty corridor, he sighed and followed.

Warrington was waiting, facing him. "Why are you still here?"

"Do you want me to leave?"

Warrington took a breath and released it. "No. I'm not saying that."

He was not saying that because his wife did not wish him to say that. The young duchess was much too hospitable and Warrington was much too in love with her to go against her in this.

Warrington continued, "I can understand the impulse for you to stop over for a night or two, but I don't understand why you are here."

Kingston nodded. Stopping in at Warrington's on the way to some house party or another wasn't new. Certainly, he had done that on occasion. It was not uncustomary. Curiosity would prompt him. Or convenience.

This time was different, though.

Those days were gone. This visit was different. This time he had stayed longer than a night or two.

From the perplexed look on his stepbrother's face, Kingston knew he was aware of that, too. It was that difference that had precipitated this awkward conversation.

Warrington continued, "Why did you come here? Why are you *still* here?"

Staring at the stepbrother with whom he had never felt any real special closeness, the strange truth welled up inside him. "I suppose I came here looking for something." *And running away from something.*

"And what is that?"

He shook his head. "I don't know."

Except in that moment Charlotte flashed across his mind. He had not come here looking for her. But he had found her.

He had found her and he didn't want to leave. Not yet.

"Not very helpful, that." Warrington frowned.

Arms still crossed in what he knew appeared a defensive stance, he gazed into Warrington's far too perceptive eyes.

"I have to say it," Warrington added rather ambiguously.

"What is that?"

"She is betrothed to be married, Kingston."

A long stretch of silence fell between them. Warrington didn't need to elaborate on his meaning. They stared at one another wordlessly.

"I know that," Kingston finally replied.

"Do you?" he asked in clear doubt.

Kingston gave a single stiff nod.

"She is a *nice* woman," Warrington added.

"Nice?" He laughed shortly at that. "And I don't deserve nice, huh?"

It was Warrington's turn to laugh. "Since when have you *wanted* nice? I did not think that was among your interests."

Kingston glanced away, thinking about that for some moments before looking back to his stepbrother. "I'm not like him, you know."

Warrington studied him keenly, understanding his reference. "I didn't think you cared one way or another what I thought."

He shrugged. "I'm not *him*."

Warrington nodded slowly. "If you're not your father, then you will leave her alone."

Because his father wouldn't.

He smiled. "Touché."

If his father wanted something, he went after it until he got it. No matter who he might hurt, he would always get his way.

Warrington stepped past him. "You know I'm right. You're not made for drawing rooms and afternoon tea and ladies with chaperones and dance cards and controlling papas."

"Because I'm his son?" he growled. "Because Norfolk is my father?"

"Because you're *you*."

"You've changed," Kingston charged in a hard voice. "You met your duchess and you changed." It could happen. It did happen. Priorities shifted. People changed.

The duke hovered in the threshold, looking back at him with a single arched eyebrow. "Is that what you're saying? Have you met your . . . duchess, Kingston?" His lips quirked in a decidedly unamused manner.

Kingston said nothing.

His stepbrother nodded slowly. "I didn't think so. Keep away from her," he announced. "It's for the best. And perhaps you should leave sooner rather than later. I see no point in you staying on here any longer. Do you?"

He didn't wait for Kingston to reply. His answer wasn't important, after all.

Turning, he departed the library as though the matter were decided. Clearly, in Warrington's mind it was.

It seemed in Warrington's mind . . . Kingston was already gone.

Chapter 17

Charlotte buried her face in her hands and moaned.

The Pembrokes had departed and she had wasted no time following Nora into her chamber to apprise her of events. "I could not do it, Nora. Clearly, it's not in me. I can't be anything other than . . . than . . ." She stopped, groping for the right words as she motioned to herself.

"Frigid, cold, repressed, drab," Nora easily supplied. Too easily. "Let me make you a cup of chocolate. You always enjoy that."

Charlotte tracked her sister resentfully as she moved about her chamber. "I was going to say *chaste*. None of those wretched words you're so quick to toss at me. I'm too *chaste*."

Or at least she had been. She frowned, recalling herself in Samuel's arms. *Chaste* was not what came to mind at that memory.

Nora gave a noncommittal grunt as she poured chocolate into a cup, tendrils of steam curling up on the air enticingly. "Let's not argue the point. Here you are." Nora placed the steaming cup in Charlotte's hands. "Drink this. It will set you to rights."

Charlotte drank from the cup, savoring the rich sweetness. "Thank you." Nora was right. The warm chocolate did make her feel better.

"Good?" Nora asked as she returned to one of the worktables.

"Yes." Charlotte nodded and sighed, rubbing at the tightness in the back of her neck.

"You're putting too much pressure on yourself. You've liked William all your life."

"That is true," she agreed.

"Certainly, he's a bit spineless when it comes to his parents. He only offered for your hand *after* Marian married Nathaniel and once his parents granted approval."

Charlotte frowned at those unwelcome reminders.

Nora continued, "Eventually you will recall whatever it was about William that enchanted you in the first place, I am sure of it." She fluttered a hand in the air.

Enchanted? Charlotte did not think William had ever enchanted her. They'd been in nappies when they first met. She could not remember *not* knowing him. Oh, all this was making her head ache.

She finished off her chocolate and lowered the cup into her lap. "You're terrible at giving words of encouragement. You know that, don't you?"

"Nonsense." Nora strode forward to collect the cup from her. "I'm bright and encouraging and cheerful." She returned to the table and faced Charlotte from across the room. "In fact, I am so encouraging that I am willing to do things for you even you yourself won't do."

An uneasy feeling came over Charlotte. "What do you mean?"

Nora started tidying the table in front of her, avoiding her gaze in a reticent manner. Nora was many things, but not reticent. Never that. "You should not have any difficulty managing that kiss now."

"Nora!" She launched up from her chair, her heart pounding a painful beat in her chest. She pressed a hand there, directly over her heart, as though that would ease the pain. "You gave me the tonic? Again? Tell me you did not! Tell me!"

Nora shrugged and waved toward the window. "If I were you I would start for William's house. Perhaps take a carriage—"

"You expect me to go out there into the world under the influence of the tonic? What if I became afflicted as I did last time? En route to William's?"

Dear heavens! That agony was to come again? The torment . . . the loss of herself . . .

The realization very nearly brought her to her knees.

"Oh, it won't be like the last time. Not at all. I gave you half the dosage as before. I'm not that careless."

"But you are! You are careless," Charlotte charged. "You did it to me again!"

Nora went on, "It shouldn't be nearly as overwhelming as before. Just enough to boost your confidence." She bit her lip in contemplation. "Still, just the same, I would not go to William's on foot. I shall accompany you, if you wish. Yes. That's probably advisable. I should like to observe you at any rate, document your symptoms as they appear."

Charlotte advanced on her, pointing to herself, tapping the center of her chest in angry motions. "Was this even about me? Or is this about you? Am I merely an experiment to you?"

It was Nora's turn to look outraged. Color stained her cheeks. "Charlotte! I take exception to that. I'm trying to help you. You're the one complaining that you can't bring yourself to kiss William. You said you wanted to kiss him. I was merely trying to help you in that endeavor. Documenting your response is just smart science. Now." She lifted off her pinafore and hung it on a nearby peg with efficient movements. "Shall I call for that carriage to be brought around?"

Charlotte shook her head fiercely, so angry, angrier than she had ever been. "No. No, I'm not going after William."

"Now you're just being stubborn, Char. This is what you wanted—"

"No," she said sharply. "This is not what I wanted. I did not want it to be like this. I did not want to have to be drugged with a love potion to simply kiss the man I'm going to spend the rest of my life with. It should not be that way."

Nora looked at her thoughtfully. "You're right, of course. It should not be that way. Perhaps you should ponder that long and carefully and ask yourself why you're marrying a man you cannot stomach to kiss."

Charlotte flinched and then swallowed back an angry sob.

Nora's expression was faintly pitying, and that only made her angrier. She did not want anyone's pity.

Charlotte charged from the room, slamming the door after her in a rare fit of pique. She told herself that her anger stemmed from what her sister had done . . . and not her parting words.

Charlotte was committed to William. She had given William her word. She had said yes . . . There would be no changing her mind now over something so shallow as . . . as *kissing*.

Or could she?

How did one even go about calling off an engagement?

Her stomach took a deep dive. It was the first time she had allowed herself to seriously consider the possibility of *not* marrying William. The queasiness was understandable. Breaking off an engagement would be an ugly business. The prospect alone would make anyone ill. Anyone who cared for their reputation, and Charlotte always cared about such things. She always cared about doing what was right and expected.

A great breath released from her lungs at the idea of *not* marrying William . . . of being free. *Free?* The word gave her a start. Was marrying William the opposite of that then? The opposite of freedom?

The Pembrokes would be furious and wish her to suffer for the humiliation. She had no doubt of that. His parents were every bit that spiteful and vindictive. And there was the matter of William. She had no wish to hurt him.

She hastened down the corridor, anxious to be alone in her chamber with her maelstrom of thoughts. She had to rid herself of the crazed notion of calling off the wedding. That was simply not done. Not done at all.

She also wanted to be safely tucked in her bed before the aphrodisiac ran thickly into her blood.

If Nora was to be believed, the torment shouldn't be as extreme this time. There was that, at least.

Up ahead the doors to the library opened.

She smothered a groan as Nathaniel emerged. She had been so close. She'd almost made it to her room without encountering anyone.

She pasted a smile on her face, a greeting on her lips withering into a croak as Samuel appeared, following close behind him.

Blast. Despite how distant he and Warrington appeared, they were together. Samuel had quit the maid's company apparently.

"Charlotte," Nathaniel hailed upon seeing her.

Her voice called back with a decided lack of enthusiasm. "Good day, Your Grace . . . Mr. Kingston."

"How was your visit with the Pembrokes? I'm sorry I could not join you." Nathaniel almost looked sincere as he said that.

She fixed her gaze on her brother-in-law. "It was lovely," she lied. "You were missed." She plucked at the collar of her gown. "It's rather warm, though. I thought I would rest for a while in my room until supper."

Not untrue. That was her plan. She was going

to strip down to her chemise and slide between the cool sheets, and there she would stay until the effects of the tonic subsided. Hopefully it wouldn't take very long.

"Ah, yes, this summer is dastardly hot." He snapped his fingers. "You should take your sisters and go for a swim in the pond."

"The pond?" she echoed numbly, sensing Kingston's scrutiny on her face. No doubt he was recalling when they had visited the pond—every wicked moment of it. Pinpricks danced down her spine as those memories beset her.

"Yes." Warrington nodded. "It's just the thing for a day like today. You ladies could take a maid with you to stand watch and make certain you are not intruded upon."

She nodded back at him, swallowing thickly. "What a . . . providential idea. Perhaps we will do that." She continued to nod as though she were truly considering the prospect, which she was decidedly *not*.

"Very good." He glanced at Kingston. She still refused to lift her gaze off the duke. She would not give Kingston's much too tempting and distracting person her attention. "We shall not keep you any longer, Charlotte. See you at dinner?"

"Yes," she eagerly replied, her face flushing. She might not be willing to look at Samuel, but she felt his gaze crawling over her like a swarm of ants. At the sensation she pressed the back of her hand to her cheek, testing its warmth. *Dear heavens.* Was the tonic already at work? Her body tingled all over.

Nora had promised she'd reduced the dosage. Certainly it wouldn't be at work this soon.

Then the duke and Samuel were gone, leaving her alone and feeling relieved. She'd stood in proximity to Kingston and scarcely looked at him.

Her chest rose and fell on sharp breaths. She hastened inside her bedchamber, closing the door behind her and collapsing against it. She was safe. Alone in her bedchamber, where she could forget all about her brush with Kingston in the corridor and combat the influence of the aphrodisiac.

It would not be like the last time. It would not be like the last time. It would not be like the last time.

The refrain gave her some comfort, even as she tugged free the fichu from her bodice and cast it aside so that her skin could breathe.

Leaning against the door, she fanned her chest. Locusts droned steadily on the air through her parted balcony doors. They'd been afflicted with swarms of them recently. This infernal summer. When would it be over?

A light knock vibrated the door at her back. "Miss Langley?"

Oh, no.

Not him. Just the sound of his voice made her tremble.

"Go away," she growled, turning her face into the door and speaking directly into the wood.

"Open the door, please. I'd like a word."

"Whatever you have to say, you can say it through the door."

"Come, come, Charlie. Let's be civilized and not speak through doors."

She yanked the door open, indignation burning through her. "I've told you not to address me so familiarly . . ."

Her voice faded away as she observed how very close his face was to hers. She could detect those tiny flecks of gold in his bourbon eyes. And the laugh lines about his eyes. The lashes surrounding those eyes were ridiculously lush and long.

She should have suppressed her outrage and never opened the door to him.

Her gaze dropped to his lips and, of course, her mind drifted to kissing. Naturally. It had preoccupied her so much of late. She had thought she would kiss William today, after all.

She had thought that, but she had been wrong.

"Are you well? You seem a little flushed," he remarked.

Her hand shot to her face, brushing against first one cheek and then the other.

"I am quite well. I just wanted a moment to myself." Before she became swept away from the effects of the tonic.

"You're staring at my mouth. Is there something on it?" He grazed his thumb along his bottom lip, and everything inside her seized and tightened.

"Just studying it for research purposes," she muttered, her hand gripping the edge of the door.

"Research purposes?" He looked bemused. "Sounds as though there is a tale in there."

"Quite so," she agreed, glancing up and down the corridor, aware that talking to him thusly was not ideal. If a staff member happened upon them, eyebrows would raise. Still, she could not bring herself to shut the door.

He angled his head inquisitively. "Care to share?"

"I merely thought I would finally be putting my lips on someone else's today." She nodded to his face, her gaze still fixed on his lips.

He smiled almost playfully and pointed to his lips. "My mouth?"

"Ha! No. No. Not you." She sent him a reproving look. "William."

"William?" His levity faded. He no longer looked amused.

"Yes. He is my betrothed. It is time we should kiss."

He blinked. "You've never kissed him?"

"No. Not yet. I was just getting around to it." She deliberately avoided thinking about how they could have kissed at any point in the past year, since they resumed their courtship and became betrothed.

"What's the delay? Haven't you known him all your life?"

Now he sounded like Nora. "Yes. I have. And there's no delay. It simply hasn't happened yet."

"Why not? As you said, he is your betrothed."

She shifted uneasily on her feet. "As I said, I plan to—"

"Perhaps you don't want to." Had he been speaking to Nora?

"Of course I want to," she said hotly. "We are getting married."

"Ah. Yes." He nodded with exaggerated sobriety. "Perhaps you do not want to do that either."

"Now you go too far, sir!"

"*Sir* is it? What happened to Samuel?"

"You are not Samuel to me. You are not *anything* to me," she insisted indignantly, fighting against the burn eating up her chest to her throat and face.

Even as the unkind words passed from her lips, she felt a stab of remorse. They were rude. Mean, even. Rudeness and meanness went against her nature, but it felt dangerous *not* to say the words.

It would be dangerous to do anything other than push this man away.

Except she had not run him off.

He still stood before her.

He stared at her intently, as though she had not just hurled hurtful words at his head.

She fidgeted uncomfortably. After a while, he asked quietly, "What are you so afraid of?"

Immediately, a reply popped into her mind. *This. You. Everything.*

Of course she didn't utter those outrageous things. She didn't dare admit them out loud. That would beg other questions. Questions like *why*.

If she answered why then all would be revealed. All would be exposed. She would be exposed . . . lost.

"You can't want this . . . You can't want Pembroke." He shook his head and dragged a hand through his dark hair, sending the locks flying in every direction. He looked distressed and that plucked at something inside her. "He hasn't one fraction of your passion or mettle. You'll perish from boredom if you marry that man."

Passion? Mettle? She sucked in a ragged breath. He described her in such a way . . . like no one ever had, and a little flutter zigzagged through her chest upon hearing him say such a thing. His description more fit Nora or Marian. Not Charlotte. Never her.

"There's nothing wrong with boredom," she defended. "Why must it be such a sinful little word? Why must everyone expect that all their days be full of entertainment and diversions?"

"You possess far too much spirit to be content with that dullard."

"I've known William all my life. We are quite suited."

"Liar. You. Me. *We* are suited."

She felt her eyes widen. "Rubbish."

"Shall I remind you then?" he challenged, a glint entering his eyes. "Refresh your memory?"

She held up a hand to ward him off. "That's not necessary. I don't long for excitement of the variety you offer."

"More lies," he hissed. "You *do* long for it."

She shook her head. "You do not know me. I'm not what you think. It was the cordial. It was an aphrodisiac. It altered me. I—I'm not that creature."

"Rubbish," he fired back at her. He stepped so close she could taste a hint of brandy on his breath. "No aphrodisiac flows through your veins now. No tonic dilates your eyes or sends your pulse fluttering at the base of your throat." His gaze drifted there then, to the area of her throat that she had exposed when she tossed aside her fichu. "That's all you, love."

"Don't call me that," she bit out in a voice far

sharper than she had ever spoken. He managed to bring out the worst in her.

"What? *Love?*"

She nodded. "It's indecent."

He laughed lightly and the sound washed ripples across her skin. "I'm not a decent man, but then you know that. You know firsthand—"

"I told you, the cordial—"

He moved suddenly then, seizing her wrist and lifting it between them. His thumb pressed against the inside of her wrist. "Your pulse. It's racing under your skin. That has naught to do with the bloody cordial you drank nights ago."

She winced. Not because of his fingers on her pulse point. Indeed, no. It was because of the cordial he referenced.

The one she had just swigged.

Certainly it was the reason his lips looked so incredibly tempting and she could only think about kissing them. About pressing her lips to that mouth of his.

Blast it! She had been doing so well resisting him . . . in working to put their unfortunate liaison behind her.

She cleared her throat. "Actually . . ."

"No. Give me no more residual-effects nonsense." A hot flush of color stained his cheeks and she knew the excuse offended him. "It's convenient, is it not?" He dropped her wrist as though the touch of her also offended him. "And how long do you think these residual effects will last and you might be able to bear responsibility for *this* . . . ?" He motioned back and forth between then with a wave of his hand. "Between us?"

She shrugged lamely, unwilling to explain she'd just consumed the tonic yet again. It was madness. The height of absurdity. As was explaining her sister had tricked her into consuming it.

He would never believe her. She could scarcely believe it herself. How had she come to find herself in this position again? "Who knows? Days? Weeks?"

He nodded with a slight narrowing of his eyes. "Then I suppose I will have to remain here for that long."

Her heart jerked and stuttered within her chest and she wasn't certain if it was with dread or excitement. "What?"

"Well, I can't very well leave you in your present condition unattended in this house. You could fall on any hapless man. A manservant or, God forbid . . . Warrington."

"I would never dare assault my brother-in-law. What do you think me?" she demanded in affront.

He shook his head and said with heavy mockery, "Oh, but you give the cordial great value.

Its effect on you can't be trusted. Surely I'll be useful to keep around should you become over-come with lust again. We've already tested the waters, so to speak. What does it matter if we have another go or two?"

Another go? The cad!

She squared her shoulders. "It does matter! I'm betrothed to another man . . . a good and decent man."

This gave him only fleeting pause. He dropped the matter of them "having another go," though. Instead, he said, "Until you *are* married, we can't leave the men in this household unprotected from your advances during that time. It's not the responsible thing to do. You certainly don't want to accost someone."

He stared at her with wide eyes and she was reminded that he didn't believe in the aphrodi-siac. He thought it was utter nonsense. Clearly he mocked her.

She mocked him in return. "So this is you be-ing considerate?"

He lifted one shoulder in a shrug.

"Your concern is misplaced," she managed to get out even as she battled the wake of prickling warmth his gaze left on her skin. It had begun. Arousal tingled through her body.

She started to close the door, determined

to place a barrier between them while she still could.

While she still possessed the power of will to do so.

His voice stopped her. "Why won't you admit the truth?" His voice rumbled through her. His expression was quite serious now. All levity and mockery gone.

She winced at his choice of words . . . for the truth was what he would not accept.

The truth being that the tonic flowed in her blood even now. But it was pointless to profess.

He would not believe her.

Even now she felt a stirring low in her belly.

She stared up at him, mesmerized by his bourbon-hued eyes.

She gave her head a single swift shake, commanding herself to turn away from him.

A kiss had been the business of the day. Or rather, it was supposed to have been. But it was not supposed to be with Samuel.

Honor demanded it not be with this man. Not ever.

Chapter 18

*N*ot this man. Not him.

The mantra rolled through Charlotte, and she wrapped the words around her mind, armoring herself with them.

Samuel's gaze crawled over her features, flitting from her eyes to her mouth and back again. She read the hunger in his eyes. She'd seen it before. He wanted to kiss her, but still, he did not inch forward. He did not close the gap between them.

He made no advance. No movement.

He waited on her.

His proximity was breaking her down bit by bit. As was the blood raging in her veins.

"Charlie," he whispered, coaxed, and it was her undoing.

She closed the distance, pushing off the edge of the door and claiming his lips with a little whimper that was part anguish, part defeat and part triumph.

Her fingers dug into his shoulders, clinging to him. She had no idea what she was about. She most assuredly lacked skill. Enthusiasm certainly did not equal prowess, but, oh, the taste of him did inflame her. Or, rather, inflame her further.

Her lips moved, caressing, exploring the shape of his mouth: cool, firm, but soft. She had not expected that. Young, virile men did not bring forth notions of softness.

She pulled back and stared dazedly into his bourbon eyes. "As far as first kisses go, that was pleasant."

Even as pleasure hummed through her she felt a pang of regret. A sense of guilt as she gazed into his face. She'd just bestowed her first kiss on this man whilst she was betrothed to another.

"Oh, that? That was not a proper kiss." His eyes glinted. "I can't have you thinking that, now, can I?"

He leaned in and this time he delivered in bold fashion. There was no withholding himself as he planted his mouth on hers. His arm looped around her waist and hauled her in.

She didn't even mind the strain in her calves

as she stretched onto her tiptoes. Her fingers curled into the fine broadcloth of his jacket as she hung on for dear life. His arm around her waist tightened as he kissed her deeper. Tasted her thoroughly with his lips and tongue. Grazed her with his teeth.

She internally cringed. A proper and honorable lady would not do this. She would not put herself in this scandalous position, and yet here she was wholeheartedly surrendering herself to this kiss over her pangs of guilt.

Clearly, things were going to be different after this. Even in her dazed and aroused state, she realized that.

She accepted that.

She should have considered where they stood— who he was, who she was . . . and that they were quite exposed to public view.

Except like her good judgment, such realization was elusive.

A small gasp penetrated the delicious fog surrounding her. She peeled her lips from his and searched the corridor for the source.

Her sister—the *wrong* sister—stood there, eyes wide, mouth agape. "Marian," she whispered, dread pooling in her stomach.

Marian looked back and forth between them, as though she could not quite believe what she was seeing. "Charlotte. Mr. Kingston," she greeted in turn, a sharp edge to her voice that was very unlike her even-tempered self.

Charlotte swallowed quickly, fighting against the sudden lump that had lodged in her throat. She disengaged from Samuel, sparing him a quick glance, certain he would be looking with mortification or apology to her sister. He was not.

Samuel's gaze was trained on Charlotte's face with what was becoming familiar intensity. He didn't look to her sister at all and Charlotte realized it was because he did not care.

He did not care that they had been caught in a compromising position—a situation made all the more awkward and untenable because she was promised in marriage to another.

A promise she could not keep.

She'd been tiptoeing around the conclusion for a while, but now there was no denial. This was the final straw. After this, she could not continue on with William.

She must end the betrothal posthaste.

The words whispered across her mind and jarred her because she felt an immediate surge of relief.

"Charlotte," Marian said again, louder, the reprimand sharp in her voice.

Samuel still did not move. He did not look away from Charlotte. She felt his gaze on her like a palpable thing, wrapping around her.

He was waiting for word or deed from her.

Marian's presence did not affect him, and Charlotte wondered if he was accustomed to this. Was he accustomed to his scandalous interactions with females being interrupted?

Charlotte nodded to him. "You'd best leave now."

He hesitated, his gaze on her still questioning.

She offered a tentative smile, hoping to convey reassurance. "All will be well. I'm fine."

Strangely, she meant that.

Charlotte suddenly felt confident that all *would* be well. She would talk to her sister. And though it would be difficult, she would talk to William, too. She'd explain her change of heart. But not because of the tonic. The tonic brought her to a state of arousal. It did not obliterate her ability to apply logic. It didn't alter her *lack* of feelings for William. She had never felt *any* overwhelming excitement to marry him.

Somehow that mattered now. Before, she had not thought much about her feelings. About the need for affection . . . for *passion* with your partner. Now she did.

Now feelings mattered. Now affection and passion for her future husband signified.

With a nod, Samuel stepped several paces back and left. She watched him go, a dull ache starting at the center of her chest. She quickly squashed the sensation. She certainly had not developed any tender *feelings* for the man. Lust did not amount to that. Especially lust derived from her sister's concoction, a source outside herself.

She turned to face Marian, who stared back at her with lifted eyebrows.

Charlotte braced herself for her sister's verbal barrage. Marian motioned to Charlotte to precede her into the library. With a deep breath, Charlotte moved ahead of her into the room.

"Charlotte, I do not even know what to say," Marian began, shutting the door behind them.

Charlotte turned to face her. "I can explain."

"Please do."

She took another breath. *Where to begin?* "No one saw us." She offered a wobbly smile.

"No one?" Marian looked decidedly displeased. "Except me, you mean." She tapped her chest. "I saw. *Me.*"

"Yes, and you're my sister. You're not going to carry tales. I'm quite safe. You've no wish to ruin me."

"Of course not, but, Charlotte—" Her gaze turned beseeching. "You are not unattached."

Familiar guilt wiggled through her.

Marian continued, "You are not free to bestow your favors, and I fear Mr. Kingston is not honorably intended toward you."

She winced. "I have been the one accosting

him, thanks to Nora's tonic. Admittedly, she gave me another dose today, albeit a small one."

"Another dose?" Marian exclaimed.

Just then, the library door opened. Charlotte sucked in a breath until she saw it was only Nora.

"Nora," Marian snapped at the sight of her. "I thought I told you to stop poisoning your sister with your questionable remedies."

Nora pulled a face. "You told me," she grumbled in agreement, looking at Charlotte resentfully.

Charlotte glared back at Nora as she admitted, "I must confess, the smaller dose was much more manageable. Not so much so that I could not resist kissing him, as you saw for yourself, Marian—" She had tried and failed. "But it was not quite as overpowering as the last time."

"What are you talking about?" Nora looked bewildered. "Did you kiss Pembroke? I did not think him still here. Weren't you going to call on him?"

"No, she did not kiss young Pembroke!" Marian's face turned bright in agitation. "That would have been much too simple." She made a sound of disgust. "No, it was Mr. Kingston. She kissed him! I caught them kissing bold as day in the corridor." She motioned toward the hall.

"Kingston!" Nora's eyebrows winged high.

"Not so shocking considering I was drugged

when I encountered him," Charlotte reminded tartly.

"Oh, indeed. I am not shocked," Nora agreed. "But not for the reason you believe."

"I don't understand," Charlotte replied.

Nora glanced at Marian almost nervously.

A sense of foreboding swept over Charlotte. "Nora?" she pressed.

"Actually . . . I did not give you the cordial this time." Nora forced a smile as though that would somehow mitigate her confession.

Charlotte could only stare at that blasted smile, thinking it misplaced and rather eerie in the after-shock of her statement.

"What?"

"I did not give you the cordial," she repeated.

A long spell of silence passed as Charlotte turned this revelation over and over in her mind. At last, she shook her head mulishly. "No, you did. Remember? You told me you did. You snuck it into my hot chocolate. A smaller dose. You said, a smaller dose . . ."

Nora shrugged. "I lied."

"Nora!" Marian moaned and pressed her fingers to the center of her forehead, as though attempting to alleviate the ache there. "You're incorrigible! Why do you do such things? Look at her." She motioned to Charlotte. "She's on the verge of apoplexy. Why must you play these games with her? She's your sister, for goodness' sake."

"I am not playing games. I was trying to help her. She wanted to kiss Pembroke, but her nerve failed her. She merely needed a boost of confidence. I thought even the suggestion that I gave her a bit of my tonic would give her the courage to kiss Pembroke."

Charlotte stared blindly ahead at the countless spines of books shelved so very correctly. Orderly. The way Charlotte's life had once been. Before she'd trysted with a rogue.

Aside of her guilt, she had thought herself mostly blameless because she lacked control of her body.

Except now there was nothing and no one to blame save herself.

She'd kissed Samuel. She alone. Nothing had made her do it. It was all her. There was no running from that truth even as difficult as it was to accept.

"I kissed him. I kissed Kingston," she admitted. "It was me."

Nora nodded, her expression sympathetic.

"Because I wanted to," Charlotte added.

There. She had declared it out loud. It felt significant—this, the final acknowledgment to herself and her sisters.

"True," Nora agreed.

Charlotte let all of it settle over her until there was no more denying, no more evading, no more hiding. It was time to put her thoughts to words.

"I don't think . . ." She stopped and swallowed. "I cannot marry William," she murmured.

"Praise heavens. She's come to her senses," Nora muttered.

"Charlotte," Marian said gently. "You're rattled. Let's not be hasty."

"I've thought long and hard on this. Deep down, I've known for a while. I acted on my own impulses with Kingston. At least today I did." There was still that first time she had encountered him under the agonizing effects of Nora's tonic. "I could not, however, even compel myself to kiss William, despite determining to do so."

"Are you saying you wish to end your betrothal because of Mr. Kingston?" Marian peered at her closely.

She shook her head slowly. "Mr. Kingston is not the only reason."

Marian gave a rude snort of disbelief.

Charlotte inclined her head. "True. It may very well be that I've developed a tendre for the man. I am . . . drawn to him. Clearly."

Marian closed her eyes in a long-suffering blink. "Oh, my dear, dear Charlotte."

Charlotte's stomach fluttered uneasily at her sister's reaction. "Don't look so alarmed. I'm not professing my love for the man," she defended, laughing nervously.

Marian's gaze shot to hers, wide-eyed with alarm. "I should hope not."

Charlotte moistened her lips, her unease only mounting. Marian's reaction seemed . . . *excessive*. "I mean . . . if I did harbor such feelings, would it be so terrible? Is Samuel—er, Kingston so very unsuitable?"

With a moan, Marian turned and sank down upon the sofa, burying her face in her hands. Her older sister's manner gave her pause. She made Charlotte feel as though she had done something terribly wrong. Something irreversibly wrong.

Marian lifted her gaze up to Charlotte. "I do understand how these things can happen. Of course I do. Mr. Kingston is a very handsome man," she allowed with a slight incline of her head.

"He is," Nora agreed, nodding. "And a sight more diverting than Pembroke."

Marian glared at Nora. "Be that as it may, he is not eligible. I can certainly understand attraction and infatuation . . . It was that way for me with Nathaniel in the beginning, but Mr. Kingston is not like Nathaniel. He will not be . . . domesticated."

"Domesticated." Nora laughed. "You make him sound like a wild animal."

Marian's gaze searched Charlotte's face. "Do you understand what I'm telling you, Charlotte?"

Charlotte gave a single uncertain shake of her head. "Not entirely, no."

"If you don't want to marry young Pembroke, then very well. Don't. You have our full support. But don't let it be because of Mr. Kingston." Marian's gaze only turned more beseeching. "He's not the manner of man whose heart you can rely on."

Charlotte bristled, disliking her characterization of Samuel and thinking it a bit unfair. "Why do you say that?"

"Nathaniel spoke to him."

Charlotte shrugged. "What does that have to do—"

"Nathaniel spoke to him about *you.*"

That gave her pause. "Oh." Her stomach tensed as she contemplated what that conversation had entailed. "And?"

"The particulars of that conversation don't precisely cast Mr. Kingston in a flattering light," Marian hedged.

The back of Charlotte's neck prickled.

"Marian," Nora said quietly, her tone one of warning, perhaps even pleading. "Don't."

Nora knew. She might be younger, but she was

clever. Intuitive. She wanted to spare Charlotte from hearing the details of that conversation . . . details she was clearly not going to like.

Marian exhaled. "When Nathaniel questioned him on why he was lingering here and whether it had anything to do with you, Mr. Kingston said he has no interest in milksop misses. I believe his words were: 'I've no appetite for milksop misses.'"

Milksop.

The description stung. She didn't know why. All her life she had been considered a boring creature. She should be fine with that designation. *Milksop* was not so very offensive.

And yet it stung.

"The cad!" Nora growled. "I'll mix him a remedy that will leave him soiling himself for a week."

Marian ignored Nora, keeping her eyes trained on Charlotte. "He said you're not to his tastes, Char." Marian looked at her intently. "I fear he is toying with you."

She nodded jerkily. Of course he was. A sophisticated gentleman like him and a country mouse like her did not suit. Even she knew that. From the start, she had known that.

Marian continued, "As I said, if you don't wish to marry, then don't. But don't toss aside the life you've planned for a rogue like Kingston."

Not to his tastes.

"Of course, you are right." She lifted her chin.

She wished he'd never come here. She wished she had never clapped eyes on Samuel Kingston. Her life would be so much simpler if they had never met.

He'd thrown her into upheaval. She'd been fine before his arrival.

Fine before the aphrodisiac.

Fine before she'd realized that she wanted more in life than what her future promised to be with William.

Kingston had ruined everything. He'd changed her, blast him. *Damn him.*

He'd changed her because suddenly nothing satisfied her anymore. Not the present state of her life and certainly not the promise of her future.

She'd been content before and now she wasn't. And it was his fault.

Chapter 19

*T*he following day, Charlotte found herself in the Pembroke drawing room. Not so surprising, she supposed.

She'd stared into the dark long into the night, pondering her future.

She'd fallen asleep at some point, waking early despite her few hours of actual sleep. She woke with a jolt. As though her slumber had only been a brief suspension on her thoughts, her mind immediately went to Samuel. The thought of him, of course, came with a frown. Yesterday's conversation with Marian had left an indelible mark.

She'd been foolish to let herself become entangled with such a rogue—a man far out of her scope, far out of anything she had ever known or encountered in her provincial upbringing in the shire.

She would take ownership of her scandalous behavior. It didn't matter why she had had dallied with Samuel. Quite simply, she had. On more than one occasion she had.

Now she had to take responsibility for her actions.

She had to take responsibility for every conversation. Every flirtation. Every lingering glance. Every touch. Every kiss. She had been a willing participant. She could blame no one but herself.

Seized with the desperate need to escape the house, she sprang from bed and dressed herself. She was never comfortable in using a maid to assist her—no matter that Warrington employed a houseful of them.

Even though they'd had servants before Papa died, that felt a lifetime ago—and Cook and Gertrude had never helped her dress herself. That did not fall among their tasks. Charlotte and her sisters usually assisted each other dressing and arranging their hair for the day. In the years since, she had learned to manage quite sufficiently on her own.

She skipped breakfast, not alerting anyone she was even awake yet, and snuck out in the murky predawn. Once outside, the fresh air did her good, allaying any lingering doubts.

She walked across the countryside at an easy stroll, the ribbons of her bonnet swinging idly from her fingers until the morning sun crested the sky. At that point, she secured her bonnet atop her head lest her nose pinken.

She took the long course to the Pembrokes', checking on her house en route, admiring Mama's flowers in the morning light before heading for William's.

She needed to get it over and done with, but she was naturally nervous. It wouldn't be pleasant, to be sure. No matter how gentle or kind she tried to be, it wasn't the kind of thing one enjoyed.

Unfortunately he was not at home.

In her eagerness to speak with William, she had called on the Pembrokes without invitation or warning, and the unexpectedness of her arrival was made patently felt. Mrs. Pembroke conveyed her disapproval with her usual scowl.

The lady glared at Charlotte over her teacup. "A little warning would not have been remiss, Charlotte. You could have sent word that you were coming and not caught us so unawares."

Sighing, she nodded. "Of course. It was thoughtless of me." She was accustomed to generally displeasing Mrs. Pembroke.

"Mother doesn't like surprises. They're not

good for her constitution." The woman gestured to her mother.

The elderly Mrs. Pembroke presently slept where she sat near the fireplace, her chin bobbing above her chest, seemingly oblivious to everything around her, including Charlotte's unsanctioned arrival.

"I will send word next time if I am not expected, Mrs. Pembroke," Charlotte promised.

William's mother sniffed haughtily as she added sugar to her tea. "Indeed. These are things upon which you need to deliberate." Pressing her lips together, she shook her head in censure. "You will certainly need to consider such things once you are married to my son. He needs a proper wife at his side, a paragon of Society . . . not some flighty, capricious creature unaware of basic comportment."

Charlotte inhaled a slow breath. The lady's criticisms had never been easy to tolerate, but she wasn't improving Charlotte's already frayed nerves.

There was a brief interlude, thankfully, as Mrs. Pembroke sipped her tea. Charlotte forced herself to drink and even nibbled at one of the biscuits on her plate despite her lack of appetite.

After some minutes, Charlotte cleared her throat and inquired, "Have you any idea when William might return?"

"If he had been aware of your impending visit, I am certain he would be here," her future mother-in-law said tartly.

Of course, Mrs. Pembroke was not yet ready to relinquish her annoyance.

Charlotte nodded and eyed the door, prepared to make her escape. Even she had her limits and she had reached them with this spiteful lady— for the day at any rate.

"Let us be clear, Charlotte." Mrs. Pembroke uttered her name with scathing precision. "You are not good enough for my son."

Charlotte blinked and leaned forward to set her teacup down with a decided clack. Well. How was that for unmincing language? There could be no confusion. Charlotte had always suspected Mrs. Pembroke felt thusly about her, but it was entirely different to hear the words boldly stated.

It shouldn't hurt.

As unsurprised as she felt, she was still baffled. *Why?*

Why was Mrs. Pembroke telling her this? It certainly didn't benefit their relationship. Was it her hopes to create animosity between them weeks before the wedding? Did she not want the marriage to go forward?

Perhaps she wouldn't be disappointed when Charlotte broke off the betrothal.

Mrs. Pembroke continued in frigid tones, "Mr. Pembroke and I have approved this match for the single reason of your newfound connection to the Duke of Warrington. Let us not pretend otherwise. You must know that. Do not think for any other reason I would allow my son to tie himself to the likes of you." Her lip curled as she assessed Charlotte where she sat.

Charlotte looked down at herself as though she might observe what it was about her that Mrs. Pembroke found so objectionable. She could detect nothing unusual about her personage. Still, she shifted uneasily, feeling as though there must be something there . . . some little sign that gave her away as less than desirable.

Perhaps the woman knew. Perhaps she could see deep inside Charlotte to all her many flaws . . . to all her recent transgressions with Kingston.

Her face burned as the memories beset her. Memories like Kingston's very hard body beneath hers, his deft hands and mouth between her thighs. Heat fired her cheeks and she reached for her teacup again. She could not have imagined such indecent love play . . . or herself a participant in it.

She knew there was joy to be found in the marriage bed. One glance at Warrington and her sister looking at each other and she knew that. They had . . . *appetites*, to be certain. The two of them were always sneaking off to their bedchamber in the middle of the day.

Charlotte gave herself a small shake. It was impossible, of course. Mrs. Pembroke could not know of her recent missteps.

She moistened her lips and cleared her throat, deciding she had nothing to lose by asking. "May I ask, Mrs. Pembroke, what is it you find so terribly objectionable about me?"

The woman sniffed. "You may ask and I will answer. You are a graceless, insipid and uninspiring female."

Charlotte almost laughed at her ready reply. Clearly these thoughts had been festering inside Mrs. Pembroke.

The lady continued, "Oh, you're fair of face, much like your mother before you." At the reference to her mother, her lip seemed to curl even higher over her teeth. "But that is hardly enough to make you a good wife to my William."

"You didn't like my mother," Charlotte concluded, the realization dawning on her. "Is that why you dislike me? Is that why you don't think I'm good enough for your son? Because you disliked to my mother?"

Mrs. Pembroke made an exaggerated sound that was part incredulity and part denial. "Do not think me so spiteful. I merely expected better for my son. A girl from a better family. Your father was a physician. A disgusting sawbones who consorted with people I wouldn't speak to, much less *touch* . . . He was little better than a blacksmith."

Charlotte sucked in a sharp breath, indignation sweeping through her. Her father had been a good man, respected and admired in the community. He often treated people who couldn't afford to pay him. That was why upon his death his daughters had found themselves without funds. He'd always been too busy tending the injured and sick to think beyond the present.

Her hands curled into fists at her sides.

Mrs. Pembroke went on, either unaware or indifferent to Charlotte's rising temper. To be certain, it was a rare thing for her to feel such anger. "Mind you, your mother was an upstart. Gave herself airs and pranced about the village as though she was the reigning queen. You should've seen the way men fawned over her. It was disgusting."

Charlotte gaped. She had never heard her mother described in such an unflattering manner.

The elderly Mrs. Pembroke suddenly spoke up from the window, lifting her silvery head and narrowing her small eyes. "Indeed. Your husband included."

Mrs. Pembroke's face deepened to a splotchy

red. "Mother," she said sharply. "You know not of what you speak." Her gaze then shot to Charlotte. "Pay you no mind to the ramblings of an old woman."

Then, as if she had said nothing particularly shattering or cruel, Mrs. Pembroke lifted the basket that sat on the floor near her feet and plopped it down beside her on the settee. She started sorting and arranging the swatches of fabric, draping them on her lap. "Now." She tapped a bright green swatch. "This is the one. We will dress the tables in linens of this color for the bridal luncheon."

It was not a question. Mrs. Pembroke was not *asking* Charlotte's opinion. She was telling her. Nora was correct. This woman would have been a miserable mother-in-law. She exhaled in secret relief to have escaped that fate.

And considering there was not going to be any wedding, she need not sit here and feign otherwise for a moment longer.

Clearing her throat, she inched to the edge of her seat. "If you would excuse me, please. I require some air."

With the woman's insults still ringing in Charlotte's ears . . . and throbbing in the marrow of her bones, she rose to her feet.

Without waiting for either woman to grant her

pardon, she fled the room through the double doors and out onto the lawn.

She sucked in a deep breath of warm air, filling her lungs as soon as she was several feet clear of the doors. She tilted her face up to the sunshine, realizing she did not have her bonnet with her. She'd left it inside. No matter. She would not go back for it. Nothing could propel her back into that room.

She would rather stand out here in the warm afternoon than endure another moment inside with Mrs. Pembroke.

She turned to look back at the house and spotted the elderly Mrs. Pembroke staring at her through the drawing room window. The old woman's lips pursed as though she had just bit into a lemon. Her wizened little face brought to mind a prisoner looking out from the bars of their cell.

Prisoner or not, Charlotte did not think it her imagination that she stared at her in pity. The irony was not lost on her. Old Mrs. Pembroke, an elderly woman confined to a wheelchair who slept the majority of the time, was staring at her in pity. She thought Charlotte was deserving of pity. Charlotte, who, to the world, was a young bride-to-be on the cusp of beginning her married life.

"Charlotte!"

She spun around at the sound of her name to spy William striding across the lawn.

Her chest immediately tightened at the sight of him.

Now it would happen.

He took her hand when he reached her and gave it an affectionate squeeze before placing it on his arm. "I didn't know you were coming. What are you doing outside? Why are you not inside with Mother?"

She smiled tremulously. "I needed some air."

He tugged at his cravat. "Some of this dreadfully humid air, you mean?"

She nodded, clinging to her smile. "And where have you been this fine day?"

Presently any conversation that did not involve his mother would be preferable. She did not want to explain to him why she was outside. She'd never complained to him about his mother before and she would not start now.

"I . . . ah . . ." He looked uncertainly over his shoulder. "I was actually next door." He nodded to the house mere yards away.

"At the Purcells?" His mother could have mentioned that.

"Yes."

"Oh. And how are they?" she inquired in what she was quite certain was an evasion. She was not certain how to begin this whole ending-the-betrothal matter.

His smile grew strained at the edges. "In truth, they were not there."

She frowned. "You were in their home whilst the Purcells were not there?"

"Ah . . ." He glanced back toward the house. "You know, come with me. I will show you." He smiled strangely. "I think you're going to like this."

Chapter 20

With her hand resting securely on his arm, William led Charlotte into the Purcells' house. Curiously, he didn't even pause to knock. He simply entered the front door of the house.

"The Purcells have gone," he announced, waving an arm as he led her through the empty foyer.

She looked around curiously. "Gone?" She gave her head a small shake. The family had lived next door to the Pembrokes for ages. "I had not heard they were leaving. Where did they go?"

He led her into the drawing room. "Apparently they were in some financial distress. They had kept it quite secret. Clearly they were eager to avoid public ridicule, but Mother had suspected, of course. She's clever that way."

She fixed a brittle smile on her face. "Of course."

William continued, "Over the last few months they let the majority of their staff go."

Her tight smile slipped. "Oh."

She knew what that was like. After Papa died, they'd had to do the same. They'd let staff go and sold off what they could. It was a horrible situation and she wouldn't wish it upon anyone.

"They simply sold the house and moved away to live with relations elsewhere." He gestured vaguely with one hand. "One day they were here and the next they were gone."

Her hand slid from his arm as he moved on to stroll through the drawing room. His steps thudded over the floor as he eyed the vacant room speculatively. Surveying the space, he dragged his fingertips over the faded wallpaper.

"Oh." She blinked and glanced around the room she dimly recalled from a long-ago visit.

She'd taken tea here once. She'd been just a girl then, sitting beside Papa. He'd sometimes taken her along on his calls. That was before Nora had proved herself to be such an enthusiastic assistant. Charlotte never really had the stomach for attending to the sick as Nora did.

She stepped forward to part the heavy damask drapery covering the window and peered outside, awarded with the familiar view of the Pembrokes' house. The Pembrokes' drawing room windows to be specific. The two houses sat in close proximity and, with the drapes drawn, one could see directly into the other house.

In fact, the Pembroke drapes were presently pulled back from the drawing room windows, and she could see directly into the house. Old Mrs. Pembroke still sat there. She sent Charlotte a small wave.

"Hopefully a nice family will take residence and be lovely neighbors for your parents." She stifled a wince of pity for that *nice* family.

"Indeed, I am quite certain of that fact."

She looked at him, curious at his conviction in the matter. "Do you know something? Has someone already let the house?"

He smiled slowly; the same smile he'd given her when he first escorted her to the house. She would use the word *slyly* if she had ever seen William look sly in all the years she had known him. "Yes. I believe it has."

"William, I don't understand." She glanced around. They were trespassing in someone's home and she didn't understand why. "What are we doing here?"

"I've acquired the house." He held his arms

out wide, a silly grin creasing his face. "It's ours."

She glanced around a little wildly, her heart accelerating in her suddenly too tight chest. "What do you mean you've acquired the house?"

"This house. It's ours."

She shook her head. "I don't under—"

"I purchased it . . . Admittedly, with a little help from Papa."

With *all* the help from Papa. William did not have wealth of his own. He lived at the grace and mercy of his parents, like so many well-bred gentlemen.

She moistened her suddenly dry lips. She knew it didn't matter. Especially now. She had come here with the intention of ending their betrothal, but indignation burned a fiery path through her. "William," she began with a slight clearing of her throat. "We had an agreement. We discussed at length where we would live after the wedding—"

"And isn't it wonderful that we can live here instead? Your family house is so far outside of town." He beamed at her, and she didn't understand that at all. He knew what she had wanted. It wasn't *this* house. How could he think she would be happy about this? Living next door to his parents?

He didn't know her.

He did not know her at all, she realized. Not truly. Not if he thought she would be happy living next door to his family. She shuddered. Every single one of her days would have consisted of Mrs. Pembroke. The woman unquestioningly disliked her. She would never have kept to herself and given them space. Of that there was no doubt.

Now she felt even *more* confident, *more* convinced that she and William were not suited. They might have been friends all their lives, but that didn't mean they belonged together.

"But that was the agreement," she said again, her anger a dull thing. She wouldn't be living here after all. She couldn't be too upset. Her relief to have escaped this fate far surpassed her anger.

William approached her and claimed both her hands in his. He gave them a squeeze. "Don't be disappointed. Our new life will be brilliant here, in this house. You will see. Trust me in this."

Trust. It was ironic for him to use that word when he had gone out and acquired this house directly against her wishes.

"I . . . No. No, William."

Confusion flickered over his face, all the delight from moments ago melting away. "Charlotte?"

The lilting question to his voice was almost comical if she wasn't about to deliver a blow.

"I can't do this."

"Do what?"

She gestured. "*This.* Us. Marriage. I can't do it."

The moment the words were out of her mouth, she breathed in a manner she had not breathed . . . in months. Even before Samuel . . . and that was a revelation. It told her she was truly doing the right thing.

It had been so long, she had forgotten what it felt like to breathe easy and clear. Her lungs lifted, expanded unfettered.

He stared at her as though she were a stranger to him, and she realized she was. He didn't know her at all.

Perhaps she was just coming to know herself.

"Because I bought this house for us?" He shook his head as though that made no sense.

"No. And you bought this house for *you*, William. But it is not only that. This house just confirms what I've come to realize."

Marriage to him would be the complete loss of herself.

"And what have you come to realize?" he asked rather stiffly, but she could still detect an undercurrent of hurt.

She had come to realize that there was someone else.

Someone who didn't want her for anything more serious than a fleeting dalliance, but she *still* preferred him over William.

"I've realized . . . that we don't love each other . . . not in the way either one of us deserves." She took a deep breath. "And I've realized I want that. I want all . . . or nothing."

Chapter 21

Charlotte returned home at an easy, relaxed stroll. She was in no hurry to confront her family and let them know she'd just ended her betrothal. Officially. She had just changed the course of her life, and, ultimately, theirs, too.

Guests would need to be notified, to say nothing of all the other plans they had made. All those plans would have to be undone. Explanations given . . . gossip to weather, stares to endure. All of that rubbish. Just thinking about it made her head ache.

When she entered the house, she noticed a certain buzz on the air. An energy that seemed proved by the staff members rushing about without sparing her a glance.

Something was afoot.

Marian entered the foyer, talking to the house-keeper in an intent manner. A pair of maids followed behind them.

"Marian?" Charlotte queried.

Her sister turned on her, looking her up and down. "Char? Where have you been? Look at your hem. I'll ring a bath for you. You need to look presentable tonight."

Charlotte frowned. "Is something—"

"We have guests."

"Guests?"

"Indeed, yes." Marian's head bobbed excitedly. "Nathaniel's mother and stepfather have surprised us with a visit."

"Nathaniel's mother and stepfather . . ." she echoed. *Samuel's father.*

"Yes. I've already spoken with Cook. She is preparing a splendid dinner for this evening. Now go on with you. Ready yourself." She smoothed a hand down the front of her dress, casting it a frown, as though realizing that she, too, needed to concentrate on that same task.

Charlotte nodded. "Of course."

Her announcement could wait. Her sister was naturally preoccupied with the arrival of their most august guests. Marian had never met her husband's mother before. Charlotte knew Marian well enough to know she wanted the visit to go smoothly.

"Now go. Make haste." She clapped her hands and gestured for Charlotte to take the stairs to her chamber. "And please see to Nora. Can you do that for me? You know how distracted she can be. She gets lost in her work and loses track of time."

Nora could lose track of *days*.

"Of course," Charlotte repeated. "Don't fret about either one of us."

Marian beamed. "Thank you." She pressed a quick kiss to Charlotte's cheek and then hurried away, the housekeeper and maids fast on her heels.

Charlotte spent the rest of the afternoon doing as Marian asked, readying herself for the evening and making certain Nora was doing the same—no easy task. As Marian had predicted, Nora was deep in one of her projects. Charlotte managed to tear her away from her work.

She felt lighter than she had in a long while. She and Nora entered the drawing room together wearing smiles.

The earl and countess had not arrived to the room yet, but Samuel stood near the fireplace, looking as stern and grim as a pallbearer. She made her way to his side.

"Good evening, Mr. Kingston."

"Miss Langley," he returned. "Come to witness the circus?"

"I beg your pardon?"

"My father and stepmother are here." His lips twisted as though tasting something distasteful. "It promises to be quite the diversion. It always is."

Charlotte was saved from replying. A good thing considering she did not know what to say. At that moment, the distinguished couple entered the drawing room. Introductions were made, and they were all soon filing into the dining room.

Marian had outdone herself. The table sparkled with the finest crystal and bone china. Candlelight sparkled throughout the room. Profuse arrangements of flowers populated the corners of the room as well as the center of the table. It was the height of extravagance, and from Marian's hopeful expression, it was clear she sought to gain the approval of her in-laws.

The duke appeared to care less. There was a certain guardedness to his eyes as he took his seat at the head of the table, the only smiles to grace his face reserved for his wife.

Charlotte felt utterly fascinated as she stared at the pair of them—both so very fashionable and handsome across the dining table.

It was easy to mark Kingston's resemblance to his father. They possessed the same bourbon-hued eyes. Except the earl's were clouded with drink and years of dissolution. She saw that at once, and those effects were not limited to his eyes. She read the evidence of hard living in the lines around his eyes and the redness to his nose and in the loose skin of his neck and jaw. He possessed none of the keen awareness so inherent in Samuel's gaze.

Nevertheless, he was a striking gentleman. The type of man one noticed in a crowded room. Dressed in dark evening attire, he was a marked difference from William's father, the last man who had sat in his seat.

She frowned at the intrusion of William and his family on her thoughts. She didn't want to think about the Pembrokes and how very angry they would soon be with her. She'd have to face that soon enough. Presently, she only wanted to watch the interesting byplay between Samuel and his parents.

She might have risen significantly in the social order of things since Marian tied the knot with a duke, but the earl and countess were the most sophisticated people she had ever met.

The countess was lovely. Her hair was midnight dark, not a gray streak evident anywhere in the strands, which made Charlotte wonder if nature had blessed her with such lustrous hair or perhaps she helped Mother Nature along with unnatural means. The countess's face was equally brilliant, a softer, less angular version of Nathaniel's face.

"I cannot believe my boy has married again," the lady proclaimed as she fed herself a dried fig from her plate with elegant beringed fingers. It was not the first time she had made such a proclamation. In the last half hour, she had expressed her astonishment a number of times.

"She's a pretty lass, make no mistake of that, but I never thought you would try your hand at matrimony a second time, Nathaniel." She nodded to Marian, who sat with a stiff smile about her lips.

Charlotte knew her sister well enough to know she did not appreciate being spoken of as though she were not even present at the table.

"*You* married a second time, Mother," the duke pointed out coolly, lifting his glass and taking a drink.

It was not lost on Charlotte that her brother-in-law's expression had only grown more dour since they sat down to dine. The line of his shoulders was tense, too, rigid as a slat of wood.

"It takes two tries to get it right apparently," the earl pointed out rather heartlessly as he stabbed his fork into the hunk of pheasant on his plate, holding it in place as he sawed at it with his knife. "This one can at least set a fine table." He paused and looked skyward. "What was the last one's name?" With a shrug, he continued as though it were of no significance. "Whatever her name, she never had quite the knack for that." He reached for his wine, taking a big gulp into his already stuffed mouth. "An accomplished cook is worth his weight in gold." He spoke around his wine-soaked food. "She never understood that."

Charlotte stared at him in immediate dislike. She couldn't help herself. Her indignation burned hot in her chest. Was the man actually insulting his late daughter-in-law's memory so carelessly?

Not only that. The two *mistakes* he referenced happened to be deceased—Warrington's first wife and Warrington's father, the late duke.

Charlotte knew next to nothing about either one of them, but that was neither here nor there. They had belonged to Nathaniel—and Nathaniel to them. You did not malign someone's father and wife—even if they were deceased.

Especially if they were deceased. It was just not done.

Marian reached for her glass of sherry. Bringing it to her lips, she took a long, fortifying drink.

Charlotte knew her well. There was nothing she could do to hide her discomfort. Her sister had wanted this evening to go so well. She had wanted these new relatives of hers to like her. As they should. Marian was lovely.

Charlotte's fingers clenched around her fork and knife.

Such insensitivity was astounding. Earl or not. Countess or not. They were appalling people.

Suddenly it seemed everyone was staring at her, and it took her a full minute to realize she had spoken aloud. She had just declared them *appalling people* to the room at large.

Nora broke into laughter. "Oh, this is rich."

Kingston leaned back in his chair and clapped slowly in approval.

The earl scowled and stabbed his knife in the air toward Charlotte. "And who is this chit?"

"This is Miss Langley, my wife's sister. We introduced you, if you recall," the duke reminded him.

Marian grinned, looking at her rather proudly.

"What do you know of anything?" the earl sniped, glaring at Charlotte. "You should keep your tongue in check rather than insult your betters."

Of course, he was correct. This was the moment she should beg for pardon. Even if he was not an earl, he was a guest in her sister's home.

Instead, she heard herself saying, "You're an unkind man."

She glanced around the table, reading the agreement in most everyone's expressions.

Except Samuel. He wasn't looking at her or anyone. She could not judge his thoughts. He was staring away from them all, through the window to the evening outside.

"Unkind?" The word rolled from the countess's lips like it was a foreign object. Laughing, she patted her husband's arm, her expression one of delight. "My dear husband is many things, but not kind. That is quite true."

His wife's agreement only made the earl's scowl deepen. Clearly he did not enjoy anyone laughing at his expense.

He waved his knife at Charlotte again in a fairly menacing manner. "I'll hazard a guess and say that you're unmarried."

"I'm yet unwed, my lord," she admitted, avoiding looking at her sisters while they still did not know the truth of her severed engagement.

"Aye, I thought as much." He took a deep swig from his glass of wine, sighing in satisfaction as he placed it back on the table. "You've the pinched look of a female in dire need of a prick between her thighs."

Gasps flew about the table. Charlotte's was one of them.

The man was an earl. She had naively thought an earl's manners would be above reproach, but now she realized that a title meant nothing. If anything, the aristocracy was given far too much forbearance.

This earl had likely lived his entire life doing

and saying whatever he wanted without consequence.

"Apologize."

The word was growled in a voice so deep
and dark that Charlotte was not certain where it
originated at first. Her gaze swept the table. One
glance at Kingston's face and she knew, of course.

His expression was brutal, the light gone from
his usually shining eyes as he glared at his father.

The earl glared back at him. "You've a yen for
the chit, is that it, King, my boy?"

"He's correct," Warrington seconded. "You
will apologize to Miss Langley for your gross
behavior."

The earl didn't even glance her way. He continued to eat with fervor, not reacting to his son's
or Warrington's apparent displeasure with him.
Picking up a leg of pheasant, he began to tear the
meat from the bone with his teeth. "I don't apologize," he said as he chewed. "Especially not to
backward country gels who have no respect for
their betters."

"You *will* apologize," Kingston cut in, his voice
battle-hard as he tossed his napkin down on the
table.

A dreadful silence fell in which father and son
stared each other down.

Everyone watched. Waited.

The duke finally broke in, "You will apologize to my kinswoman or take your leave of this house."

"Your *kinswoman*," the countess interjected, her hand fluttering to her throat, all levity gone. Her eyes sparkled indignantly, as bright as the jewels at her throat. "And what am I? Am I not your kinswoman? He's my husband. If you cast him out, you cast me out. I am your *mother*, Nathaniel."

"It takes more than blood to be family," Kingston quickly cut in. "'Tis a lesson I've learned long ago."

The earl and countess both wore expressions of bewilderment at this comment.

"What rot are you spouting?" the earl demanded.

"What's gotten into you, Kingston?" the countess added.

"Neither one of you understands what makes a family." Fury vibrated from him.

The earl banged a fist on the table. "Have I not supported you? Did I not pay for your schooling? Get you started with a parcel of land, which you later sold to that rail company? You made a tidy sum from that." He wagged his leg of pheasant, sending bits of meat flying.

Kingston shook his head and looked down at his plate. When he next spoke, his voice was hoarse with emotion. "Do you even know?"

"Know what?" His father looked at him blankly.

"What's become of her? Do you even know? Do you care?"

"Her . . . *who*?" the earl asked in bafflement. He pulled a face and glanced around the table as though seeming to say: *My son has gone daft.*

"Good God . . . my mother!" Kingston slammed his palm flat on the table, rattling the dishware. "Are you even aware what's become of her?"

"Ah. Her." The earl reached for his glass and brought it to his lips, taking a drink. "Should I be aware?"

"Indeed, Kingston. Why would he know anything about her?" The countess sniffed. "He has had no communication with her in years."

"Because she is *my mother*. And my father was with her for three years. Three years before he severed all ties with her, taking back the house he had given her and sending her off with a pittance, forcing her to find another protector, and then another after him, and then another . . ." Hot emotion glittered in his eyes.

A lump formed in Charlotte's throat as she watched him, afraid to move as Samuel unleashed himself. She couldn't breathe at the glorious visage he made, angry and hurt . . . a seething cauldron of emotion. He was a man who felt deeply, and she ached for him. Ached for the wounds he bore deep.

"I believe that is the nature of a whore's work, is it not?" The earl spoke so calmly, indifferent to the gasps around the table. "I saw to your care, did I not? It's more than some men would do. I should be commended, not forced to suffer your puerile temper."

"You should be horse whipped," Samuel hissed.

For the first time, Norfolk looked uneasy. Leaning back in his chair, he asked rather bewilderingly, "Why are you so angry, son?"

Son.

One look at Samuel's face and she flinched. She knew. She understood. Samuel did not want it. He did not want to be this man's son. He did not want this man to be his father. With one look at his face, she knew all of that.

"You took everything you wanted from her, used her until you were satisfied, and then cast her aside like rubbish. Did it never occur to you what would become of her? Did you care at all? Did you think what it might mean to me?"

The earl cleared his throat. "King, now is not the time—"

"When is the right time? After she's dead? Will the time be right then? Because that will be any day now."

"Samuel," Charlotte whispered. He was too far from her—across the table—but she wanted to reach him.

He continued, "She has the pox. Did you know that?"

Silence met the shocking declaration. There was a rustle of clothing as people shifted uncomfortably in their seats.

Charlotte did not look away from his face. He'd mentioned an ill mother. She could not have imagined the awfulness of this, though.

"Did you know?" Samuel thumped his fist on the table again.

"No, I did not." For a brief moment, the earl looked guilty. "How should I know that? I haven't communicated with her in years."

"Exactly. She's blind now. I don't suppose you knew that either. And quite mad. She doesn't even know me. I sat at her bedside for weeks. Hoping she might remember me . . . or herself . . . as she withered away."

The earl shrugged. "I do not see how this is my fault. I did not . . . infect her."

"No. But you didn't protect her, did you? When you released her, you never gave her another thought. As the mother of your only child, you might have cared enough to look out for her. Provide her with even a modest allowance."

"She was not his responsibility," the countess dared to insert.

"Indeed." Samuel's father nodded stiffly. "You cannot blame me for her lack of discernment."

Samuel laughed then. "Discernment? Discernment is for those who have the luxury, the privilege, of choice."

The countess pushed up from the table then, her slender frame quivering in outrage. "We will not stand for another moment of this abuse. To think we came here all the way from Town. We had countless invitations and chose to come here! We could be at a house party in the Lake District right now. I've never been treated so abysmally. And by family, no less." Her glare swept the table, falling pointedly on the duke and then Samuel. *"You."* She pointed a damning finger at her stepson. "You are fortunate your father even saw fit to acknowledge you. You're naught but a bastard Son of a whore. You should thank him for not casting you into the nearest stream."

"Out," the duke growled from where he sat at the head of the table, his lean frame deceptively relaxed. His locked jaw attested to his tension.

"Gladly." The regal lady lifted that haughty chin of hers. "We will gladly take our leave." She cast one last fulminating glare at her daughter-in-law. "Your Grace, the pheasant was dry."

That said, she swept from the room.

The earl did not even look in the direction of his son before following.

"Well," Marian announced after some moments. "Shall I ring for dessert?"

"Forgive me, Your Grace," Samuel murmured as he pushed back his chair. "The meal was delicious."

Without another word, Charlotte watched him depart the room at a steady stride, aching to follow, to go after him even though it was not her place to lend him comfort. Should he even need or want it from her, he was not hers to console.

She looked around the table at the others. They, too, looked after him, watching him go, Marian and Nora with varying expressions of pity. The duke's expression was more ambiguous.

Samuel departed the room, a servant shutting the door after him, but moments later the sound of a cry alerted everyone.

They all surged as one body from the table and spilled out into the corridor—just in time to observe Samuel standing over his father, his hand knotted tightly in a fist. Clearly he'd just delivered a blow.

"You never apologized," Samuel said tightly over the man sprawled on the floor, clutching his bloody nose.

The countess screeched and squatted beside her husband, attempting to help him into a sitting position.

Charlotte blinked rapidly as Samuel gestured in her direction. "I said, apologize to Miss Langley."

The earl cast a dazed glance her way. "Apologies . . . Miss Langley."

She nodded dumbly, astonished at the brutish display and uncertain what to think.

Samuel looked at her and the anguish was etched into his features. He didn't feel better. Hitting his father had not cured him of his anguish.

He didn't linger. Without another word, he turned and strode away.

Her sisters turned their attention to her, assessing for her reaction.

Charlotte fought to school her features, certain her heart was in her eyes.

Impossible, she realized. She hurt for him because she knew he was hurting. As long as he hurt . . . she hurt. This awareness settled over her in jarring impact, robbing her of breath.

There was no hiding the emotion from her face because she was very much in love with him.

Chapter 22

*S*leep would not come.

Through the mullioned window of his bed-chamber Kingston watched his father flee the house with his countess, servant after servant carrying out what seemed to be their endless amount of baggage. They gave no thought to the fall of night shrouding them. They simply wished to be gone. He'd effectively run them from his brother's home.

Kingston watched them go and felt nothing. Even as he realized he might never see his father again, he felt nothing inside. Only numbness. A great void. There would have had to be something there in the first place for him to feel any sense of loss.

He did not know what he had hoped to gain from his outburst. Perhaps he had hoped to see regret in his father's eyes. To hear words that even vaguely resembled remorse.

Of course, he'd been foolish in that hope. He knew what kind of man his father was. In truth, he had not been so very different from him a year ago—before he visited his mother and came face-to-face with her condition.

He had cared only for his comfort and baser pleasures. When he heard his mother was ill, he had called on her, but he had no notion at the sight waiting to meet him. He'd had no idea the gravity of her illness.

The pox was an awful way in which to perish. It was a long, lingering disease, eating away at both body and mind.

The sight of his mother afflicted like that had killed something in him. His ardor for women had swiftly died. He'd had no interest in the fairer sex.

Until Charlotte.

With a curse, he sprang from the bed. No sense lounging about. There would be no sleep for him. At least not any time soon.

He left his chamber. He'd had no appetite at dinner and while that had not greatly changed, he could eat something. Better that than staring into the shadows of his chamber.

Tomorrow he would leave.

Tomorrow he would find a place to go.

Somewhere. Anywhere other than here, near the brother who didn't want him, who was not even his real brother but rather a connection made through the father with whom he'd just severed all ties.

Anywhere other than near a woman he wanted but could never have.

CHARLOTTE DRESSED FOR bed, but it was pointless. She didn't even attempt to sleep. A maid had pulled down the counterpane for her, but she didn't bother slipping inside the waiting comfort of the bed.

There would be no comfort for her. Not while the newfound realization that she'd fallen in love with Samuel Kingston bounced through her like a marble set loose.

Perhaps she had known for a while, since their first encounter, but it wasn't something she could admit until she'd freed herself from commitments and entanglements.

She didn't know. She didn't know anything except she had to see him. The urge was too strong to resist. The man had her aflutter.

Charlotte grabbed her dressing gown from the foot of the bed and slipped it on, belting it at the waist. She crept from her chamber, gliding down the near-dark corridor, looking over her shoulder for fear that she might be caught. She had no desire to explain what she was about to either one of her sisters. She could scarcely explain it to herself. She loved a rogue—a rake who had no desire for the type of life she wanted. She might not be quite the dull creature she once was, but she still craved all the same things for herself. A home of her own. Hearth. Love. Family.

Samuel wanted none of those things. He'd never said as much, but she knew. He eschewed convention. He was no typical gentleman looking for a wife. In all their trysts, he'd never asked her to end her betrothal. Never suggested that they marry, and it wasn't honor that kept him from uttering those words. He simply was not interested in such traditional trappings. He was not that man . . . not that person.

She noticed a thin line of light beneath Samuel's door. Apparently she was not the only one unable to sleep. Considering the events of the evening, she was unsurprised.

Knocking gently so she did not wake anyone else, she waited, glancing up and down the corridor surreptitiously.

After a few moments, Charlotte turned the latch and entered the chamber. It was empty. He was not in the room.

She rotated slowly and glanced around as though she could find him hiding in some dark corner of the room. Silly. Of course he was not. His bed was mussed, the counterpane tossed back as though he had left hastily. His boots were sprawled haphazardly near the foot of the bed. He had not left the house then. He was somewhere under this roof.

She left his room and began a search of the house, checking first the library and then the drawing room. Nothing. No one.

She moved on to the kitchens next and there she found him, sitting at the large rough-hewn worktable dominating the center of the large space.

He did not notice her arrival. His attention was fixed on the drink and plate of food before him.

"Mr. Kingston?" She stepped closer, clearing her throat. "Samuel?"

He lifted his head, resting a bleary-eyed gaze on her. He looked inebriated, but she knew that was not the case. Alcohol had not done this to him. The ravages of the evening, of his father, had done this to him.

He had scarcely touched his drink or food at dinner, which could explain the assortment of bread, cheese and dried fruit before him now. Evidently, he'd come down here at this late hour to find something to eat.

"Are you . . . unwell?" She moistened her lips, her words echoing lamely in her own ears.

Of course he was not well. Who could be well after tonight? After that dinner with his wretched father and stepmother? The ugliness of that scene was imprinted on her mind. Her heart had ached for him then and it still did.

She wanted to comfort him just as much as she wanted to go after his father with a crop and give him a good thrashing. The man did not deserve a son like Samuel. Indeed not. He deserved a beating.

Her violent thoughts unsettled her. It was not in her nature.

She had been raised among siblings. Of course, there had been times when she had been pushed to the brink of madness. Nora especially had pushed her. Indeed, her youngest sister could vex her as no one else could. But even amidst all their squabbles, she had never been prompted to violence. She had never felt the urge to strike anyone before.

Until tonight.

When she had stared at the earl's face. When his foul words had vibrated on the air. She'd longed to deliver a good slap to that man. A novel experience that, and all because of Samuel Kingston. Because of these deep feelings she harbored for him.

Confronted with the wretchedness of his father, learning the dreadful truth of his mother, she had not felt like her calm, quiet self. She did not feel like herself even now, staring at Samuel looking so broken at the kitchen table.

"Shall I fetch my sister? Nora can mix you a tincture to calm your nerves. She's quite useful to have around. At least most of the time."

He snorted. "This being the same sister who you claim drugged you with an aphrodisiac? No. No, thank you. My nerves are fine."

"That was a rare case," she protested, perfectly aware that he still thought her sister's aphrodisiac to be rubbish.

"Forgive me if I remain skeptical."

She rubbed her palms together and glanced around the kitchen, moving toward the kettle. "I can make you some tea."

"No," he barked, startling her.

"I don't need tea and I don't need you." He glared at her. "Why are you even here? Should you not be abed? Dreaming of your upcoming wedding?"

She paused, her face warming. His animosity was new. In all their encounters, he had never been like this toward her. Never caustic or biting. Never one to make her feel unwanted. Indeed. It had been quite the opposite. He had pursued her with warmth in his voice and fire in his eyes.

"When is it?" he added roughly.

She shook her head. "When is what . . ."

"Your wedding? When is the grand occasion? Is it not soon?"

"Oh." He was asking about the wedding she had called off, the *grand occasion* that would never be.

She released a shuddery breath, but did not answer. Now did not feel like the time to explain there would be no wedding. This moment was not about her. It was about the wreck of a man before her.

Yes. It would have been soon. It would have been the eighteenth of July. All the more reason to break the news to her family that it was not happening so that they could begin coping with the many consequences most assuredly to come.

His expression turned faintly mocking. "How thrilled you must be."

It was on the tip of her tongue to tell Samuel that she would not be going through with it, but she stopped herself with a bracing breath. Not now.

There would be no talking about herself right now.

This was about him.

She wanted to be a friend to him, absurd as that was, perhaps. After tonight's debacle, she suspected he could use one of those. A friend to listen and talk to. Someone who cared.

Something told her he had not had many friends in his life. Not beyond those who caroused with him on raucous nights of revelry. Not true friends.

She had always been fortunate enough to have people in her life who cared about her. Papa. Her sisters and brother. Samuel likely did not even realize what he was missing. How could he if he had never had those things?

"I... uh. I am so very sorry about your mother."

He groaned. "Are we really going to do this?"

"Do what?"

"Talk about tonight," he supplied. "Talk about my tragedy of a family."

She lifted one shoulder. "Talking about it might make you feel better."

"Might it?" His features twisted in skepticism. "Talking of my wastrel father who abandoned my mother and left her to barter her body for a roof over her head, leaving her disease ridden, dying in agony and madness? Should talking about that make me feel better?"

She flinched. "I . . ." She suddenly felt very foolish. What did she know of his particular experiences? His misery was out of her realm of knowledge.

"Can you understand that perhaps I do not want to talk about that? That I don't want to talk at all?" He stood as he uttered this question, the wood stool clattering to the floor behind him.

She jerked a little at the sound of the stool hitting the floor and the suddenness of his movement, but she didn't move. He didn't scare her. She wasn't alarmed.

A tremor of excitement chased down her spine, and that was when she realized the truth.

This was as much about *her* as it was about *him*.

She wasn't being fully truthful with herself. She didn't want to tell him she had ended the betrothal because he would want to know why and that would be getting into dangerous territory.

She would have to give him a reason—and so much of that reason was wrapped up in him. In how she felt about Samuel, in all her tender and desperate longing for him and her inability to keep her distance from him—something she would have had to do if she remained with William.

No. She could confess none of that to Samuel.

She watched him, her eyes unblinking as he rounded the table, moving with the ease and grace of a predator, a slowly advancing jungle cat.

He stopped in front of her, all tightly coiled energy. She felt the same tension echoed inside her.

Still sitting, she craned her neck to look up at him. "I . . . Yes. I can understand that."

"Sometimes the opposite of talking is what one needs." His hands reached out to close around her arms. The heat of his palms singed her skin as he pulled her to her feet.

She went willingly. Gladly.

His hands moved from her arms to her waist.

Everything faded into a dizzying blur.

He pulled her in closer, lifting her up in the air with a warm huff of breath, plopping her down on the table before him, bringing them satisfyingly eye level.

For long moments their heaving breaths collided, mingling as they gazed at each other. Fire burned in his eyes.

"What are you doing?" she whispered.

"You need an explanation?" he growled.

She waited a beat before replying, "No."

She knew what he was doing. She knew what *they* were doing. Perhaps the moment she had come to him, she knew. She wanted this to happen.

Never looking away from her, he shoved her dressing gown and nightgown up around her thighs so that he could wedge himself between her splayed knees.

The callused rasp of his palms squeezed her tender flesh. Firmly. As though testing himself of her solidity, her durability.

She could think of nothing more thrilling

than his big strong hands on her bare limbs, squeezing, kneading her, branding her with his desire.

A heady exhale slipped from her lips and she covered his hands with her own, prompting them to squeeze harder.

"I won't break," she encouraged.

His eyes dilated.

She was out of control. There was no considering propriety. The world failed to exist. It was only the two of them right now, in this moment, in this kitchen.

Irritation flashed across his face. "You're not his," he growled. "Not tonight. Tonight you're mine."

His head dipped. He claimed her mouth swiftly, with surety and finesse. She sank into the kiss, drowning in it. In the pure pleasure of it.

She moaned as his lips devoured hers, reaching for him with greedy hands, skimming her palms over his hard shoulders, making their way down the flat plane of his chest, despising the barrier of clothing between them.

He broke away with a gasping breath.

"Samuel?" Her fingers curled, tightening on him, digging into the fine lawn of his shirt, desperate to touch, to feel, to seize him and bring him back to her.

He gave a single hard shake of his head. "Not here. Not like this."

His arms came around her, enveloping her and sweeping her off her feet.

Then they were moving.

Chapter 23

*I*t crossed Charlotte's mind that she was being carried in Samuel's arms through a house full of people. Staff and family alike. Certainly, all were presumably abed, but in the house nonetheless. Under this very roof. There were plenty of people within these walls who could discover them like this.

She should care. She *should*.

And yet she did not.

She, Charlotte Langley, astonishingly, could not summon forth the will to care about propriety.

Tonight was not like any other night. Truthfully, it had started this morning, with the end of her betrothal to William.

Earlier today she had been attached, bound,

shackled. Her future had been mapped out for her like the lines etched on the palms of her hands. Her fate had felt so defined, so very decided. Now that future was gone—washed away.

She was a free woman. No longer bound in betrothal. She was free and she would allow herself this.

She was caught in a dream. Living the moments of a life that didn't even feel like her own. She was someone else now. Someone new. Not that girl from a fortnight ago. Not even the girl from last night or upon waking this morning.

She was someone else. Someone unknown. Someone who could do this. Someone who could be carried through a house in a lover's arms with no fear.

They advanced up the stairs. He walked them directly into his room.

Soon she was descending onto the bed, the delicious weight of him coming over her. He kissed her. She met the slick glide of his tongue with her own.

He shrugged her dressing gown off her shoulders and down her arms, never breaking the kiss. His hands found the hem of her nightgown and tugged it up. His mouth broke from hers, tugging it over her head and sending it flying like a dove through the air, landing somewhere beyond her vision. It mattered not.

Her gaze was riveted to his starkly handsome face. To the way his hot gaze dragged over her body, leaving fire in its wake as he surveyed her nakedness, missing nothing in his heated examination.

Naked under him, not a moment of embarrassment seized her.

A growl of approval rumbled from his throat, and the sound emboldened her.

Her hands set to work on ridding him of his shirt, pushing it up until he helped her and pulled the garment over his head.

She came up on her elbows so that her hands and mouth could explore the expanse of his chest.

His hands were buried in the thickness of her hair, her scalp tingling as his fingertips speared through the strands, curling around the shape of her skull, holding her to him. She kissed and licked and scraped her teeth over his firm warm skin. She found the small dusky circles of his nipples and licked them, scoring them with her teeth.

He cursed, thrusting his hips against her bared sex, grinding into her.

"I can feel you, Charlie . . . so wet."

She whimpered, nodding desperately, falling back on the bed.

He watched her, eyes burning, scalding her as

she parted her thighs wider and thrust that most vulnerable part of her into the hardness of his member, barred to her through the barrier of her breeches.

He swallowed visibly, throat muscles working. "You're wanton."

"I am what you've made me."

"Charlie," he said hoarsely.

She wiggled, her body twisting on the bed. "Touch me, Samuel."

His hot gaze fixed on her body. He lifted his hand.

She almost imagined that it trembled ever so slightly as he lowered it to her rib cage. Or perhaps it was she who was shaking.

Air hissed out between her teeth as his hand landed beneath her breast. Her breasts were not big, but they felt heavy and aching right now.

One of his hands closed over her breast and she gasped, overcome with a want so sharp and achingly deep that she couldn't stop the keening cry from tearing loose of her throat.

Her cries grew louder and he smothered her mouth with a kiss, muffling the sound. They kissed as he continued to massage her breast until she was arching into him.

She was lost. A slave to her passion. His for the taking, and she wanted him to take her.

He left her mouth, his head lowering, claiming her breast. His lips sucked on her, pulling her deep into the wet cavern of his mouth. His tongue swirled around her nipple and hot sensation ripped through her. His hand shot to her mouth, muting her scream of pleasure.

The hard press of his hand over her mouth thrilled her even more. Her sex clenched, desperate for pressure, to be filled with his thickness.

His head lifted from her breast, eyes burning. "You're going to be a screamer, aren't you?"

She might be new at this, but she understood his meaning.

He lifted his hand from her lips and she felt a small pang at the loss. "That could present a problem."

"Take me . . . and keep your hand over my mouth." His eyes widened at her invitation. "I can't wait anymore."

His member grew harder, swelling between her thighs. She rubbed against him.

"You are certain?" There was hesitation in his eyes, and she knew it was because he was thinking of her . . . thinking that she was planning to marry another man.

Of course, she wasn't, but he did not know that.

She didn't want to think about that right now. That was a conversation for later. Tomorrow they would talk. Tomorrow she would tell him everything.

Right now she simply wanted to *feel*.

Her hands moved down between their bodies. She was an accomplished seamstress. She knew her way around men's trousers. She had him freed and in her hands in no time.

She familiarized herself with the shape of him. He was big, and as much as that alarmed her, it thrilled her, too. *More*. Her sex tightened, squeezing.

As she continued to explore him, a bead of moisture rose up to kiss her thumb, rolling over the head of him. Want twisted deep inside of her.

With a curse, his hand delved between them, finding her sex, and his fingers did a hurried exploration of his own that had her writhing and gasping. He parted her folds, his finger dipping inside her channel, testing her, stretching her.

"Samuel," she pleaded.

"God, you're ready, Charlie."

She knew that . . .

Tested beyond all endurance, she closed her fingers around the pulsing length of him and guided him toward her, placing the head of him at her entrance, trusting he would take over at some point. The man was skilled. He clearly knew what he was about. He had gotten her to this point, after all. No aphrodisiac pulsed through her blood, just stark primeval need. Hot and thick as syrup in her veins.

Groaning, he collapsed over her, his elbows coming on either side of her head as he drove inside her, lodging himself deep.

His hand shot to her mouth, smothering her cry. Gratification mingled with pain and pleasure.

She held herself motionless, stunned at the strangeness of it all. He was inside her body . . . *Samuel*. They were connected, merged, linked by his member, pulsing in rhythm to her own heartbeat.

She was not the only one motionless. He was not moving either. As the pain ebbed, he continued to hold himself still.

"Sorry," he gasped near her ear. "It's been so long . . . and you're so sweet . . . so perfect."

Enough.

She murmured against his palm, encouraging him to move, to continue. She widened her legs in welcome. Without a voice, it was the most obvious thing she could do to suggest he continue . . . that he give her more.

She tilted her hips and took him in as deeply as she could, whimpering into his palm as she stretched, molding around him.

Her hands came up to claw at his back. Her palms swept down, latching on to the tight swells of his buttocks, urging him on.

She needed this. Him. His body working over her own.

He moved, pumping his bigger body between her thighs, driving hard, harder. Her whimpers turned into cries buried in the cup of his hand.

The salty taste of his skin against her mouth, the press of his fingers into her cheeks added to the intensity of the moment, twisting the ache tighter and tighter within her.

His head fell into the crook of her neck and his teeth bit down on her shoulder as he choked out her name. "Charlie . . ."

He rode her, and she took it all, desperate for more, for everything, an end to the anguish. An end to the twisting throb.

She arched under him, the mounds of her breasts pushed into his firm chest, the chafing pressure against her nipples incredibly erotic.

Her vision blurred and darkened at the edges as her body let go. Snapped in an explosive release.

The muscles of her sex squeezed in a searing flash of pleasure and pain.

Sensations rippled through her. Too powerful, too intense, too everything.

A stinging curse fell from his lips as he drove into her several more times before stilling over her, freezing as he poured the proof of his desire into her.

He collapsed over her, his hand slipping free from her mouth.

She lay still for a moment, his bigger body still cradled between her thighs, his member still lodged inside her.

Her muscles felt like jam. She was nothing more than a puddle.

As her pleasure ebbed, a great lethargy stole over her.

He rolled off her and she turned, curling into his side with a contented sigh. His arm draped over her waist.

Had she not been sleepy earlier? Amazing considering how very tired she was now.

Her eyes drifted shut. So tired . . . so tired she could just sleep an eternity with Samuel's arm wrapped around her.

Chapter 24

Charlotte fell asleep almost instantly and Kingston was left gazing at her beside him. Propped up on one elbow, he watched her chest rise and fall in slow even breaths. He could watch her like this all night.

She was in his bed.

He should probably wake her so that she could remove herself to her own bed. She couldn't possibly want to be discovered here like this. Even if she wasn't betrothed to another man, it would be scandalous.

The reminder of her betrothal stung—had him scowling and killing off the glorious aftermath of his own release.

The Samuel Kingston of a year ago would not

have cared if the woman sharing his bed was attached or not.

He would gladly have been used by any lady—attached or unattached. He would have thrown himself at the altar of desire and not cared one bloody damn about where his bed partner spent the rest of her days.

Now he cared. Damnation, he cared. He cared too much.

In the lamplight, her features were soft and relaxed. She looked so young. Innocent. Far too innocent for the likes of him. He might not be indiscriminate when it came to his bed partners any longer, but he was still jaded, still unworthy of her.

With that final thought, he crept from his bed. No. Not his bed. This was Warrington's house. This bed was not his. Nothing here was his. He didn't belong in this place.

He dressed quietly, the whisper of fabric the only sound in the chamber. He watched her where she slept, so still and peaceful in slumber. Fully dressed, he paused at the foot of the bed. Staring down at her, he almost willed her to wake so he could admire her lovely eyes one last time—see them seeing him.

He wasn't that selfish. He knew what that would lead to—just another tumble in the sheets. Shaking his head, he gathered his things and slipped silently from the room, closing the door behind him.

He took the servants' back staircase and was almost to the door when a voice stopped him.

"Leaving without saying goodbye?"

Kingston turned with a tight smile for his stepbrother. "I did not think it would matter greatly to you. You've wanted me gone since I arrived. I suppose I should thank you for not tossing me out the first day I showed my face here."

Warrington shrugged. "My wife would not have allowed that." He paused, but his gaze held tight on him. "Are you certain you want to leave?"

A smile played on Kingston's lips. "Don't tell me you will miss me?"

"I won't . . . but someone else might."

Kingston's smile slipped. "No." He shook his head. "I won't be missed."

"Is that what you think?" This last question was dropped heavily. There was no mistaking his implication. Warrington knew exactly how he had spent his evening . . . and with whom.

Deciding not to play at denials, he said, "She will be better off without me."

Warrington nodded slowly. "You might be right, but I'm not certain *she* would agree with that."

"She's for someone else."

He snorted. "Pembroke? She won't go through with that. She told as much to Marian. Said she was going to end it."

Exhilaration swept through him before he quelled it. As gratified as that made him, it didn't change the fact that she deserved someone better. Someone who could give her the life she wanted.

He hefted his satchel higher on his shoulder and held out a hand for the duke to shake. "Thank you for your hospitality."

Warrington hesitated before taking his hand. "I'm sure we will see each other again soon."

Kingston did not bother disagreeing. It was not worth arguing.

Turning, he left Haverston Hall, certain he would not be coming back.

CHARLOTTE WOKE ALONE in the haze of early dawn.

She stretched out a hand on the bed to find nothing. Only empty space. No Samuel.

She lifted her head to look over the bed, assuring herself that she was not mistaken. He was gone. Truly gone. Samuel had left. She was alone.

She vaulted from bed, having no desire to be caught in his bedchamber by the staff. She could well imagine the horror of one of the maids discovering her.

As she hastily slipped her nightgown over her head, she moved toward the armoire, flinging open the doors, only to find it empty. No clothes. All of his things were gone . . . as she had feared.

He was truly gone. Not just from the room, but from the house.

And could she blame him?

He thought she was still going to marry William. He didn't know the truth. As far as he was concerned she was still betrothed to another, but he'd pursued her even knowing that. She thought she'd have time to tell him in the morning. She'd meant to tell him of her change in circumstances then.

Although she did not know if it would have mattered. After all, he had left.

He hadn't stayed for her. And perhaps even more hurtful . . . he had not stayed for himself. She had not been enough to compel him to remain.

She inhaled a steadying breath.

Resolve filled her, flooding through her and finding every tiny little corner where doubt and hurt dwelled.

All those little hollows hurt a fraction less now. She felt better. Stronger. Emboldened. Undefeated by life.

Everything was fine. *She* would be fine. She had not broken it off with William with the expectation of anything lasting with Samuel. She knew better than that. She knew what manner of man he was. Last night had been wonderful. She did not regret it. She'd done it for herself. A newly freed Charlotte had done it for herself.

She marched from Samuel's room, returning to hers, where she dressed herself.

Once appropriately attired for the day, she strode down the corridor to her sister's bedchamber. Day had barely begun to break. She doubted either her sister or Nathaniel had left their bedchamber yet. They were not early to rise. Interestingly enough, her sister had been early to rise. Before she married Nathaniel.

She never would have dared to disturb them before. Before she became this new person. A gloriously resolved person as she was now.

She knocked briskly on the door.

Indistinct voices carried through the wood.

When she was not immediately awarded with a bid of entrance, she knocked again, this time louder. She was not in a patient mood.

Marian opened the door wrapped tightly in her dressing gown, her hair tousled in charming disarray, her cheeks flushed an equally charming pink.

Clearly Charlotte had interrupted something. Something she now understood firsthand after her night with William, and she could not help the swift stab of envy because her sister was fortunate enough to have that whenever she wanted.

Charlotte wouldn't have that ever again. At least she could not imagine she would. Samuel was gone. She could not imagine wanting anyone else.

Pushing aside inappropriate thoughts of shagging, she focused on the task at hand and what had brought her to her sister's bedchamber so early.

"Charlotte? Is everything—"

"I've broken my engagement to William," she blurted, eager to have the words finally out.

Marian blinked and glanced back inside the room. Charlotte tracked her gaze to where her husband reclined in the bed.

The duke had not bothered to cover himself. He was defiantly sprawled upon the bed, his well-formed chest bare, the sheets tugged up to his waist in the barest nod to modesty.

Marian turned wide eyes back on Charlotte. "Oh. You did then. How . . . um, when?"

"Yesterday," she announced. "I did not want to distract you from your guests, but now that they're gone I don't want to wait another moment. I imagine the Pembrokes will call on you today. They will be very unpleasant, I am sure. You shall have to endure that, and for that, I apologize."

"Don't fret about that." Marian sent another

quick glance to her husband. "I have to ask, Char . . . did you do this because of Mr. Kingston?" Her sister lifted her chest on a breath, looking almost in fear of her answer.

Charlotte lacked the heart to tell her the truth.

It had *everything* to do with Kingston.

He'd changed her. Changed her for the better. She might have fallen in love with him, and he might have left, but she would never regret ending her betrothal. Just as she would not regret their night together.

"It has naught to do with him," she lied, knowing her sister would otherwise hold him to blame. She might even go after him. She did not wish for her sister to be at odds with her brother-in-law for some imagined slight to Charlotte.

"He is gone," Nathaniel announced from the bed.

Charlotte's gaze whipped back to him. He knew that then, did he? She forced her expression into stoic resolve, revealing none of her inner turmoil, none of her aching heart.

"He left in the middle of the night," he elaborated. "I—er . . . happened upon him in the corridor."

"In the middle of the night?" she echoed, wondering if he knew how Samuel had spent the night. She looked to Marian, wondering if she knew, too.

Marian looked intently at her husband. "Did you know he was leaving?" she demanded. "You didn't say anything to make him leave, did you?"

He looked mildly affronted. "No. I would not do that."

"Whatever the case, it does not matter," Charlotte insisted with a wave of her hand. She knew Samuel well enough to know that no one made him do anything. He'd left because he'd wanted to leave. "I simply wanted you to know that I ended the betrothal, and I wanted to ask a favor of you . . ."

Charlotte paused, realizing in that moment how very important it was to her that her sister agreed to her request.

"Yes?" Marian prompted.

"I'd like the house. You promised it to me upon marriage to William, and I'd still like it. I want it for myself." She moistened her lips. "I want to live there."

Marian blinked, staring at her.

Charlotte continued, "I don't expect you to fund me entirely. At least not forever. I can open my own dressmaking shop and conduct business from home. The Hansens operate the only shop in the area and they have more business than they can manage. The shire is large enough to support more than one seamstress."

"Of course, Char. The house is as much yours

as it is mine. You needn't my permission to move in."

"Nor must you press yourself into work . . . unless you want to," her brother-in-law spoke from the bed.

Relief blossomed in her chest at their kind and generous support. "Thank you. I shall begin moving my things back home posthaste."

"So soon? You need not rush."

She shrugged. "It will always be home to me. I am eager to return."

"It was rather nice having you here with us."

"It was . . . and I thank you for your hospitality, but I miss home."

"It's only down the road, Marian," Nathaniel gently assured her. "She is not moving across the country. I am certain you will see each other often."

Charlotte nodded in agreement. "Of course we will." Smiling in promise, she backed away, keen to begin packing and start living her life. Her life as a free woman.

Chapter 25

Kingston reached the next village well before
the doubts settled over him like a dark pall.

He forced himself to keep going, however,
pushing his mount through that first village and
on to the next one, calling himself all kinds of
fool. Weak. Delusional.

He was simply enamored. Last night had only
whetted his appetite for her.

The act of congress had been familiar. Something missed. It was only that. That was the
cause of this bewildering longing.

Sex had always been about using someone for
gratification. For pleasure. He admitted that to
himself with no sense of pride. After seeing his

mother . . . he'd had no taste for empty pleasure. It held no allure. It did not tempt him.

Until Charlotte.

She might have only been about pleasure seeking, but it was more than that for him.

Certainly there had been physical pleasure, but there had also been more. For him, for the first time, strange as it seemed, it had been about need. Closeness.

She did not feel what he felt. That much was evident.

He might be good enough for a dalliance but nothing else. Not anything lasting and significant, otherwise she would not have come to his bed whilst bound to another man.

He knew enough of *this* particular woman to know that.

She may very well be marrying another man. Or she may not.

He didn't know, and it didn't matter, and she had not seen fit to tell him either way.

She didn't view him as a matrimonial prospect, as someone she could build a life with, because he wasn't. He wasn't worthy of her.

He'd left to preserve himself. To protect what dignity he had left . . . and what little heart he possessed.

He'd be damned if he stuck around Brambledon

to watch her walk down the aisle into the arms of another man. He wasn't a sadist.

Never once had she given him the impression that he was worthy.

Except she had.

The sudden realization assaulted him like a blow.

When she'd found him in the kitchen she had been looking for him. She had tracked him down to see how he was faring. He was the one who had turned the encounter into something of a carnal nature.

When she'd kissed him back and joined him in his room, in his bed, she'd surrendered herself to him in complete trust.

That meant something.

For a woman such as she, it meant everything.

This thought had him lurching upright in the bed of a room of an inn whose name he could not recall, in a village whose name also eluded him.

He stared blindly into the dark, seeing so very clearly now what had been obscured to him before.

She would not have come to his bed void of emotion.

He should have stayed. He should have waited until she woke and asked her what she felt for him.

He should have asked her not to marry Pembroke.

He should have told her he loved her.

Bloody hell.

He rose from bed and hastily dressed. Leaving the inn, he fetched his mount from the nearby stables himself. He'd have to ride carefully in the dark, but with any luck he'd be back at Haverston Hall before tomorrow night. Well before her wedding.

Well in time to persuade her to take a chance on loving him.

CHARLOTTE MOVED ALL her things into her house, returning them, as far as she was concerned, to their proper place.

Her clothing. Her books. Her small collection of mostly paste jewelry.

Her knitting and sewing, including the basket of fabric scraps that had belonged to her mother. The large basket contained buttons and swatches that had come from Mama's frocks, from dresses Charlotte and her sisters wore as girls. There were even some pieces that had come from her brother's old vests and shirts. She knew these were only things, but to her it was her family's legacy. More valuable than jewelry or the most costly heirloom.

Once the decision had been reached and all the details arranged, it had taken only half a day to move it all. A testament to the fact that she didn't possess much. Not much save her dignity. She'd felt that particular trait in full abundance as she'd packed up all her worldly belongings. She was claiming her life. Claiming her future happiness.

Future happiness.

While she could not claim to be fully happy yet, she felt its impending arrival deep in the marrow of her bones.

Happiness was coming.

For now there was contentment. Peace in knowing she was in full control of her fate and would accept nothing less than what she deserved.

The sting of Samuel's rejection would fade. The ache of waking up to find him gone . . . The knowledge that she wouldn't see him again, that he could never be all that she needed . . .

That pain would fade.

She guided the carriage down the lane to Haverston Hall with a snap of the reins. Nora sat beside her. She'd accompanied her, insisting on helping her settle in. Nora had worn a smile ever since she learned Charlotte had called off the wedding.

"Thank you for bringing me home."

"No problem at all."

"Will you stay for dinner?"

Charlotte shook her head. "Cook gave me a basket of food. I have more than enough to eat until I get the kitchen outfitted once again."

"You really intend to stay the night?"

Charlotte nodded. "I do."

"That will be strange. I don't think we've ever slept in different houses before."

Charlotte angled her head contemplatively. She had not considered that, but Nora was correct. They had always slept beneath the same roof. Before they'd moved in with Marian and Nathaniel, they had even shared a room. A bed. It had been an adjustment simply having a bed to herself.

"It will be strange," she agreed. But life went on, continued, changed, evolved. This she knew, as bittersweet as it might be.

Nora looked out at the countryside. "It was destined to happen. If you hadn't called off your engagement, you would have been leaving me soon then."

Charlotte inclined her head in agreement. "I suppose so."

"This way is better. You'll be living close. I can visit you any time I want . . . And I don't have to see the Pembrokes on those visits." Nora sat a little straighter, clearly delighted at this.

Charlotte smiled. "That is a perk."

"Indeed."

Marian had insisted she keep one of Warrington's smaller carriages for herself, so that she might convey herself with ease back and forth to Haverston Hall or to the village as needed.

It was a kind gesture, and perhaps too generous, but Marian and Nathaniel had insisted. Just as they insisted they would help staff her house.

Charlotte could not dispute them. It was the only way they would agree to give her the house. They had ultimately negotiated and agreed upon two servants. She'd chosen Gertie and Thomas. Even now Gertie and Thomas were back at the house, arranging things for their new lives.

"You know, Nora . . . you are welcome to stay with me," Charlotte offered.

"I have considered it." She shrugged, staring straight ahead at the road. "I think I'll stay at Haverston Hall. For now. I've quite settled in and am enjoying my laboratory. It's a vastly grand space—"

"Uh, that's your bedchamber, you realize."

Nora continued as though Charlotte had not spoken. "And I admit I am passing fond of Cook's biscuits." She patted her middle. "I think I've added a stone since we moved in."

"Well, the offer is there. You can join me at any time, if you so choose."

Nora nodded and gave a small satisfied sigh.

"I will keep that in mind. Thank you. Marian is married. You've found your situation. I need to find my own way as well."

"You have time aplenty. You may wish to marry—"

She made a scoffing sound. "Doubtful. Can you imagine a gentleman choosing me for a wife? Or me choosing a gentleman? No man could be more interesting than my work." She shuddered as though the prospect repulsed her.

A smile played about Charlotte's lips. "One never knows." She had certainly not been looking for passion or love, but it had managed to find her nonetheless. Unfortunately, it had not ended as merrily as Marian's own foray in romance.

"Oh, I know. I will never marry."

"Perhaps a taste of your tonic will persuade you otherwise?"

Nora harumphed. "As it changed your mind? Now you are not marrying at all. Although I imagined . . ." Her voice died away.

"You imagined what?" she prompted.

"I imagined that you and Mr. Kingston . . ." She wiggled her eyebrows meaningfully at Charlotte.

Charlotte's levity faded. "I do not know what you are implying," she lied. She had a good notion of what her sister was implying. She simply did not want to discuss Samuel with her. Not yet. Perhaps never. The wound was still much too raw.

"Oh, you know what I mean. You and Kingston. Together. As in married. I thought there was a very strong likelihood of that happening. When the two of you were together the air fairly crackled . . . as it does when Marian is with Nathaniel."

"We are not like Marian and Nathaniel. *They* are in love."

Her sister and Nathaniel loved each other. Undoubtedly. It was not a one-sided love. It was lasting. Forever.

A year ago, when Marian was abducted, Charlotte had never seen a man so overcome, so lost at the prospect of losing his wife.

Nora sighed. "I suppose I was mistaken."

"Quite so."

They topped the hill and started the descent to Haverston Hall. The house sprawled out below them in grandeur. Even though she had been living in the place for a while, it still took her breath away. It was a marvel to her that Marian had married into this world.

"Oh," Nora said with heavy emphasis. "Maybe not *quite*."

Charlotte sent her a curious glance. Her sister was gazing steadily at the house ahead. Charlotte followed her gaze and her stomach plummeted. She pulled up on the reins, hard, stopping the carriage.

"What are you doing?"

Charlotte could only stare.

Nora pressed. "Well, we can't sit here all day and gawk at the fellow."

Charlotte shook her head. "What is he doing here?"

He left. He wasn't supposed to be here.

"I could hazard a guess as to what he is doing here. Can't you?"

"He left."

He left me.

It appeared as though they had just happened upon him as he, too, arrived at Haverston. He was dismounting from his horse. A groom hastened forward, reaching for his reins.

He had not noticed her yet, and she was heartily glad for that.

Charlotte was tempted to make her sister climb down from the carriage so that she could leave her here, so that she could turn around without him ever seeing her.

So she could get on with her life and get on with forgetting him.

That would be cowardly, however. She would not run. This place was her home. Well, in a manner. It was more her home than his at any rate.

"He came back. Obviously, he came back for you. I was not mistaken at all. I was right. He loves you."

"There is nothing obvious about this to me," she snapped.

Nora's bright expression fell. "Well, whatever the case, no sense dawdling here."

Charlotte flicked her wrists and sent the carriage lurching forward. She sat stiffly on the bench as they advanced.

The groom spotted them, nodding his head in their direction.

Samuel whipped around. She felt his gaze land on her, the hot intensity not softened by the distance between them.

The distance soon closed.

She pulled the carriage to a stop before the steep steps leading to the front door and braced herself. It was not helpful that he was so handsome. His hair was windblown from his ride, his strong features ruddy from sun and the exertion.

"Good day, Mr. Kingston," Nora greeted cheerfully as she hopped down from the carriage, not waiting for assistance. She shot a quick glance to the late-afternoon sky. "Or should I say good evening?"

He nodded at Nora, his lips moving in some distracted fashion of greeting. Charlotte could not make out the words. Not that it mattered. She needed to be on her way. Especially considering the manner in which he stared at her.

His gaze fastened on her, his bourbon-hued

eyes starkly fierce, liquid-deep . . . an ocean trying to pull her in.

Those eyes brought her back to the night she'd spent in his bedchamber, in his bed.

It was not a good idea for him to be looking at her in such a way.

He moved around to her side of the carriage and she knew he meant to help her down.

"I'm not staying," she said tersely. Addressing Nora, she added, "Thank you for spending the day with me. I will see you soon."

"What do you mean you're not staying?" Samuel asked.

She battled the impulse to ignore his question. Again, it would be cowardly of her. She looked down at him. "I have moved into my old house."

"You moved?" His gaze swept over her and the carriage. "I've only been gone for a few days and you've moved into your former house?"

"That is correct."

"I don't understand. You decided to move in earlier? Before the wedding?"

"There is not going to be a wedding."

He blinked and sent a quick glance to Nora as though for verification. Nora gave a single nod, a small smile on her lips.

At that moment, the front door opened. Marian and Nathaniel stepped out, exchanging knowing looks.

Charlotte continued, "I don't need to be married to follow through with my plan."

"Good."

"Good?" she echoed.

"Good for you." He extended a hand toward her.

She exhaled, for some reason feeling . . . *disappointed*. She wanted him to declare that it was good for *him*. Good for him because he didn't want her to marry anyone else. Because he wanted her.

He didn't say that. He didn't say any of those fanciful things she should not be thinking.

She shook her head, ignoring his proffered hand. "As I said, I am not staying."

He dropped his hand, frowning. "I came back . . ."

"Yes. I see that." She lifted an eyebrow. "And why is that? Why did you return?" *Why did you return to shake up and upset my life?*

He stared at her for a long moment. She held his stare, even as she felt the weight of her family's focus on her. They were watching everything unfolding with rapt attention.

"I came back for you."

Her heart gave a treacherous little leap. She inhaled and gave her heart a firm push, attempting to settle it back in her chest. "You left."

Heat glinted in his eyes. "That was my mistake. I should not have done so. Not after . . ."

He stopped himself, but she knew what he

had wanted to say. What he would have said if they were alone. *Not after they had spent the night together.*

He went on, "I soon realized it and turned around." He paused. "I came back to ask you not to marry Pembroke."

"Why?" she demanded, tightening her grip on the reins as the horses shifted restlessly.

He let out a breath of frustration. "You wanted to marry Pembroke. If that was your wish, I told myself it was not my right . . . that I should respect your decision."

Nora made a strangled sound in her throat, as though she was trying to suppress speech.

Charlotte glared at her before looking back at Samuel. "Very noble of you," she said with full scathing bitterness. "What changed your mind?"

"I'm not noble." He held out his arms wide. "Not in the least. I don't want you to marry anyone . . . except me. I came here to convince you of that. Even if I had to steal you away to stop you from marrying Pembroke."

The world darkened, tunneling to the solitary sight of his face. There was nothing beyond it.

It was the only thing she could see. Handsome and stark and so very compelling.

Her heart wasn't inside her chest anymore. It had burst free.

"Charlotte?"

She couldn't find her voice. Perhaps it was a consequence of losing one's heart.

"Charlotte?" Nora added her voice. "Did you hear him? Say something!"

Charlotte shook her head as though returning to herself. "I heard you." She adjusted her weight on the bench. "I appreciate the offer. I cannot accept, however."

Of course she couldn't. He'd said nothing of love, and now she knew she would settle for nothing less.

Even if she loved him. She would not have him unless he loved her.

She had ended one betrothal because it had not been right. It had lacked love.

She would not agree to another one without the all-important ingredient of love. Affection. Passion.

"Charlie . . ."

No. She would not do this. Not stand here and be tempted by his seductive voice.

"I have said all I am going to say on the matter. There is nothing more to discuss. Good day, Mr. Kingston."

She would not do this with him.

She especially would not do this in front of her family.

She shook her head firmly and snapped the

reins. She was dimly aware of her sisters calling out farewells behind her. She did not slow down. She did not look back. She pressed on, advancing through the burn of her tears.

He had come back. He had come back and asked to marry her.

And yet he had not said the one thing that mattered. The one thing that would have made all the difference and made her think that perhaps he was doing this because living without her was an impossibility for him.

There had been no romance or affection or sentimentality as he tendered his proposal. All things she had not thought she needed before. But now she knew she did. She needed those things. She wanted them. She would have them or nothing.

She drove the rest of the way home in relative composure. She would not weep. It would not do to be seen crying by one of the neighbors. As though she had conjured her, Mrs. Pratt, the biggest gossip in the shire, waved at her from her garden. No doubt the farmer's wife would credit any tears to her broken engagement. News of that had slowly started making its way through the village.

She could never fathom the truth. Charlotte could scarcely fathom it herself.

She, dull and proper Charlotte Langley, had a liaison with a renowned rogue, and he was still hanging about, complicating her life with public proposals. Hopefully none of the staff at Haverston Hall had overheard. She did not wish for this bit of her private life to be bandied about town.

As she passed the Pratt farmhouse, she lifted her face to the breeze. Today had not been as dreadfully hot as the weeks prior.

She took dinner in the kitchen with Gertie and Thomas. Together they made a list of things to do the following day to get the house back to rights. It was a useful distraction and a nice way to rein in her still galloping heart.

She settled into bed in the master bedchamber that night with a sense of accomplishment. She'd come far. She'd seized her life and was making good choices.

Even though she had fallen in love with Samuel, she had not accepted his offer of marriage because it was less than right . . . less than she deserved. After William, she wanted a marriage that had it all—*everything*.

Even though a gnawing ache persisted in her chest . . . she would not accept anything less than a love match. Nothing else. She didn't have to marry. No one required it of her. Her sisters had long operated under this belief. Now she did, too.

This was her consolation as she drifted to sleep.

When she woke disorientated in the gloomy hours of predawn, it was not to the memory of this, however.

It was to the acrid smell of smoke.

Chapter 26

*T*he distant tolling bell from the village woke
Kingston with a jolt. The barest hint of day broke
the skyline through the parted damask drapes of
his bedchamber.

He flung back the counterpane and hastily
donned his breeches and boots. He snatched his
shirt from where he had discarded it upon un-
dressing the evening before when he had gone
to bed crushed and confused over Charlotte's rejection. He didn't understand why she'd refused
him. Her betrothal to another no longer stood in
the way, barring them from being together.

He didn't know what the bell signified. Villages
used the bells to alert everyone in the countryside of some manner of emergency. A lost child.

A dangerous criminal on the loose. Some kind of disaster was afoot, that much was evident.

As he hastened down the hall, he slipped the shirt over his head. By the time he reached the first floor, most of the household was up and assembled. He approached his stepbrother in the foyer just as a footman burst through the front door.

"'Tis fire! A fire!"

Warrington flew to action. "Hines, fetch buckets!"

Marian and Nora stood on the stairs in their dressing robes. At this announcement, they turned and hurried up the steps, presumably to dress.

The servant who burst through the door added, "At the old Langley place!"

Everyone froze. Except Marian and Nora. They whipped back around. "At my old house?" Marian demanded.

Nora gasped and reached for her arm as though needing support. "Charlotte!"

Samuel didn't wait for confirmation.

He vaulted through the front door and raced to the stables, fetching his mount and saddling it. Every moment felt an eternity.

The wind tore at him as he rode through the burgeoning dawn to Charlotte's, the force making his eyes tear. At least he thought it was the wind. He couldn't be sure. Fear coated his mouth and lodged in his throat like a stone.

Myriad thoughts flashed through his mind. Mostly how his horse couldn't move quickly enough, and how had he ever thought this beast fast?

Dark smoke rose in great plumes against the lightening sky and panic clawed at him at this evidence that Charlotte's house was burning. *Please, God. Not with her in it.*

It felt like forever before he reached the house. Flames licked out its left side. He recalled the kitchen was in that area.

There were already people there, a dozen or so passing buckets of water from the nearby well. It was all they could do, but staring at the blazing flames jutting from the kitchen's window, he knew it would not be enough. The house was lost.

Charlotte.

He jumped from his horse. She couldn't be in there. She couldn't!

He stood in the yard, wildly looking around, calling her name with a desperation that burned deeper than the fire in front of him. "Charlotte!"

He didn't see her.

With a curse, he rushed through the front gate and up the steps, ignoring those calling him to stop, pushing through the men who tried to bar him entry, barging past them as if they were insignificant gnats. Nothing could keep him from reaching Charlotte. Not mere men. Nor fire.

He charged through the door, shouting for her amidst the blinding smoke.

"Charlotte!" He held an arm up in an attempt to shield his eyes from the stinging air. His throat quickly grew hoarse, as though scraped from the inside with a blade.

Coughing, he bent low and pressed on, searching for the stairs, his mind feverishly trying to recall the layout of the house—and guessing which bedchamber she might have taken for herself.

Suddenly a hand clamped down on his wrist. He swung around, ready to strike and deflect anyone who kept him from going up the stairs to retrieve Charlotte.

Only when he swung around, it was to see Charlotte. Her sweaty, soot-smeared face was the most precious sight he had ever beheld.

With an exultant shout, he hauled her to his side and turned them for the door.

Hunkered low, they pushed out into the fresh air, both coughing violently.

They staggered past people—there were a good dozen more now and still more coming—trying to put out the fire. He led her several yards away, beneath a tree. She gasped for breath amidst her sobs.

"Easy," he soothed.

There was no easing her. She wept, tears leaving clean trails down her sooty face. "My house . . ."

He knew what this house had meant to her. He felt her sorrow keenly.

She rocked side to side. "The house . . . it's gone."

He pulled her into his arms. "But you're here. You're alive. That's all that matters. Houses can be rebuilt."

He felt the dampness of her tears at his throat. "I was going back for the basket."

"What basket?"

"The basket my mother left me. Of all the scraps of fabric from her dresses . . . and our dresses as girls. It was . . ." Her voice broke on another sob. The sound twisted like a knife into his heart.

"Where is it?"

"I left it in the front drawing room. Near the settee. The smoke was too thick. I could not see my way."

"Your life is more important," he said firmly. "*You* should not have gone back for it," he admonished her even as he set her from him.

She blinked at him in confusion, wiping at her nose. "What are you—"

"Wait here."

He rushed back to the house, resolute. Determined that she not lose everything today.

He heard her shouting his name, but he ignored her, searching the yard for something to aid him. Spotting a discarded bucket, he lifted it and rushed around to the side of the house, swinging the bucket and crashing it into the glass of the drawing room doors several times, clearing the shards enough so that he might ease himself through—and inside the burning house.

CHARLOTTE STAGGERED FORWARD, screaming as Samuel disappeared inside the house, his shape swallowed up in the deadly inferno that was once her home. She started to go after him, but was suddenly restrained on all sides.

"Samuel!"

What was he doing? He was mad . . . risking his life for a basket? It was one thing for her to take such a risk. It had been for herself.

What was he thinking doing such a thing for her? She should never had said anything to him.

He could die. For her. To fetch something for her. *God. No.*

"Samuel!" She fought, too weak against the men holding her and she hated them for it.

She watched the house burn helplessly—her only thought for the man inside. The man she loved. The smashed drawing room door through which he'd leaped was engulfed in black smoke. It was impossible to see within the room. How could he even see to locate her basket?

Simple. He could not. He was in there even now, likely lost in the smoke and fire. Dying.

Crying out, she surged against her captors with renewed vigor, determined to break through. He could not die.

She could not lose him.

Suddenly her sisters were there. They grabbed hold of her with comforting hands, shooing aside her captors. It was the opportunity she needed. They were no match for her. She managed to escape—only to be caught up by Nathaniel. Apparently, he'd been ready for her. He lifted her off her feet, indifferent to her swinging fists.

"Nooo! Let me go! Samuel's in there!"

Because of her.

Because of her and her wretched tears for something that didn't matter.

Not as he did. Not as he mattered to her. He was everything. The house was just stone and timber. It could be replaced. He never could.

"Char! Look!" Nora pointed to the house.

Charlotte went limp with relief, following the direction of her sister's gaze.

Samuel emerged from the broken door, her basket tucked under one arm.

Nathaniel released her and she ran. She ran until she was at his side, looping one arm around his waist. He was hot to the touch—all of him, his skin and clothes—and she winced.

Someone confiscated the basket of fabric from him, but she didn't care. She didn't spare it a glance. His weight fell against her. He coughed fiercely as she led him clear of the house.

"Water," she shouted, motioning for several bucket bearers to douse him. Five or six buckets were dumped over him. She never left his side, getting soaked herself in the process.

She pushed the hair from his forehead and wiped the water and ash from his face, looking him over critically. "You daft fool! What were you thinking?" A sob choked out of her at this last question. She knew what he had been thinking.

"*You*," he answered thickly, his voice hoarse as he collapsed against a tree. "I was thinking of you. Only you. I only ever think of you. Your peace. Your happiness. You . . . you are everything to me, Charlie."

A sob swelled up in her throat, and it had nothing to do with grief or fear or sadness.

"Like I said . . . you're a daft fool." She sniffed back the burn of tears and wiped at her runny nose. She knew she looked a fright, but here he was telling her the most profound words she had ever heard in her life. And she was a wreck. "Promise to me that you will never do anything like that again. Not for me."

"I can't promise you that."

"You stubborn man." She shook her head, her heart overflowing with emotion.

"I can promise you anything else. The world. A new house. Jewels to drape around your lovely neck. Anything, but I can't—"

"Promise me your love," she cut in, staring at his smoke-ravaged face. "That's all I've ever wanted."

A slow smile spread his features, his teeth shockingly white against the stain of ash and soot on his skin. "That is easy. Don't you know? You have that. For some time now, you have had that, my love. My heart is yours."

Her own heart expanded, swelling to the point of pain in her chest. Was love supposed to ache like this? "I needed to hear it," she whispered, stroking his cheek.

He pressed a kiss to her lips, slow and lingering. "You'll hear it every day, love. For the rest of our lives, I will be telling you this."

Epilogue

Ten months later . . .

The summer day was overly warm with the sun burning high overhead. Charlotte guided the wagon beneath a stretch of trees, seeking the shade. She lifted her face to the dappled light that made its way down through the leaves and branches. The shroud of trees shielded her from the worst of the sun's rays.

The lemonade she transported in the back of the cart sloshed loudly inside its barrel as she drove across the countryside. It would be a welcome treat, no doubt, for the thirsty crew busy at work.

Charlotte cast a glance over her shoulder to assure herself the lid was still safely secured and the barrel had not tipped over. A wood crate packed with no less than two dozen ham sandwiches, their aroma rich on the air, sat beside the lemonade.

Satisfied, she faced forward again and continued to guide the cart across the countryside, clicking her tongue to encourage the mare.

"Nice of you to join me," Charlotte addressed Nora, seated beside her on the bench.

"I've been cooped up long enough." She, too, sent a glance to the back of the cart. "Those sandwiches smell heavenly. I skipped breakfast."

"Yes, we missed you this morning."

Lately Nora had become more reclusive, spending long hours in her chamber or outdoors, hunting for plants and herbs. She lost all sense of time when she was busy at her work.

As a result, Marian had forbidden the servants from taking meals to Nora in her bedchamber in an attempt to encourage her to emerge to eat with them in the dining room. Unfortunately, now that the servants weren't allowed to bring her food Nora often worked right through meals. Skipping breakfast was not uncommon these days.

Of course, Nora hardly looked as though she

were wasting away. She probably bribed servants to bring her food. Nora could be tremendously persuasive.

Charlotte was certain that if Nora lived alone she would be perfectly content going days, weeks, without seeing anyone.

"If you can reach the box, you can have one now," Charlotte offered.

"No, I will wait." Nora smiled and then tilted her face up to the sun, clearly enjoying the jaunt outdoors. "What kind of sandwiches?" she asked.

"Ham."

"Hm. Delicious."

Cook had suggested cucumber sandwiches as though Charlotte were delivering food to a ladies' garden party, but she had insisted on filling the sandwiches with thick wedges of ham. The men rebuilding the house were hard at work in the sweltering heat and deserved hearty sandwiches stuffed with plenty of Cook's honey sweet ham.

"Oh, my," Nora exclaimed as the cart cleared the copse and rounded the turn leading to what had once been their childhood home—before it had burned to the ground. "You and Kingston have been busy," she said over the song of hammers as the house came into view. "Just think," Nora mused. "This all started because of me."

"You mean because of the tonic?"

Nora shrugged and then nodded. "Same thing."

"You know, Samuel still doesn't believe your tonic works as an aphrodisiac."

"Pessimist." Nora sniffed.

"It would be interesting to see if it worked on men the same way," Charlotte mused.

A thoughtful look came over Nora's face. "Why, yes, it would. Why didn't I think of that? It would be an interesting experiment . . . interesting indeed."

Charlotte chuckled. "Don't get any ideas, Nora."

Nora looked indignant. "Have a little faith, if you please."

Charlotte left it at a "hmph" and turned her attention back to her house.

It was coming along nicely. A complete rebuild. They weren't able to salvage any of the original house. The fire had destroyed it all.

The structure was slightly larger than before, designed for their preferences, but it still possessed a similar aesthetic with the same elevation and facade and scalloped trim.

Similar but still new. Something she and Samuel could make their own.

Samuel had hired an architect from London and included Charlotte in every meeting.

At first, she had been hesitant to speak up, but her reticence quickly faded. Samuel wanted her opinion . . . he wanted her mark on the house.

Now her enthusiasm bubbled over. She could hardly contain her excitement and was full of ideas she had no trouble voicing.

This house was more than anything she had ever wanted because it was everything *they* wanted.

It would be their house—*their home*.

It was strange. While she and her sisters would forever mourn the loss of their childhood home, there was no regret in this new house.

She and Samuel were building it together. It would be theirs. For their family.

Her hand drifted to the slight swell of her stomach and a small smile played about her lips.

"They've made much progress," Nora remarked approvingly.

"Haven't they?"

"The last time I was here there was naught but beams. Not even a roof. When will it be finished?"

"The initial projection was October, but now Samuel thinks the house might be ready for us in September."

"September?" Nora lifted an eyebrow. "Just don't move in on the day of Pembroke's wedding. You promised him you would attend."

"Ah, of course." She nodded as she climbed down from the wagon.

William was marrying Delia Smith. Delia

had long mooned after William, and the couple seemed very happy.

Most important, William was happy.

He'd come to Charlotte the day after he proposed to Delia to thank her for ending their betrothal. *For doing what I didn't have the courage to do.*

His words had served as a release. A blessing. She had not known she needed to hear them until he had uttered them.

Samuel emerged from the house. His eyes alighted on her and a smile stretched his lips.

Her heart swelled at the sight of her husband, virile and too handsome to believe, and hers. He strode across the yard toward her.

With no care for their many witnesses, he embraced her and kissed her, long and deep.

"Ick. You two," Nora muttered. "You definitely need to finish this house so I don't have to see so much of that anymore."

They came up for air to watch Nora start for the house.

Charlotte chuckled and shook her head.

"And how are you, my beautiful wife?" His hand went to the slight mound of her stomach.

"I am wonderful." She motioned to the cart. "I've brought food and drink for everyone."

"Brilliant." His hand shifted on her stomach. "And this little one? How fares the baby?"

"Snug and happy, too," she replied.

"Well, my two happy girls—"

"Girls? Are you so certain it's a daughter?"

"Yes." He kissed her nose. "Just as beautiful as her mother. Now. Shall I show you to the nursery? The molding is up and they've started papering the walls."

"Oh! Yes." She bounced excitedly on her toes.

He slid an arm around her waist and guided her forward, up the walk, through the door and into their waiting home.

Sophie Jordan continues her
scintillating Rogue Files series with

The Duke Effect

On Sale
October 2020

*Next month, don't miss these exciting
new love stories only from
Avon Books*

Sit! Stay! Speak! by Annie England Noblin
Tragedy sent Addie Andrews fleeing from Chicago
to the shelter of an unexpected inheritance: her
beloved aunt's home in Eunice, Arkansas, population
very tiny—but *very* interesting. Most surprising of
all, she's got a bedraggled puppy she discovered
abandoned and in desperate need of love. Kind of
like Addie herself . . .

How to Catch a Queen by Alyssa Cole
When Shanti Mohapi weds the king of Njaza, her
dream of becoming a queen finally comes true. But
while Shanti and her husband may share an
immediate and powerful attraction, her subjects see
her as an outsider. When turmoil erupts in their
kingdom, Shanti goes on the run, and Sanyu must
learn whether he has what it takes both to lead his
people and to catch his queen.

Nothing Compares to the Duke by Christy Carlyle
Rhys Forester, the new Duke of Claremont, lives his
life by four words: Enjoy All, Regret Nothing. He's
devoted to the pleasure of his wild soirees and
reckless behavior. The debts that come with his title
don't fit the carefree lifestyle he's created and when
he's forced to return to his family's estate, he's also
forced to confront his one and only regret: the
beautiful girl he left behind.

REL 0520

The Wildes of Lindow Castle

Wilde in Love
978-0-06-238947-3

Too Wilde to Wed
978-0-06-269246-7

Born to Be Wilde
978-0-06-269247-4

Say No to the Duke
978-0-06-287782-6

EJ6 0719

At Avon Books, we know your passion for romance—once you finish one of our novels, you find yourself wanting more.

May we tempt you with . . .

- **Excerpts** from our upcoming releases.

- Entertaining **extras**, including authors' personal photo albums and book lists.

- Behind-the-scenes **scoop** on your favorite characters and series.

- **Sweepstakes** for the chance to win free books, romantic getaways, and other fun prizes.

- Writing **tips** from our authors and editors.

- **Blog** with our authors and find out why they love to write romance.

- **Exclusive content** that's not contained within the pages of our novels.

Join us at
www.avonbooks.com

AVON

An Imprint of HarperCollins*Publishers*
www.avonromance.com

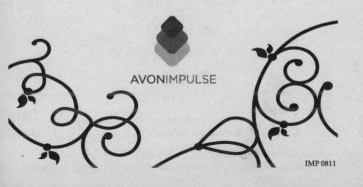